07

SHAKEN

07

TIM LaHAYE
JERRY B. JENKINS

with CHRIS FABRY

TYNDALE HOUSE PUBLISHERS, INC., CAROL STREAM, ILLINOIS

Visit Tyndale online at www.tyndale.com.

Discover the latest Left Behind news at www.leftbehind.com.

TYNDALE, Tyndale's quill logo, and *Left Behind* are registered trademarks of Tyndale House Publishers, Inc.

Shaken is a special edition compilation of the following Left Behind: The Kids titles:

Cover designed by Mark Anthony Lane II

Interior designed by Jacqueline L. Nuñez

Published in association with Alive Literary Agency, 7680 Goddard Street, Suite 200, Colorado Springs, CO 80920. www.aliveliterary.com.

For manufacturing information regarding this product, please call 1-800-323-9400.

Library of Congress Cataloging-in-Publication Data

Shaken / Jerry B. Jenkins, Tim LaHaye; with Chris Fabry.
   p. cm.
  Summary: Special edition compilation of the following three previously published works: Horsemen of terror; Uplink from the underground; Death at the gala.
   ISBN 1-4143-0268-1 (hc)
[1. End of the world—Fiction. 2. Christian life—Fiction.] I. Jenkins, Jerry B. Horsemen of terror. II. Jenkins, Jerry B. Uplink from the underground.   III. Jenkins, Jerry B. Death at the gala. IV. LaHaye, Tim F.   V. Fabry, Chris, date.   VI. Title.
PZ7.J4138Sh 2005
[Fic]—dc22   2004013512

ISBN 978-1-4143-9956-0 (sc)

Printed in the United States of America

21   20   19   18   17   16   15
7   6   5   4   3   2   1

VICKI Byrne stared at the man. She couldn't believe he was actually Buck Williams's brother.

"I live with my dad not far from here," Jeff said. "We've tried to keep the business going, but it's been tough."

"Business?"

"Dad owns a trucking company. We bring fuel into the state, mostly from Oklahoma and Texas. At least we used to. With everything that's happened, we're just scraping by."

Jeff explained that he had worked his way up in the family business and now handled the day-to-day operations. "Dad always thought Buck would come back and help us out, but he went away to school and we haven't seen much of him since. He wasn't here when Mom died. . . ."

As others left the house, Jeff moved toward the door. "Better get back. Nice talking to you."

"Wait," Vicki said. "You must have come here for a reason."

"I heard about this church from a guy. This is only my second time."

"Do you have any other family?"

Jeff looked away and took a deep breath. "A wife and two children. They're gone."

"I'm so sorry," Vicki said.

"My wife was picking up our kids at a retreat in the mountains. There was an accident. Her car flipped. The state police never found her body, just her clothes."

"The night of the disappearances?"

Jeff nodded. "They found a late-night snack burning on the stove and a hundred sets of pajamas, but my kids were gone. I took the four-wheel drive up there to see for myself. Then I went to the cabin where all those kids were."

Jeff sat and put his face in his hands. "Thought I was over this. I told Dad I was finally moving on, but hearing you brought it all back."

"What was your wife like?" Vicki said.

"Sharon and I had our problems before the kids came along. We even split up for a while but got back together after she got religion. She really changed. Losing her and the kids has been the hardest thing I've ever gone through."

"Have you talked to the pastor here about this?"

Jeff glanced at the man. "Dad would have a fit if he knew I was here. He doesn't agree with Buck that we're not Christians."

"What do you think?"

Jeff looked away.

"Your wife and children didn't die that night," Vicki said.

"Buck talked to my dad and told us his theory."

"It's not a theory. The Bible is coming true all around us every day. . . ."

"At first I thought this whole thing was like the last judgment of God. But if he took all the good people and left the bad ones, why were my dad and me left behind? What did we do to deserve this? Earthquakes, meteors, and stinging bugs. This can't be from God."

"God cares about you, Jeff. He gave his life for you, and now you've been given a second chance to follow him."

Jeff scowled. "Promise me something."

"What?"

"Don't ever tell Buck or anybody else that you saw me here."

Vicki glanced at Conrad and Shelly, who seemed to be listening. "We won't. But we'll be here another couple of days. There are answers that you and your father should hear."

Jeff shook his head and walked toward the door. He turned and said, "Leave my dad out of this."

Conrad, Shelly, and the pastor joined Vicki. The pastor said he had seen Jeff only once before. "I tried to talk with him myself, but he slipped out before I had the chance."

"Buck has tried to get through to him, hasn't he?" Conrad said.

"Sounds like they haven't had a very good relationship," Vicki said.

"Maybe we should try to find him and his dad," Shelly said.

The pastor shook his head. "I don't want to scare him away. Let's pray and ask God to work on him."

Judd listened as Sam told more about being questioned by the Global Community. Sam didn't know for sure why he had been released, but he thought his father might have been involved. Plus, he had spoken so much about God that many prisoners had believed in Jesus. The most troubling part of Sam's story was that Nada and her family had been taken into custody. Judd and Lionel pulled Sam aside and asked to hear the whole story.

"The guards brought Kasim and Jamal inside and treated them roughly," Sam said. "Kasim got the worst of it. They put them in separate cells so they wouldn't be able to talk. Kasim was near me."

"Did Kasim talk with you?" Judd said.

Sam nodded. "Kasim wanted to be careful. His lip was bloody and he was in a lot of pain. But he whispered that the GC came a few nights ago. Kasim and Nada slipped out a window and thought they had gotten away, but a squad car cornered them in an alley."

"How could the GC have found them?" Lionel said.

"Kweesa," Judd said.

Sam nodded again. "Kasim told me about calling his old girlfriend in New Babylon. He was sure she was the one who gave his family away. They probably traced Kasim's call."

"Then the GC know who he is," Judd said.

"Kasim thinks they'll try him as a deserter," Sam said. "And you can bet the deputy commander recognized Jamal and the rest of the family as soon as he saw them."

Judd put a hand to his forehead. "You're right. Woodruff was questioning them in the apartment when he got stung. He'll fry them."

"We have to get them out," Sam said. "Our only chance is my dad. We should pray for him to believe the truth and then somehow release them."

"There might be another way," Judd said.

Mark Eisman tried calling Vicki throughout the day but didn't connect until late evening. Vicki said the trip to Arizona had been interesting, but she wouldn't go into detail.

"A lot's been happening here too," Mark said. "Have you heard the news?"

"What news?"

"They're starting up school again."

"What school?"

"The Global Community Department of Education made a statement today. They're setting up satellite schools around the country. I just heard a couple days ago about the final decision."

"Let me guess," Vicki said. "Carl found out about it in Florida."

"Bingo," Mark said. "He was going through some top secret GC files and found a memo from the GC's top guy in education, Dr. Neal Damosa. He's handpicked by Carpathia for the United North American States."

"What did the memo say?"

"They've been planning this for a long time, but with each judgment, they've had to put it off."

"Put what off?"

"Requiring everyone under the age of twenty to go through what they're calling continuing education."

"Brainwashing," Vicki said.

"Exactly," Mark said. "There are thousands of sites across the U.S. where they'll register kids and have them go through training beamed by satellite."

"What are they going to teach?"

Mark pulled up the memo on his computer screen and read parts to Vicki. *"We exist to make our students better members of the Global Community. We will teach tolerance and the ideals represented by our leader, Potentate Nicolae Carpathia.*

"Our hope is to also identify those who might be candidates for our Morale Monitor squad. Each location will be asked to screen students for this elite team of committed young people."

Vicki sighed. "I had hoped after Commander Blancka that the Morale Monitors would end."

"It gets worse," Mark said. "Listen. *Not only will we identify those loyal to our cause, but we will also target those against our goals. Some would like to see the downfall of the Global Community. No doubt they have been brainwashed by*

parents, friends, or heretics such as Tsion Ben-Judah. Young
people who refuse to attend our learning facilities will be
rounded up and processed."

"Processed?" Vicki said. "Like we're slabs of meat."

"They mean business," Mark said. "We showed the
announcement to everybody here today, and a bunch of
unbelievers left."

"Melinda and Janie?"

"No. Janie's worried about getting sent back to prison.
Melinda says she's waiting until you get back before she
decides what to do."

"Then we have to come home right away," Vicki said.

"You have more meetings."

"We've been gone too long. Cancel our other meetings and tell the groups we'll do our best to reschedule. I
need to clear up a couple of things here, and we'll hopefully make it by the end of the week."

"I'll tell Melinda," Mark said.

"One more thing. How close is the nearest GC learning center?"

"A few miles from the town where we found Lenore,"
Mark said.

"Sounds too close," Vicki said. "If those people who
stayed with us rat us out, we're dead. We need a plan in
case the GC come looking."

"I'm on it," Mark said.

He hung up and wrote e-mails to the groups who had
requested teaching from the Young Tribulation Force. He
said he hated letting them down, but he hoped they
would understand.

Lenore sat by Mark and looked over his shoulder. "Maybe having all those people stay with us wasn't such a good idea."

Mark kept typing. "We all agreed to take care of them. What we need is a backup plan in case any of them inform the GC about us. Any suggestions?"

———————————

Judd closed the bedroom door and huddled with Sam and Lionel. He pulled out a sheet of paper and drew a diagram. "They held me in the same jail. I know how the offices and cells are laid out. Sam, you were just there. If we can figure a way in, I think we can get them out."

Lionel shook his head. "We've done enough damage. If the GC catch us . . ."

"Damage?" Judd said. "If it were you in there, Nada would try to get you out."

"That's what's wrong with her. She shouldn't try that kind of thing."

"I'm not leaving her in there!" Judd shouted.

Sam started to speak, but the door opened. Mr. Stein walked in and sat on the bed. "I know what you're thinking, and I don't blame you. I can't imagine what Jamal's family is going through. But I can't let you attempt an escape—"

"We have to get them out," Judd said. "Kasim's life's at stake."

"I know that. Allow me to finish. I can't let you attempt an escape without *my* help."

"You'll help us?" Sam said.

"We must come up with a plan we all agree on," Mr. Stein said. He looked at Judd and Lionel. "That should be no small task."

They laughed, then spread out several sheets of paper on the bed. They worked until early the next morning.

Vicki looked for Jeff the next day but didn't see him. She sped up the teaching and told the participants that she and her friends had to leave that night. When Vicki opened the floor for questions, kids asked about the start-up of the Global Community satellite schools.

"What should we do?" a girl asked. "They could brain-wash us, and we'll lose the mark of the believer. But if we don't go, they'll know we're against the Global Community."

"You don't have to worry about losing the mark." Vicki explained that the kids who believe in Jesus are held not by their own power, but by God's. "Each of you has to make up your own mind. By going you might be able to reach some people who don't know about God. But it might be too much for you to listen to the GC's blather."

"What are you going to do?" another teen said.

Vicki glanced at Conrad and Shelly. "I'd like to ask you all to pray for us as we head back tonight. We have to resolve some issues about the place we're staying and some people we've taken in."

Kids stood and held hands. The pastor led them in a prayer and asked God to protect Vicki and her friends as they traveled. Other kids prayed simple prayers and thanked God for bringing Vicki and the others to help them learn.

As they were praying, the door opened. Vicki looked up and noticed Jeff Williams slip into the back of the room. When they were finished, Vicki walked up to him. "I'm glad you came back."

"What you said makes sense, but I'm not sure I can believe it."

"Why?"

Jeff frowned. "It would mean Buck was right." He sat and leaned back in his chair. Shelly, Conrad, and the pastor joined them. "I'm ticked off at Buck right now. I mean, I'm proud of him and everything. He's accomplished a lot. But he didn't even come to Sharon and the kids' memorial service."

Vicki started to speak, but Jeff held up a hand. "I know he was probably busy with a story or something. I also know I shouldn't base a spiritual decision on what Buck did or didn't do."

The pastor leaned forward. "Jeff, you know the truth now. You were left behind because you didn't have a true relationship with God like your wife did. Give your heart to God right now."

Jeff stood. "I need more time."

"I understand," the pastor said. "But don't wait too long. We don't know how many will make it through the next judgment."

Jeff turned to Vicki. "You promised not to tell my brother or anybody else that you saw me here."

Vicki nodded. She felt bad as she watched Jeff leave.

She wanted him to pray right then and bring his father to the church. But she knew no one could make the decision for Jeff. He had to make it himself.

Before they left, the pastor gave the kids some extra food to take on their trip. Since the man's computer had been destroyed in the earthquake, Conrad suggested they let him have theirs. Vicki and Shelly agreed.

Vicki's phone rang. "I just heard from Carl," Mark said. "Are you sitting down?"

"Just tell me."

"Remember the guy who helped you out in Tennessee?"

"Omer?"

"Yeah. He and a bunch of others from Johnson City stormed the GC prison to try and rescue the believers."

"Is he—?"

"The GC killed most of them. Omer's gone, Vick."

Vicki slid to the floor. Shelly knelt beside her and put a hand on her shoulder.

"The worst part is that the GC were getting ready to release Omer's mom. Carl said if they had waited a few more days, everything would have been all right."

VICKI stretched out in the back of the van and thought
of the disaster and death that had become so common.
The world had changed on the awful night of the disappearances, but with each passing day things got worse.
Losing her parents, sister, and brother was only the start.
She had been adopted by Bruce Barnes, the pastor who
had helped the kids know God. Bruce had died in a fiery
explosion at the start of World War III. Then, Ryan Daley,
one of the original members of the Young Trib Force, had
been killed during the wrath of the Lamb earthquake.

With each day, Vicki grew numb. She didn't want to.
She wanted to feel alive. With each person who prayed
and asked God for forgiveness, she felt a spark in her
soul. Then something else would happen, like the news
of Omer, and she would become preoccupied again. She
knew the Bible taught that things would get worse and
worse. In four months they would reach the halfway

point of the seven-year tribulation. Then would come the Great Tribulation. Vicki trembled. Nicolae Carpathia was bad enough now, but the Great Tribulation would make this seem like a picnic.

She wanted to survive all seven years and see the Glorious Appearing of Christ and his victory over evil. But how? In time, the Global Community would force people to identify with Nicolae or face the consequences. That was something she simply would not do. Rabbi Tsion Ben-Judah believed only one-fourth of the population alive after the Rapture would survive until the end. Would Vicki be among them? And what of her friends? What about Judd?

Vicki prayed for Jeff Williams and his father. She prayed for each group she had met over the past few weeks and asked God to continue raising up house churches around the country. She felt exhausted but kept praying and pleading with God for believers she knew. She thought of Chloe Williams and her new baby. How difficult it must be bringing up a child in a world like this. Chloe had a lot of work to do with the commodity co-op. Now she would need to care for little Kenny. Vicki prayed that Chloe would have new strength each day.

Vicki pulled out a flashlight and a printout the pastor in Arizona had handed her before they left. It was the latest copy of *The Truth,* a cyberspace magazine. The articles were written anonymously, but the kids had heard this was Buck Williams's new writing project. Buck told the truth about Nicolae Carpathia and the Global Community. The latest edition gave more information about the so-called satellite schools.

The article included photos of locations ready for students. "These schools will not teach reading, writing, and arithmetic," Buck wrote. "Instead, they will soak young people with Global Community propaganda. We can only hope the next generation will see through the smoke and mirrors and find the truth found in the Bible."

Buck sure wouldn't have been able to write that in Global Community Weekly, *Vicki thought.*

The next few pages were printed from www.theunderground-online.com. Mark had posted Tsion Ben-Judah's latest Internet offering.

> *My text is from Revelation 9:15-21. "And the four angels who had been prepared for this hour and day and month and year were turned loose to kill one-third of all the people on earth. They led an army of 200 million mounted troops—I heard an announcement of how many there were.*
>
> *"And in my vision, I saw the horses and the riders sitting on them. The riders wore armor that was fiery red and sky blue and yellow. The horses' heads were like the heads of lions, and fire and smoke and burning sulfur billowed from their mouths. One-third of all the people on earth were killed by these three plagues—by the fire and the smoke and burning sulfur that came from the mouths of the horses. Their power was in their mouths, but also in their tails. For their tails had heads like snakes, with the power to injure people.*

"But the people who did not die in these plagues still refused to turn from their evil deeds. They continued to worship demons and idols made of gold, silver, bronze, stone, and wood—idols that neither see nor hear nor walk! And they did not repent of their murders or their witchcraft or their immorality or their thefts."

Vicki shivered as she read. She pictured the frightening beasts and riders and the millions who would die.

This passage has puzzled me for some time. For centuries scholars have looked at prophecy as symbolic. These symbols have been explained in different ways by different people. But why would God make it so difficult? I believe when the Scriptures say the writer saw something in a vision, it is symbolic of something else. But when the writer simply says that certain things happen, I take those literally. So far I have been proven right. This passage says John sees 200 million horsemen in a vision. I doubt these men and animals will be flesh and bone since John mentions a vision, but they will have a terrible impact on the world. They will indeed kill a third of the population. Friends, I don't know how this will happen or even how long it will take. God could make it occur in an instant. It appears to me that it will take several weeks. I ask you to read the account in Revelation and ask God to make it clear to you.

Vicki folded the pages and stuffed them in her pocket. She rubbed her eyes and asked Shelly and Conrad if they needed anything.

"Rest," Conrad said.

Vicki awoke in what seemed like a few minutes. She looked at the clock on the dashboard and saw that she had been asleep four hours. Conrad glanced in the rear-view mirror.

"Are they still back there?" Shelly said.

"Yeah," Conrad said.

Vicki sat up. "What's wrong?"

"Somebody's following us," Conrad said.

Vicki turned but didn't see any cars. In the moonlight she spotted a mountain range and a butte in the distance. "Where are we?"

"South of Denver," Shelly said. "Mark showed us a highway that should take us straight to Illinois, but—"

Conrad whipped the van to the left as a car parked alongside the road suddenly pulled out in front of them. Shelly screamed and hit her head against the side window. Conrad veered inches from the car and struggled to regain control. He nearly went off the side of the road but managed to get the van back on the pavement.

"They must be working together," Conrad said.

Vicki glanced behind them and saw two sets of headlights. "They're gaining on us."

"Is it the GC?" Shelly said, putting a hand over a knot on her head.

"It might be worse," Conrad said.

Judd and the others considered several plans to help Nada and her family. Judd wanted to create some kind of diversion outside of headquarters. Sam suggested they slip sleeping pills into the station's coffeepot.

Finally, Mr. Stein said he was going to bed. "I think we should all pray about what we're going to do."

Judd shook his head as Mr. Stein left. "How can we sit here and pray when we know they're in trouble?"

Sam put his arms behind his head and stretched. "I understand how you feel. You want to get in there and get them out."

"If we don't, they're toast."

"If we don't come up with something soon, I'll go to my father."

"You can't do that."

Sam sighed. "Part of me wants to run in there with pepper spray and disable the guards. But I still hold out hope that my father will believe. I don't want him to think we're some kind of radical military group. I want him to see Christ in what we do."

The morning sun was coming up as they each fell asleep. Mr. Stein awakened them. "It's time."

"Time for what?" Judd said.

"God has spoken. He revealed that we should go to the station quickly."

18

"What are we going to do?" Sam said.

"Get dressed. We must go."

Vicki watched the two sets of headlights rapidly approach. One set was an old truck. The other was a smaller sports car. "Can't you go faster?"

"There's no way we're going to outrun them!" Shelly screamed.

"We're going uphill," Conrad said. "I'm going to try something."

Conrad jerked the wheel to the right, and the van ran into a ditch and up the side of a gully. Even though she was buckled in, Vicki's head hit the ceiling. Finally, the van reached a dirt riding path that ran parallel to the road.

Vicki glanced behind them. The truck was a few hundred yards behind. The sports car was still on the main road.

"I'm going to try something else," Conrad said. He turned off the headlights, plunging them into darkness. Vicki could barely see the lights of the truck through the dust they had kicked up. The sports car slowed and pulled to the side of the road.

"Maybe they'll think we went off a cliff or something," Conrad said. "Hang on!"

He jerked the van to the right and drove straight through a wooden fence and onto another road. They found an overpass and headed west. Conrad drove wildly across an open field. He slowed as they hit a winding stretch of road. He turned his headlights on for an instant to get his bearings. They crossed railroad tracks and turned into a gravel parking lot. Vicki spotted old playground equipment and a lake. Conrad drove onto a jogging path and parked the van behind an abandoned picnic shelter.

The three got out and kept watch. A few minutes later the sports car flew over the railroad tracks and wound its way around the lake. The truck followed moments later.

"You think we're safe?" Vicki said.

Conrad turned. "Let's get back to the main—" He stopped midsentence and grabbed Shelly by the shoulders. Shelly stared straight ahead, shaking.

"What's wrong, Shel?" Vicki said.

Shelly dropped to her knees and gasped for air. She pointed toward the lake.

Vicki and Conrad looked but didn't see anything. The cars were out of sight now.

"They're gone," Conrad said. "Don't worry."

Shelly trembled, as if she had just walked out of a freezer. She rubbed her arms and shook. Vicki knelt beside her and looked into Shelly's eyes. Total fear.

"I think she's going into shock," Vicki said.

"Get her in the car and let's get out of here."

Judd followed Mr. Stein, Sam, and Lionel through the narrow streets that led to the GC headquarters. Judd asked several times what they were going to do, but Mr. Stein merely shrugged.

When they neared GC headquarters, Mr. Stein took

them to a small café across the street. The four sat, and Mr. Stein ordered each of them something to drink. When the waiter left, Mr. Stein scratched his beard. "I have felt such a strong urge to be here, but I don't know why."

"This happened a lot on your trip, didn't it?" Lionel said.

Mr. Stein smiled. "There were many times when I didn't know my next move, but I simply trusted God. This feels the same. I know God wants me to speak about him, but I have no idea how this could gain the release of your friends."

The kids studied the headquarters building. Sam said, "We don't even know if they're still—"

Sam stopped as the front door to headquarters opened. Deputy Commander Woodruff and Sam's father stepped outside. Woodruff was yelling at Mr. Goldberg.

Mr. Stein turned. "I believe this is it. I have to go."

Judd stood, but Mr. Stein held up a hand. "Please. I have to go alone."

Vicki held Shelly in the backseat as Conrad drove back to the main road. Shelly shook violently, and Vicki couldn't calm her.

"I think we're okay now," Conrad said. "We're leaving those guys behind."

"Good," Vicki said. She pushed Shelly's hair from her face. "See, you don't have to worry about those guys."

"I-I-I'm not," Shelly managed. "Th-th-that's not what scared me."

"Then what on earth did?"

"Not what *on* earth, but what was above it."

"What do you mean?"

"You didn't see them? They were hovering over the water by the mountain. It was the most awful thing I've ever seen." Shelly put her face in her hands.

Vicki glanced at Conrad in the rearview mirror. He shrugged. Vicki turned to Shelly. "What scared you?"

Shelly swallowed hard and closed her eyes. "Horses. Huge horses that looked like lions."

3

VICKI leaned close to Shelly. "Are you sure you didn't fall asleep and dream about it?"

"They were there, I swear. Just as real as you and me."

"We believe you," Conrad said. "We just didn't see anything."

"You said they were above the ground?" Vicki said.

Shelly nodded. "It was like they were walking on air. And they were huge."

Vicki felt confused. Tsion had written that the horses would be some kind of angelic beings, unseen to the human eye. If Shelly had seen them, they were real and the next judgment was about to begin.

Conrad hit the accelerator. Vicki turned and saw the same car and truck. "These guys don't give up."

The truck pulled along their right side, and the car raced on their left. The driver of the truck wore a hat and had a stubbly beard. He pointed and yelled.

"Whatever you do, don't stop!" Vicki said.

A woman rode in the passenger seat of the sports car. She rolled down her window and yelled, "Pull over!" When Conrad didn't obey, she turned to the driver.

"She's got a shotgun!" Shelly screamed.

Conrad swerved into the truck, but it was too late. The gunshot blew out the left front tire and sent the van reeling. Vicki and Shelly screamed as Conrad fought to keep control. He slammed on the brakes, and both vehicles shot past them. The van skidded into a ditch and toppled over.

Vicki unbuckled first and checked Conrad and Shelly. Shelly was bruised but okay. Conrad lay slumped over the steering wheel, his air bag deployed.

"Are you okay?" Vicki said.

Conrad grabbed his neck and put his head back. "I think so. But I can't say the same for the van. We're stuck."

"Look!" Shelly shouted.

The car and truck were turning. Shelly tried to open the side door, but it was stuck. Conrad pulled himself free and pushed the front passenger door open. The three crawled out and hit the ground just as the truck skidded to a stop in front of them.

Judd prayed as he watched Mr. Stein walk toward the Jerusalem Global Community headquarters. The man seemed fearless.

Sam stared at his father and stood. Lionel and Judd grabbed him and pulled him into his chair.

"We don't need anybody else getting arrested," Lionel said.

Mr. Stein walked into the street, his face turned toward the steps of the station. A car passed him and honked, but Mr. Stein continued, staring at the deputy commander and Sam's father. Mr. Stein stopped in the middle of the street and raised his voice. "You who walk in darkness, behold, you will see a great light—a light that will shine on all who live in the land where death casts its shadow."

Deputy Commander Woodruff and Mr. Goldberg turned and glared.

"This is what the Lord Almighty says," Mr. Stein continued. " 'Every word that was written, every promise given, will be fulfilled.' "

Deputy Commander Woodruff walked down a few steps and yelled back, "And this is what I say; you are under the arrest of the Global Community!"

Judd looked at Lionel. "What's he doing?"

Lionel shrugged. "Looks like he wants them to take him away."

Mr. Stein stood his ground as GC officers walked outside to see what was going on. The deputy commander pointed and ordered them to arrest Mr. Stein.

"The captives will be released and the prisoners will be freed!" Mr. Stein shouted.

"And you will be behind bars where you belong, you stupid fool," Woodruff said. "No more of your lies after today."

The officers reached the bottom of the steps and

moved into the street. Sam shook his head. "I don't understand."

Suddenly, officers coughed and gasped for air. One pulled a handkerchief from his back pocket and put it over his face. The two near Mr. Stein fell to their knees, sputtering and panting.

"What's that smell?" the deputy commander said. Everyone in front of the GC station coughed and waved their arms.

The waiter at the restaurant ran inside. "Sulfur! It's sulfur!" He closed the door behind him and collapsed in a heap.

A woman ran by them on the sidewalk shouting, "We're going to die! It's poison!"

"I don't smell anything," Sam said.

Then Judd saw them. The huge beasts rode over a building in front of them. Judd pointed. Lionel and Sam couldn't speak.

The horses approached the street where Mr. Stein stood. They hovered as if walking on air. These were not ordinary sized horses. These were monsters. Judd had seen Clydesdales close up, but these were enormous, at least twice the size of any he had ever seen.

Lionel gasped. "Look at their faces!"

Judd couldn't keep his eyes off them. Their heads looked like lions with flowing manes and huge teeth. Flames and thick yellow smoke shot out of their mouths and nostrils, but Judd didn't hear anything. No hoofbeats or snorting or any sound.

The horses were so frightening, Judd almost didn't

notice the riders. They were every bit as large as the animals. They looked human, but each one was at least ten feet tall and five hundred pounds. Every horseman wore a shimmering breastplate. Their biceps and forearms rippled with muscles as they worked to control the enormous horses. Judd thought they might stampede at any moment.

Judd jumped out of his chair. "Come on!"

"I'm not going out there," Sam said.

"These have to be the horses from Revelation 9. Tsion teaches that they won't hurt believers."

"How can we be sure? They look pretty mean."

Judd raced into the street. Lionel and Sam followed. Mr. Stein put up a hand as the three came near. One of the horses was only a few yards away. It turned and for the first time they saw the tail.

"Sick!" Lionel said.

Instead of hair, a snake's head writhed on the end of the tail. It bared its fangs and looked at the kids.

"So this is why you came out here," Judd said to Mr. Stein. "You knew this was going to happen."

"I had no idea," Mr. Stein said. "I felt God wanted me to speak and I did. Follow me."

"We can walk right through the horses?" Judd said.

"These are not physical beings. Their effect is real. They will cause the deaths of many, but we have no reason to fear them."

Sirens wailed throughout the city as Judd and the others walked up the steps. The deputy commander lay on the steps, clutching his throat. As Judd passed, Woodruff reached out and grabbed his leg. Judd quickly jerked away. The man summoned his strength and stood, finally recognizing Judd. He reached for the radio on his shoulder and clicked the button.

Woodruff gasped and tried to speak. Before he could utter a word, a horse moved toward them and turned, its tail crashing into Woodruff's back. The man flew into the air like a child's toy and crashed into the building. His limp body fell to the sidewalk.

Judd shuddered. How could the horses strike with such force when they weren't physical beings? He and the others had walked directly through them!

Lionel reached the deputy commander's body and checked his pulse. He shook his head.

"Let's go," Mr. Stein said.

Vicki started to run, but Conrad grabbed her arm.

"Stay right where you are!" the man in the truck said. Vicki noticed a gun rack in the rear of the pickup. The man stepped out and walked in front of the headlights. He was thin and had a long face with a stubbly beard. His arms were gangly, and he walked with a slight limp. He cocked a pistol and held it out as the car arrived.

"How many are there?" the woman said as she stepped out of the car. She was short and wore a leather jacket. She waved the shotgun as she talked.

"Three," Long Face said. "Two girls and a guy."

The driver of the car was a man in his mid-thirties. He was stocky with curly hair. He got out and eyed Vicki and Shelly. Something didn't seem right about him.

The woman threw a bag in front of Conrad. "Put all your Nicks and valuables in there and step away from the van."

"We don't have much," Vicki said. "This isn't even our car—"

"Shut up and do what you're told!" the woman screamed.

Conrad turned to Vicki and said, "Give them what they want. Main thing is getting out of here alive."

"Why didn't you think of that back on the road?" the woman yelled.

"Yeah," the man by the car whined. "You almost scratched my car."

Conrad shrugged. "The stuff's going to be hard to get. Van's all smashed and—"

The woman pointed the shotgun at Conrad. "Shut up and get out of the way."

Long Face crawled inside the van and rummaged around. He threw out Vicki's notebook, and papers flew everywhere. Vicki started to retrieve them, but Conrad held her back.

"I've got a bad feeling about this," Shelly whispered.

"Hey, look what I found!" Long Face said from the van. He handed a metal box to the woman.

"So, you were holding out on us!" the woman said. "Where's the key?"

Conrad pulled a key from his pocket and tossed it to her. She tried to catch it, but it pinged off the side of the car. The curlyheaded man glared at him.

The box held enough Nicks to get the kids back to the

schoolhouse, but not much more. The woman stuffed the money in her jacket pocket.

"Van's torn up," Long Face said. "Probably couldn't drive it even if we got it out of the ditch."

The woman kicked the van and cursed. "We could have sold it, no problem. Now it's a hunk of junk."

"Better make 'em pay for their mistake," the curly-headed man said. He stepped forward and reached for the shotgun.

The woman pushed him away and waved the gun at the kids. "If you hadn't tried to get away, we'd have let you go."

"We won't tell anybody what happened," Shelly said.

The woman frowned and pointed to the field. "Start walking."

"What are you going to do?" Conrad said.

"Move," Curly Hair said.

"You think we should make a run for it?" Vicki whispered.

"I don't think we have much choice," Conrad said.

Shelly gasped. "Wait. They're back!"

Vicki's mouth dropped open when she saw the horses and riders. A herd was moving effortlessly across the field behind them. Fire blew from the horses' nostrils, and great clouds of black and yellow smoke came from their mouths. Vicki guessed they were a half mile away.

The woman glanced behind her when Shelly gasped. The men did too. Both turned and laughed.

"You're not going to get us to fall for that," Long Face said.

"You don't see them?" Vicki said.

"Real cute," Curly said. "Just keep moving."

"If I were you, I'd get out of here fast," Conrad said.

"This is far enough," the woman said. "I'm tired of your games. Let's get this over with."

Vicki looked at the horses. They were right behind the three bandits, hovering over the field. Vicki cringed when she saw their faces. The locusts had been hideous, but these horses and their riders were even scarier.

"Whoa, what's that smell?" Long Face said.

Curly took a deep whiff of air and coughed violently. One of the horses blew a plume of smoke toward the three, and it engulfed them. The woman dropped the shotgun and fell to her knees. She grabbed her throat with both hands and gasped.

Long Face ran toward the kids, his face turning blue. He nearly knocked Shelly over as he pushed past them. One of the horses followed and snorted a blast of white-hot fire. Long Face burst into flames and went rolling headlong onto the ground.

Curly ran toward the road and jumped in the pickup truck. He gunned the engine and shot past several horses. One turned and flicked its snakelike tail and smashed the windshield. The truck went out of control, ran up the side of an embankment, and hit a tree. One snort from the horse's nostrils and the pickup was engulfed in flames.

The woman tried to stand but couldn't. Finally, she cried and stretched out on the ground. Her body twitched and jerked for a moment; then she lay still.

Shelly put her head on Vicki's shoulder and cried. "I never dreamed it would be this awful."

Conrad checked, but the woman was dead. He found their money in her jacket and walked toward the road. "Come on, let's get out of here."

MARK Eisman and the others at the schoolhouse sat in front of the small television their friend Z had recently sent. Mark usually monitored the computer for the latest news, but everyone wanted to see the local coverage. Darrion had alerted Mark about the horses and riders. Now they all sat before the flickering television.

"Reports from Rockford to downstate Illinois have officials concerned," a nervous reporter said. "But it's not just the Midwest that's being affected. We're hearing about fires and deadly fumes from around the globe. As of yet, there is no explanation for this lethal outbreak that has killed thousands. We have no word yet on the exact number of casualties, but some experts believe hundreds of thousands might lose their lives."

"Try millions," Darrion said.

Charlie sighed. "I'm sure glad I got the mark before any of this happened."

Someone handed the reporter a piece of paper. "We're going to join live coverage from the international head-quarters of Global Community Network News."

The feed switched to a newscast already in progress. The anchor was better dressed than the local reporter but equally baffled at the unfolding events. "Emergency medical professionals are at a loss, frantic to determine the cause. Here's the head of the Global Community Emergency Management Association, Dr. Jurgen Haase."

Dr. Haase looked composed, almost too calm for the situation. He spoke slowly and with great poise. "If these deaths were isolated, we might say they were caused by a natural disaster, a rupture of some natural gas. But they seem random, and clearly the fumes are lethal. We urge citizens to use gas masks and work together to put out the fires."

The news anchor asked, "Which is more dangerous, the black smoke or the yellow?"

Haase said, "First we believed the black smoke was coming from the fires, but that doesn't appear to be the case. It can be deadly, but the yellow smoke smells of sulfur and has the power to kill instantly."

"Has the Global Community considered the possibility of terrorist action?"

"It's very early," Haase said. "We've ruled nothing out. We do know there is a group of religious zealots who would love to create more suffering, but I won't speculate on that. To be honest, we simply don't know what we're dealing with."

"Great," Darrion said. "Now we're being accused of germ warfare."

The reporter put a hand to his ear, then read from a bulletin. "This just in. While there are pockets in which no fire or smoke or sulfur has been reported, in other areas the death count is staggering, now estimated in the millions. His Excellency, Global Community Potentate Nicolae Carpathia, will address the world via radio and television and the Internet inside this half hour."

"What do you think Carpathia will say?" Lenore said.

Mark shook his head. "He'll find a way to look good. He'll probably get more people to worship him because of this."

The report switched to a feed from Jerusalem. Smoke rose from the old city, and fires were everywhere. Another report came from New Babylon, where Nicolae Carpathia was about to speak. People lay motionless in the street. Once sparkling buildings were shrouded in black and yellow clouds. Fire and smoke appeared on every continent, in every major city, but no one knew how it was happening. People throughout the world panicked. Airplanes filled with passengers plunged from the sky after choking pilots radioed their Maydays.

"They even have power to affect airplanes?" Charlie said.

Melinda walked in, rubbing her eyes. "What's going on?"

Lenore stood and let the girl have her seat. "The next judgment is here. Nicolae's about to put his spin on it."

"How do you know this is from God?" Melinda said.

Lenore showed her the passage in Revelation. Melinda read it and glanced at the television. "If this is supposed to be caused by horses, how come they haven't shown any?"

Mark said, "My guess is they're not visible. But believe me, they're real. And we don't know how long they'll be here. You could be in danger."

"Just me? Why wouldn't you guys be worried?"

Darrion turned down the volume. "When things like this happen, those who believe in Jesus are immune. The locusts didn't sting believers, just unbelievers. It's the same with this."

Melinda seemed in a daze. She stood and walked up the stairs to the balcony. Mark followed. The moon was bright, but there was no sign of horses and riders.

"You've heard the message every way we can think of telling you," Mark said. "We've all been praying for you."

"I want to talk to Vicki. I trust her, and I don't want to do something simply because I'm scared of dying."

"I understand. The problem is, we have no idea where she is. We haven't been able to reach her."

"I'll wait."

Darrion yelled that Carpathia was about to speak. Mark and Melinda sat just as the potentate was being announced. Carpathia looked into the camera and did his best to calm viewers.

"I want to assure you that this situation will soon be under control," Carpathia said. "We are working around the clock and using every resource to stop the fires and smoke. Meanwhile, I ask citizens of the Global Community to report suspicious activity, particularly anyone who is making or transporting toxic chemicals. Sadly, we have reason to believe that religious rebels may be behind this massacre of innocent lives. We have extended every courtesy to these people, and this is how they react."

Carpathia bit his lip. "Though they cross us at every turn, we have defended their right to dissent. Yet they continue to see the Global Community as an enemy. They feel they have a right to maintain an intolerant, close-minded cult that excludes anyone who disagrees with them.

"You have the right to live healthy, peaceful, and free. While I remain against war, I pledge to rid the world of this cult, beginning with the Jerusalem Twosome, who even now express no remorse about the widespread loss of life that has resulted from this attack."

"Who's he talking about?" Melinda said.

"Jerusalem Twosome must be his new nickname for the two prophets, Eli and Moishe," Mark said.

Carpathia pushed a button, and a video of Eli and Moishe appeared. They were speaking in unison near the Wailing Wall. Words flashed across the screen underneath the video clip.

"Woe to the enemies of the most high God!" they said. "Woe to the cowards who shake their fist at their creator and are now forced to flee his wrath! We beseech you, snakes and vipers, to see even this plague as more than judgment! Yea, it is yet another attempt to reach you by a loving God who has run out of patience. There is no more time to woo you. You must hearken to his call, see that it is he who loves you. Turn to the God of your fathers while there is still time. For the day will come when time shall be no more!"

Carpathia turned off the video and smiled. "The day will come, my friends, when these two shall no longer spread their venom. They shall no longer turn water to blood, hold back rain from the clouds, send plagues to the Holy Land and the rest of the globe. I upheld my end of the bargain negotiated with them months ago, allowing certain rebels to go unpunished. Now this is how we are repaid for our generosity.

"But the gift train stops here, loyal citizens. Your patience and steadfastness shall be repaid. The day will yet come when we will live as one world, one faith, one family of man."

"Yeah, one big happy family," Darrion said. "What a loser."

Carpathia continued. "We shall live in a utopia of peace and harmony with no more war, no more blood-shed, no more death. In the meantime, please accept my deepest personal condolences over the loss of your loved ones. They shall not have died in vain. Continue to trust in the ideals of the Global Community, in the tenets of peace, and in the genius of an all-inclusive universal faith that welcomes the devout of any religion.

"Just four months from now we shall celebrate in the very city where the preachers now taunt and warn us. We shall applaud their demise and revel in a future without plague and disease and suffering and death. Keep the faith, and look forward to that day. And until I address you again, thank you for your loyal support of the Global Community."

"What does that mean?" Melinda said.

"Tsion has taught us all along that the two witnesses will one day be killed by Carpathia. It looks like Nicolae has done his homework. The 1,260 days of their preaching ends in four months."

———————————

Mr. Stein led the kids inside the Global Community police station. Many of the officers had rushed outside when Mr. Stein began to speak. A few were still inside now, coughing and sputtering.

"Where's Sam?" Judd said.

"Outside with his dad," Lionel said. "I'll get him."

Mr. Stein pointed to a locked doorway. Judd found the keys on an officer's desk. Inside, they heard more coughing and wheezing.

"Can't breathe!" someone shouted. "We need air!"

Judd found Nada's cell. She was huddled in the corner with her mother. "Thank God you've come!" Nada said. She hugged Judd and pointed toward the back of the building where her father and brother were being kept.

As they rushed past the cells, several believers called out from behind the bars. Judd freed those with the mark of the believer on their foreheads. Most of them believed because Sam had given them the gospel.

Judd opened the last door on the corridor and found a guard on the floor, gasping for air. Kasim and Jamal cried when they saw Nada. She took the keys from Judd and released them. They had bruises on their faces, deep circles under their eyes, and they looked like they hadn't eaten for days.

"Let's get out of here," Jamal said weakly.

"Wait!" someone said as he rushed through the door.

Judd turned and spotted the jailer pointing his gun at them. "Stop or I'll shoot!"

Vicki crawled into the van and handed Conrad and Shelly as many supplies as they could pack into the sports car. The cell phone had crashed into the windshield and was fried. The sports car was a tight fit for the three of them, but they were grateful to have something to drive.

"I feel guilty taking this car," Vicki said.

"They're not going to use it anymore," Conrad said.

"I know, but they probably stole it."

Shelly pointed out the window at another cavalry of fiery horses and riders. They were moving north along an abandoned railroad track. As they ran, they breathed great clouds of black and yellow smoke over rows of homes and ranches nearby. In some homes, lights came on and people burst through the front doors, falling on lawns and rolling. In other places, the horses snorted enough fire to send whole blocks up in smoke. Conrad pointed to the other side of the road where another herd stood perched on a butte overlooking a small town.

"There doesn't seem to be any method," Shelly said.

"They're just putting that smoke and fire wherever they find people."

"I'm glad they came when they did," Conrad said. "I feel like a cat who's just used up two or three of its lives."

"How long will it be until we get home?" Vicki said.

"Before the roads were torn up during the earthquake, we'd have been able to do it in less than twenty hours," Conrad said. "Now it's going to be at least two days, and that's if we push it."

Vicki sat back and watched the herds run. She had no idea how long they would stay, but when they were through, the world would never be the same.

Judd held up his hands and begged the man not to shoot. The others stood back, waiting to see what would happen.

The guard choked and gasped for air. "If they find prisoners missing from here, they'll have me shot!"

Mr. Stein moved forward and knelt beside the man. "Many of your fellow officers are dead or are dying because of this judgment."

"You're one of those crazies!"

"I bring you good news. You don't have to die. Believe on the Lord Jesus and you will be saved."

The jailer frantically looked around. Some of the prisoners were coughing uncontrollably. Others lay motionless in their bunks. "Why aren't *you* coughing? Is this some kind of spell you've put over the jail?"

Mr. Stein shook his head. "This was predicted thousands of years ago in the Scriptures. A third of those still living will die because of this terrible judgment. But you can be saved from it if you will—"

The jailer stood and waved the gun frantically. "All right, everybody back in their cells."

Mr. Stein moved back. He motioned for the others to leave the cellblock. "The Lord has provided a way of escape. I won't allow our friends, who are innocent, to suffer any longer."

The jailer coughed again and put his hand to his mouth. Mr. Stein turned to leave. The jailer raised the gun.

Before Judd could react, Nada lunged at the man. People screamed and fell to the floor as muffled gunfire echoed through the jail.

FOR A few seconds, everything went into slow motion for Judd. Nada staggered backward and slumped to the floor. The jailer coughed and waved the gun around. Mr. Stein subdued the man and took the gun away.

Judd rushed to Nada's side and pulled her close. He pushed the hair from her face and saw a red spot appear on her shirt.

Jamal knelt beside his daughter and screamed, "No!"

Nada's mother burst into tears.

Judd felt Nada's neck. "She's alive. I can feel a pulse."

Nada coughed and struggled to breathe. Jamal leaned over her. "Daughter, speak to us."

Nada's eyelids fluttered. "Hard to . . . breathe . . ."

"Lie still," Jamal said.

"Somebody get a doctor!" Kasim shouted. "She's losing blood!"

Jamal and Kasim ran into the next room. Judd shook with fright. He didn't know what to do.

43

"Judd?" Nada whispered.

"I'm right here."

"I can't feel anything. My legs and arms won't work."

"You're going through a big shock. Just . . . we'll get some help."

Nada opened her eyes. "I had it all planned. We were going to spend . . . the rest of our lives . . ."

"Why did you do that?" Judd said.

Nada ignored his question. "Promise me you won't forget."

"Don't talk like that! You're going to be all right. We'll get a doctor and . . ."

Nada took another painful breath. "Go to your friends . . . take Sam and Lionel."

Nada's mother knelt and wept by the girl's side. She took Nada's limp hand and kissed it. A trickle of blood ran from the corner of Nada's mouth. Judd dabbed it with his shirt.

Nada looked at her mother and smiled. A tear ran down her cheek. She tried to speak but couldn't.

Nada let out a breath and rested her head on Judd's chest. He felt Nada's neck, then her wrist. Nothing. He held her body tightly and cried.

The air seemed to go out of the room. Judd's mind spun. He wanted to run, to hide, to get away from this awful scene. But here he was, holding the body of his friend. She had given her life for him and the others. How could he ever thank her? Or forgive her?

Jamal and Kasim rushed in with a stretcher. They stopped when they saw Judd's face. Nada's mother lay on the floor, weeping. Jamal and Kasim both collapsed beside Nada's body.

"I'm so sorry," Judd managed.

Mr. Stein, who had been standing nearby, knelt beside the group and placed a hand on Nada's head. "Father, we commend the spirit of our sister to you. We are thankful you allowed us the privilege of knowing her. She was filled with courage and truth. You have said that there is no greater love than for someone to lay down their life for a friend. Surely, Nada has done this today. Comfort us now with this loss, and we look forward to the day when we will be united again when you return to rule and reign."

Jamal picked up the prayer through his tears. "Oh, God, we were not worthy to have had her as a daughter. But we thank you for giving her to us. Now we give her back to you."

"If she hadn't found me, Lord," Kasim said, "I'd still be in New Babylon. Forgive me for rejecting your message through her for so long."

Nada's mother couldn't speak. She shook her head and wept at the girl's side. Judd squinted and tried to speak. Mr. Stein put a hand on his shoulder. Finally, Judd managed a few words. "God, she cared so much for her family. I thank you that I got to know her." Judd paused, then said, "If I'd only. . . ."

Jamal put a hand on Judd when he couldn't continue. The man whispered, "It's okay, my brother. It wasn't your fault."

The jailer appeared behind Mr. Stein, walking like a

drunk man. He approached the group staggering and coughing, clutching his throat. Mr. Stein turned and stood in time to catch him as the man collapsed.

Jamal and Kasim brought the stretcher, but it was too late. The jailer had been overcome by the smoke of the horses.

Jamal took Nada from Judd and carried her body outside. When Lionel saw them, his mouth dropped open. Judd told him briefly what had happened and asked about Sam.

"Over there." Lionel pointed.

Sam sat on the sidewalk, cradling his father's head. The herd of horses had moved on, leaving the street littered with bodies. Lionel put an arm around Judd. "I'm really sorry about Nada."

Judd nodded.

"I've been trying to get Sam to move, but he won't budge."

"I'll talk with him."

Judd sat by Sam and put an arm around his shoulders.

"I prayed for him every day," Sam said. "I thought for sure he would believe . . ."

After a few moments, Judd said, "I don't have any more answers than you. I know God's in control, but I sure don't know how this all works together."

Mr. Stein said, "We should go."

"I can't leave my father like this!"

"The surviving GC will be back to lock down the jail," Kasim said.

Judd held up a hand. "We'll use the stretcher to carry his body."

Judd and Lionel carried Sam's father on the stretcher, and Jamal and Kasim carried Nada. They walked through streets littered with the dead. Some buildings were on fire, but there was no one to put them out. The massacre got worse as they neared Yitzhak's home. Those who hadn't been killed ran into the streets, wailing and crying over the dead.

Yitzhak contacted a funeral director about the bodies. "If you want a burial, you'll have to do it yourself," the man said. "The Global Community says they're going to burn the bodies to reduce the risk of contamination."

While Nada's mother prepared the bodies, Judd and Lionel found a pair of shovels in a utility building. The men took turns digging in the small backyard. Judd was numb. Each shovelful of dirt was a painful reminder that Nada no longer lived. When the holes were dug, everyone gathered outside.

"We have said our good-byes," Mr. Stein said softly. "But I need to add something. The time is coming when the Antichrist will take full control of the world system. The judgments will get worse. Before us are two people— one who knew God and one who didn't. One who showed the love of God, who gave her life so that we would be saved. May these two lives renew our resolve to live for God. We must let nothing stand in our way in telling others the truth. Even if it costs our lives."

"Amen," Sam said.

"Amen," the others said.

Sam grabbed a handful of dirt and tossed it on his father's body. Each person did the same.

Before Judd went into the house, Nada's mother came to him and put something wrapped in cloth in his hand. "She would have wanted you to have this."

Judd couldn't speak.

Nada's mother said, "She told me some things about you two. I encouraged her to tell you what was in her heart, but she never had the chance. Some of it is in this letter. Take it."

Judd stuffed the package in his pocket and went upstairs. He sat on his bed and thought of all that had happened since the disappearances. Losing his family was tough. It had thrown him together with brothers and sisters of a different kind. Now that family was being torn apart. He closed his eyes and thought of each person, believer and unbeliever, who was no longer alive. The longer he lived, the more people he would lose.

When will it be my turn? Judd thought.

He let his mind wander until it finally came to rest on Nada. He had been so excited to free her. She was so close. Judd thought through the series of events. If he had only been quicker and lunged at the jailer before Nada, she might be alive. A wave of guilt swept over him. He hadn't pulled the trigger, but he felt responsible for Nada's death. Then came the anger. Maybe the man wouldn't have fired at all. If Nada had stayed where she was, perhaps no one would have been hurt.

Judd remembered the first time he had met Nada. He

thought of their exercises and discussions on the roof of her father's building. They loved to talk late into the night. A lump rose in his throat. *Gone. Nada is really gone, and she isn't coming back.*

Judd pulled out the cloth-wrapped package. Inside was a folded piece of paper and Nada's necklace. On the gold chain was a cross. Judd turned it around and saw Nada's initials on the back. He held the cross to his lips, then slipped the necklace around his neck. The paper was worn and somewhat faded. Judd looked at the date at the top of the page and realized Nada had written the letter soon after her family's arrest.

> *Dear Judd,*
>
> *My mother suggested I write this down so I won't forget. Maybe the GC is going to execute us, and if that happens, you can take comfort in the fact that I'm in a better place. Being with Christ is what our lives are all about. If they've killed me, I'm there, so don't be sad for me. I love you very much. From the moment you came to our family, I felt close to you. You were like a brother to me. Then, as my feelings grew deeper, you were more than that.*
>
> *But I have to tell you something. I feel it's only fair that I express this. As close as we became, in our talks and the time we spent together, I always felt there was something missing. I couldn't put my finger on it until we came back to Israel and you backed away. I feel what I'm about to say is something that God wants me to say. I have prayed many nights about this. . . .*

Lionel knocked on the door and walked in. "Care for some company?"

Judd folded the paper and put it in his pocket. "Sure."

Lionel sat on the bed. "Sam's taking it pretty hard about his dad. How about you?"

"I'm not exactly throwing a party."

"Yeah." Lionel put his hands on his knees. "Well, I've got something to say. It might not be the right time, but with the way things are going, we don't know what's going to happen next."

"Say it."

"I rode you pretty hard about getting back to the States. Said some bad stuff."

"You were right."

"Maybe. But I shouldn't have questioned your motives about Nada. I can't tell you how sorry I am about what happened."

"Thanks."

"However long it takes, whatever kind of time you want to spend with her family, even if you decide to stay, I'm with you."

Judd's lip quivered. He and Lionel had been together since the disappearances. Through the tough times with Lionel's uncle André, to the first printing of the *Underground*, and all that had gone on afterward, Lionel was there like a rock. Judd threw his arms around his friend and hugged him.

Judd told Lionel the full story about Nada and the jailer and how he was feeling.

"Man, you can't blame yourself."

"Who else?"

"It was instinct. She moved a little faster, that's all. Her family doesn't hold it against you. They're down there talking about you like you were their son."

"What kind of son would let his sister get killed?"

Lionel put a hand on Judd's shoulder. "We're going to get through this. You and Sam and Nada's family are going to come out on the other side."

"I don't know how."

"Time. Take as much as you need. Come get me if you want to talk."

When Lionel closed the door, Judd pulled out Nada's letter. What was it she was trying to tell him? Judd read:

> I have prayed many nights about this. I've asked God to show me why I'm feeling this way. Honestly, I think something is holding you back. At first, I thought it was God. You're so sold out on him, and you want to live for him. But the more I thought and prayed, it became clear that God wasn't coming between us. I really believe there is someone else. You've never talked much about your friends in the States, but I sense there is someone there you care about deeply.
>
> Maybe I'm making this up. If so, I apologize. But if I'm right and you find this letter, go back to her. You're a wonderful person with so much to offer. I have loved being your friend. I'm sorry for the trouble I caused you in New Babylon. I'm sorry for being difficult at times. (You had your moments too.) I'll look forward to seeing

*you again, whether it's in this life or the next. May
God bless you.*

*Love,
Nada*

Judd folded the letter and shook his head. A thousand
thoughts swirled in his head. *Is she right? Did I hold back
in our relationship? Why?*

Judd lay back on the bed. The shock of seeing the
horses and the experience at the jail had drained him of
emotion and strength. He didn't think he could sleep, but
when he closed his eyes, he drifted off and dreamed of
Nada.

6

VICKI listened closely to the reports about the deadly horses as they drove east. Through Nebraska they saw the effects of the latest judgment. Houses in Lincoln were charred. The kids drove through billowing yellow and black smoke that floated through the area. They spotted herds of horses and riders in Omaha.

"I hope I never see those horses again," Shelly said.

Conrad turned the news down. "I don't get it. Those beasts are evil. They must want to hurt believers."

"God's using those killing machines for his own purpose. Somehow he's put a hedge around those who are his, and those beings know it."

Though it was a lot smaller than the van, the kids slept in the car as much as they could. In Iowa City, they rented two motel rooms with most of their remaining money. Conrad staggered to his room. "I'm going to sleep, and I'm not waking up for a week."

Vicki and Shelly tried to order a pizza, but they couldn't get an answer at any restaurants. Instead, they walked half a block to a convenience store and bought snacks.

"This used to be my favorite thing to do on vacation," Shelly said. "My mom would give me a few dollars and send me to a store next to the hotel. I'd get all kinds of soda and junk food, then stay up all night watching television."

Vicki smiled. "We used to have fun at the vending machines. I'd take my little sister, and we'd get pop and candy. Sometimes the machines would give us more than we'd paid for, and we felt like kings."

Shelly flicked on the television as Vicki spread their food on one of the beds. Many of the channels carried updates on the incredible world situation.

"Scientists are still speculating on the cause of this worldwide death plague," one news anchor said. "Hundreds of thousands are reported dead; millions have been sickened by the mysterious smoke that seemingly came out of nowhere."

"They can't see the horses," Shelly said.

Vicki shook her head. "Somehow God made them visible to us but blinded unbelievers."

Reports from overseas showed horrific scenes in major cities on every continent. People lay dead in the streets. One amateur video showed a man standing on a street corner in Brussels. Smoke rose in the distance, and people ran in fear. One second the man stood by a lamppost. The next instant he was flying through the air, smashing into a huge window. They showed the video again in slow motion, but there were no clues as to how the man had moved so quickly.

One expert guessed that the earth was going through "a strange gravitational change, which makes some areas at risk for life-threatening events."

"They don't have a clue," Vicki said.

Shelly tried other channels. Those that weren't showing the news were disgusting. One program featured a man in a desperate search for a family member who had been buried alive. A ticking clock was positioned at the bottom of the screen. At first, Vicki thought it was a movie.

"This is real," Shelly said in disbelief.

"Turn to something else."

Shelly switched to the next channel. A man in black robes and a mask stood inside a five-pointed star. It looked like he was praying.

"Turn it off," Vicki said.

Shelly did. "What was that?"

"Exactly what Tsion Ben-Judah predicted. People love themselves and their sin too much. Tsion said we'd see more drug use, murder, gross sexual stuff, and . . ."

"And what?"

"I think that guy was leading people in a prayer, but it wasn't to God. I think he was praying to demons."

Shelly shivered.

"The other channels are probably worse."

The girls lay in the dark, talking and trying to fall asleep, but the images they had seen on television were too much.

When the sun came up, Vicki and Shelly dressed and put their things in the car. They waited until they thought they heard Conrad moving around and knocked.

The kids ate some snacks and got back on the road. Vicki sat in front and let Shelly have the backseat so she could rest.

"You guys didn't sleep?" Conrad said.

Vicki shook her head. "How much longer until we're at the schoolhouse?"

"If we push hard enough, we could be there tonight."

———————————————

Judd awoke to a quiet house. Yitzhak had asked everyone who was staying there to keep as quiet as possible out of respect for Nada's family and Sam. Judd found Nada's mother at the kitchen table alone. She pulled out a chair and said, "Sit."

The woman had said very little in Judd's presence since he had met her. He wondered if it was cultural or if she was ashamed of her English. Judd said, "All this time I've never known your first name."

The woman smiled. "Lina."

Judd nodded. "I read Nada's note. Did she write it in jail?"

"Yes. She told me a little about her concerns and said she wanted to talk to you when we were released. I told her she should write down her feelings so she would remember everything. I never dreamed she would die." Lina looked away and closed her eyes.

"I don't know if she was right," Judd said. "Maybe I

was concerned about what your husband thought about us—"

"What about her belief that there is someone else?"

Judd sighed. "I have friends back home that I met after the Rapture. But I'm not sure—"

Lina put a hand on Judd's shoulder. "Forgive me. I do not like to give personal advice when it's not asked for."

"Go ahead."

"Nada spoke very highly of you. She said you were a gentleman in every way. But she had a gift for knowing things. The longer you two knew each other, the more she felt like there was someone standing between you and her. If this is true, you must return to your home and find out."

Judd ran a hand through his hair. The only person he was remotely interested in was Vicki, and they had fought so much. He didn't know what to think.

"Jamal and I agree that you should stay here as long as you need to. Frankly, it may take a while to get back to the States with the judgment that has come."

"Does your husband know about this?"

Lina shook her head. "All he knows is that he has lost his only daughter. She was such a joy to him. When she was a little girl, he would take her everywhere. When he was at work, she would wait at the window until afternoon watching for him. It was very difficult for him when she became interested in you."

"That's why I tried to be careful. The trip to New Babylon was totally Nada's idea."

Lina smiled. "I understand. Even when she was small,

she had wild ideas. She collected kangaroos. Stuffed. Porcelain. She cut out pictures of kangaroos and taped them to the wall of her bedroom. It was no surprise to me that she disappeared one day. We found her walking on the street, several blocks from our house, with a suitcase full of clothes and her kangaroos."

"Where was she going?"

"Australia. She had read an article in the newspaper that said there are many kangaroos there. She said she was prepared to take a bus if she got too tired."

Judd laughed out loud. That was Nada all right. Stowing away in a Global Community airplane was a piece of cake compared to her trip to Australia. "How old was she?"

"Seven, I think," Lina said, the tears starting again. "I believe you when you say it was her idea."

"I'm not sure how soon we'll go home. So if it's okay with your family then, I'd like to stay here awhile longer until we've arranged the flight."

Lina hugged Judd. "May God bless you and keep you safe."

Mark Eisman was excited to read anything Tsion Ben-Judah had posted on his Web site, but when Tsion sent him a personal note late one night, Mark was thrilled. The file attached was Tsion's latest message to fellow believers around the world.

I am sending you this a few hours before this hits the Web site, Tsion wrote. *Please work your magic to make it understandable to young people.*

Mark went to work and was almost finished when he heard Darrion sound an alarm. "There are headlights coming up the road!"

"Maybe it's Vicki and the others," Mark said, rushing to the balcony for a better look. Lenore wasn't far behind. Tolan cried downstairs.

"It's not them," Charlie shouted from the kitchen. "It looks like a small car. Could be GC!"

"Everybody to the basement," Mark yelled. "We take no chances."

As the others ran downstairs, Mark unplugged the laptop and grabbed the important files.

"What's all the commotion?" Janie said, rubbing her eyes.

"Unknown car's coming up the road. Get to the hide-out."

"Not me. I'm not going to that dungeon again."

"Fine. If it's the GC, you'll be the first one they catch."

Janie scrambled down the steps behind Mark. They were almost to the basement when Mark heard the car's horn. "The signal! It's Vicki!"

The kids rushed upstairs and greeted their friends. Vicki took Tolan in her arms and squeezed him tightly. "You're getting so big!"

Janie headed back to her room while everyone else settled in the kitchen.

"Don't you want to hear what happened?" Vicki said.

"Tell me in the morning," Janie said.

Vicki found Melinda and gave her a hug as she squeezed in with the others. She couldn't believe she was finally back among her friends.

Conrad explained what had happened to the cell phone and the computer. Shelly described what had happened with the bandits in Colorado and how their van had been totaled.

The newest believer, a girl named Jenni, laughed and said, "I'll take the car over the van any day."

"Did they take your money?" Lenore said.

Vicki described the interaction with the three thieves. The kids gasped when they heard the story of the horses and riders and what they had done to the thieves.

Vicki took over and went through many of the stops they had made across the country. She wanted to tell the others about Jeff Williams, but she knew she couldn't. "We met a relative of someone in the Trib Force," Vicki said. "We need to pray for this guy and his dad."

"Who is it?" Darrion said.

"I promised I wouldn't say."

Mark excused himself and returned a few minutes later with a stack of pages an inch thick.

"What's that?" Vicki said.

"Read it," Mark said. "It's feedback."

Vicki read the first page but couldn't continue. She passed the stack to Shelly.

"These are messages from people we met?" Shelly said.

"All but the last few pages," Mark said. "Those are more requests for you to come teach."

Vicki took the stack back and glanced through the pages. She recognized most of the names. Each person had a story to tell about how God had used Vicki, Conrad, and Shelly in their lives. "I don't know what to say," Vicki finally said.

"You can read those tomorrow," Mark said, pulling out another printout. "This is even more exciting."

"What is it?" Melinda said.

"Tsion Ben-Judah's latest message to believers." Mark looked at his watch. "It's supposed to be released on the Web in a few minutes. But I have an advance copy. And you're not going to believe what's in here."

7

VICKI wanted to sleep, but she wanted to hear what Tsion had said even more. As Mark read the letter, changed slightly for younger readers, she felt like she was taking a drink of cold water after a long journey across the desert.

> *"My dear brothers and sisters in Christ, my heart is heavy as I write to you. While the 144,000 evangelists raised up by God are seeing millions come to Christ, the one-world religion continues to become more powerful and—I must say it—more revolting. Preach it from the mountaintops and into the valleys: There is one God and one Mediator between God and man, the Man Christ Jesus.*
>
> *"The deadly demon locusts prophesied in Revelation 9 finally died out after torturing millions. Many who were bitten at the end of that plague have recovered only three months ago.*

"While many gave their lives to God after seeing this horrible judgment, most have become even more set in their ways. It should have been obvious to the leader of the Enigma Babylon One World Faith that followers of that religion suffered everywhere in the world. But we followers of Christ, the so-called rebels—enemies of toler-ance—were spared."

Darrion shook her head. "Makes you wonder why anyone wouldn't believe the truth about God."

Vicki glanced at Melinda. The girl looked down at the table as Mark continued.

"We can be thankful that in this time of turmoil, our beloved preachers in Jerusalem continue to prophesy and win converts to Christ. They do this in that formerly holy city that now must be compared to Egypt and Sodom.

"By now you know that the sixth Trumpet Judgment, or the second woe of Revelation 9, has begun. I was correct in assuming the 200 million horsemen are spiri-tual and not physical beings. But I was wrong to think they would be invisible. I have spoken with people who have seen these beings kill by fire and smoke and sulfur as the Scripture predicts. Yet unbelievers charge we are making this up."

"I saw them, and I never want to see them again," Shelly said.

"It is helpful to know this current plague was created by the releasing of four angels bound in the Euphrates

River. We know that these are fallen angels, because nowhere in Scripture do we ever see good angels bound. These were apparently bound because they wanted to create chaos on earth. Now they are free to do so. In fact, the Bible reveals they were prepared for a specific hour, day, month, and year."

Melinda raised a hand. "I don't get it. I thought angels were good."

"They were all created by God to follow him," Vicki said. "But a third of the angels followed Satan and became demons. Angels only got one chance to choose."

"I'm glad I'm not an angel," Charlie said. "It took me a long time to decide to follow God."

"What's the deal with the river Tsion mentioned?" Shelly said.

"I'm getting to that," Mark said. He turned a page and read:

"It is significant that the four angels have been in the Euphrates. It is the most prominent river in the Bible. It bordered the Garden of Eden, was a boundary for Israel, Egypt, and Persia, and is often used in Scripture as a symbol of Israel's enemies. It was near this river that man first sinned, the first murder was committed, the first war fought, the first tower built in defiance against God, and where Babylon was built. Babylon is where idol worship started. The children of Israel were taken there as prisoners, and it is there that the final sin of man will culminate."

"That means Nicolae is going to get clobbered one day," Charlie said to Melinda.

Mark smiled and continued.

> *"Revelation 18 predicts that Babylon will be the center of business, religion, and world rule, but also that it will eventually fall to ruin, for strong is the Lord God who judges her."*

Mark moved to a blackboard and wrote:

R
25%
75%
25%
50%

"What do those numbers mean?" Shelly said.

"I studied what Tsion wrote and came up with this chart," Mark said.

"I'll bet the *R* is for Rapture," Darrion said.

"Right. Tsion told us the horses and riders will kill a third of the population alive right now." He pointed to the *R*. "After the Rapture came a great war, an earthquake, and meteors. All of that killed 25 percent of the people alive after the disappearances. That left 75 percent of the people who weren't taken away by God. Follow closely. One-third of 75 percent is 25 percent, so the current wave of death will leave only 50 percent of the people left behind at the Rapture."

Vicki shook her head. "And the worst is yet to come."

"This next section is a little difficult," Mark continued. "Tsion thinks God wants people to come to him, but this latest judgment might be preparation for the final battle between good and evil. He's weeding out the people who won't accept him."

"I don't understand," Shelly said.

"Let me read," Mark said.

> *"The Scriptures foretell that those unbelievers who do survive will refuse to turn from their wickedness. They will insist on continuing worshiping idols and demons, and engaging in murder, sorcery, sexual immorality, and theft. Even the Global Community's own news operations report that murder and theft are on the rise, and idol and demon worship are actually applauded in the new tolerant society."*

"So God is taking away people who would be against him in the big battle?" Charlie said.

"Exactly," Mark said.

"So how much longer will the horsemen be around?" Darrion said.

"Tsion believes it may continue four more months, until the three-and-a-half-year anniversary of the treaty between Nicolae and Israel."

"Which will also be the end of our friends Eli and Moishe," Vicki said.

"They're going away?" Charlie said.

"In the due time, the Antichrist will execute them," Vicki said. "But they won't stay dead."

"Here's the bad news for us," Mark said, finding his place in the letter.

> *"This will usher in a period when many more believers will be martyred."*

"What's that mean?" Charlie said.

"Killed because you believe in Jesus," Conrad said.

The room fell silent. Vicki thought of the adult Tribulation Force and those believers who even worked inside the Global Community. Could they survive for long when they were employed by the enemy of God? What about Buck Williams and Rayford Steele? Vicki closed her eyes and wondered how many in this room would make it to the Glorious Appearing of Christ.

"Let me finish the rest of this, and we'll get some sleep," Mark said.

> *"Many of you have written and asked how a God of love and mercy could pour out such awful judgments upon the earth. God is more than a God of love and mercy. The Scriptures say God is love, yes. But they also say he is holy, holy, holy. He is just, as in justice. His love was expressed in the gift of his Son as the means of salvation. But if we reject this love gift, we fall under God's judgment.*
>
> *"I know that many hundreds of thousands of readers of my daily messages must visit this site not as believers but as searchers for truth. So permit me to write directly to you if you do not call yourself my brother or sister in*

Christ. I plead with you as never before to receive Jesus Christ as God's gift of salvation. The sins that the stubborn unbelievers will not give up will run out of control during the last half of the Tribulation, referred to in the Bible as the Great Tribulation.

"Imagine this world with half its population gone. If you think it is bad now with millions having disappeared in the Rapture, children gone, services and conveniences affected, try to fathom life with half of all civil servants gone. Firemen, policemen, laborers, executives, teachers, doctors, nurses, scientists . . . the list goes on. We are coming to a period where survival will be a full-time occupation."

Vicki glanced at Melinda. She was hanging on every word of Tsion's letter.

"I would not want to be here without knowing God was with me, that I was on the side of good rather than evil, and that in the end, we win. Pray right now. Tell God you recognize your sin and need forgiveness and a Savior. Receive Christ today, and join the great family of God. Sincerely, Tsion Ben-Judah."

Mark folded the pages and put them in his pocket.

Lenore said, "You did a great job making that understandable." All the kids agreed, then, one by one, stood and headed off to bed.

Shelly hugged Conrad. "Thanks for all the driving you did."

"My pleasure, little lady," Conrad said in a mock cowboy voice. He laughed, and Shelly winked at Vicki.

"Wait a minute," Vicki whispered. "Are you interested in Conrad?"

Shelly yawned. "I'd love to stay up and talk, but I'm pretty tired."

"Not fair!" Vicki said, but Shelly was already out of the room.

Melinda sat alone at the table. Vicki put an arm around her. "You want to talk?"

"I don't trust the others like I do you."

"I'm glad you trust me."

"When they told me about those horses and riders, I freaked. Getting stung by the locust was bad enough, but this next thing sounds awful."

"It will be. It is. But you don't have to be afraid. If you'll just—"

"I know. All I have to do is believe like you guys." Melinda turned. "I don't want to do this simply because I'm scared."

"Understood, but God's trying to get your attention."

"He's doing a pretty good job of it." Melinda looked out the window. "I had nightmares after they told me."

"Nightmares?" Vicki said, stifling a smile.

"What?"

Vicki put a hand to her head. "I'm sorry. I'm just really tired. We were talking about the horses, and you said you had night*mares*. Bad joke."

Melinda smiled. "You're crazy. That's one thing I like

about you. A lot of church people I met would never laugh."

Vicki snorted and put a hand over her mouth. "My mom used to call this the tired sillies. We'd laugh our heads off late at night at the dumbest things."

When Vicki settled, Melinda said, "Maybe that's one thing that scares me. If I believe like you guys, I'm afraid I'll never have any fun again."

"I used to think the same thing. Church people seemed so stiff and uptight, like if they cracked a smile their face would break. But the believers I've met since the disappearances are the real deal. They're serious about their beliefs, but there's something different."

"They're happy on the inside."

Vicki nodded. "Yeah. God can give you joy, even in the middle of the worst things anyone on earth has faced. He puts something indescribable in your heart. He gives you hope."

Melinda nodded and looked away. "I want that," she whispered. "I don't want to live scared anymore. In my dreams, those horses had big hooves, and they were tromping all over people. One stood by my bed and breathed on me."

"To be honest, those horses and riders were even worse than your nightmares." Vicki described the heads of the horses, the tails, and the fire and smoke that came from their mouths and noses.

The more Vicki said, the more worried Melinda looked. "How can you see that and not be terrified?"

"I was. And so were Conrad and Shelly. But after we

figured out it was a judgment from God, we knew we wouldn't get hurt."

Melinda brushed hair from her face. "You've done a lot for me. You helped me when Felicia died, when my feet got frostbitten, and even after those locusts bit me. I know you care."

"Believe me, God cares so much more for you than I ever could."

"Maybe I'm one of those weeds God's getting rid of," Melinda said.

"What do you mean?"

"In that letter from Dr. Ben-Judah, Mark said there were some people who would reject God and just go on doing what they wanted. Maybe I'm one of them."

Vicki put a hand on Melinda's shoulder. "I've seen how you listen when I teach. I saw you listening to the letter. I think you want to know God."

"I could never be as good as you and the rest."

"You don't have to be good—"

"If somebody came and tried to arrest me and threatened to kill me like I did to you guys, I'd never let them stay here. I'd have sent me back to the GC as fast as I could."

"Let God work on your heart, Melinda. You'll be surprised at what he can do. I was just like you. I thought religion was for people who had it all together. But God takes you like you are. He wants to come in and help change you from the inside out. He can take away the fear."

Melinda closed her eyes and clenched her teeth.

Vicki knew there was a battle raging. She felt Melinda needed a challenge. "What do you believe about Jesus?"

Melinda sighed. "I think . . . I think he was God, like you've said."

"Do you believe he died in your place, to take away your sin?"

"Not if I'm one of those weeds."

"Stop it," Vicki said. "Don't pass up this chance. I can tell God is working on you. Let him do it."

"Okay," Melinda said. She rolled up her sleeves and put her hands on her knees.

"Do you believe Jesus died for you?"

"Yeah, I think he did."

"He's offering you a gift right now. Do you want to accept it?"

Melinda paused, then looked up. "I'd like that a lot."

"Then pray with me."

As Vicki prayed, Melinda repeated the words. "God in heaven, I'm sorry for the bad things I've done. I believe you died in my place to pay for my sin. Right now I want to receive the gift of eternal life that you offer. Make me a new person. Be my Lord and my Savior from this moment on. In Jesus' name. Amen."

Melinda looked at Vicki and gasped. "When did you get that thing on your forehead?"

JUDD kept to himself and tried to deal with Nada's death alone. He awoke in the middle of the night, sweating. The whole experience felt like a bad dream. Surely Nada would walk through the door any minute, and everything would be all right. But what had happened wasn't a dream. Each time he awoke and realized she was gone, he felt a stab in the heart.

Mr. Stein asked to speak with Judd. "When my wife died, it was very difficult. Since my daughter had left my faith and had become a believer in Christ, I felt alone. I responded to my wife's death by withdrawing. That wasn't all bad, but there came a point when I had to talk with someone."

Judd nodded. "I guess Sam is going through the same thing."

"Yes. He came to me yesterday, and we had a long talk. It is difficult for him since his father never responded to the message of Christ."

"That's a tough one. I know it'll be good to talk with someone, but I just don't feel . . ." Judd's voice trailed off.

"I am available when you're ready."

Lionel came in the room. "Did you hear what happened to Mac McCullum?"

"Mac who?" Mr. Stein said.

"The pilot who flew us to New Babylon," Judd said. "What's up?"

"A few days ago Mac's plane was attacked," Lionel said.

Judd raced to the computer and looked at the information Lionel had downloaded. The first reports were sketchy. Officials feared that the supreme commander, Leon Fortunato, and the others on the Condor 216 had all been killed by the mysterious smoke and fire. Later reports told a different story. The plane had landed in Johannesburg, South Africa, for a planned meeting with one of Nicolae Carpathia's regional potentates. It was ambushed by gunmen who believed Carpathia was on the plane. Mac McCullum was hailed a hero by Leon Fortunato.

Judd pulled up a video clip from a news conference Fortunato had held not long after the incident. "I was prepared for a meeting with Regional Potentate Rehoboth, but what I received was nothing short of an assassination attempt. Though there was a hail of bullets, I was able to escape. If it had not been for the quick thinking of myself and the flight crew, we would all be dead right now."

Fortunato praised Mac McCullum for "putting his body between the would-be assassins and myself."

Fortunato promised a ceremony honoring the pilots as heroes as soon as they had recuperated from their wounds.

"Why would Mac save Fortunato's life?" Lionel said.

"I can't wait to talk to him and get the inside scoop," Judd said.

Vicki slept until late the next afternoon. She wanted to tell the others about Melinda. She went to the kitchen to get something to eat but found no one. The front room was empty as well. Finally, Vicki discovered a group of kids in the computer room. Mark was leading them in a review of all of Tsion Ben-Judah's Internet messages. Melinda was in the middle of the group, listening intently.

Mark welcomed Vicki, and Melinda beamed. "I asked to hear some of those messages again," Melinda said. "I think a lot of it went over my head the first time, but now it's making more sense."

Janie walked by and spotted Vicki. She yawned and said, "So, you're back. Great."

Melinda stepped forward. "I did it, Janie. I finally became a believer. You should too."

Janie shook her head. "Just what I need. Another Holy Roller who wants to sign me up." Janie looked at Vicki. "You guys don't quit, do you?"

Vicki bit her lip and kept quiet.

"You know the mark they've talked about?" Melinda said. "It's real. As soon as I finished praying, I saw it on Vicki's forehead."

"Sure you did," Janie said. She looked at the others and cursed. "Don't you think it's bad enough that we get stung by the worst-looking creatures ever to fly over the earth? Now you scare this girl into joining your little religious club."

"I don't believe this," Vicki muttered.

"It didn't happen that way," Melinda said. "I asked God to forgive me, and he did. He loves you, and he wants—"

Janie held up a hand. "Give it a rest. Haven't you seen all the people dying around the world? You think a loving God would allow that?"

"He's trying to get your attention," Melinda said.

"No. He's not there or he'd do something about all this. The only person you can trust right now is Nicolae Carpathia."

Melinda stood, a frightened look on her face. She went to the window.

"What is it?" Mark said.

"Something outside . . . I was right. There they are."

A herd of horses stood on the other side of the river. The riders looked toward the schoolhouse. Suddenly, a few of the horses moved over the water.

"They're coming!" Melinda gasped.

Janie looked out the window. "Who's coming? I don't see anything."

"We have to get her downstairs!" Melinda said. "It's her only hope."

Vicki reached for Janie, but the girl jerked away. "You're not taking me down there!"

Melinda grabbed Janie's arms and held them behind her. Janie struggled to get free, but Mark and Conrad grabbed her legs. Together they rushed the screaming girl down the stairs and into the lowest chamber of the schoolhouse.

Vicki watched in horror as the horses and riders moved effortlessly across the surface of the river. It was like seeing a horror movie. The riders didn't speak. They simply stared at the schoolhouse. The horses snorted smoke, but no fire. Vicki heard coughing and screaming below and rushed downstairs.

"She's having a hard time breathing!" Mark yelled. "Bring some wet cloths."

Vicki ran to the kitchen and found some towels and ran them under the water faucet. She jumped back as a horse stuck its lionlike head in the window. It gnashed its teeth and snarled.

Vicki took the cloths below. Janie grabbed them from her and put them over her mouth. The smoke had penetrated the walls of the house. The kids could see it, but they couldn't smell it.

Janie's tongue stuck out of her mouth as she coughed. It was clear the girl wouldn't last long if the smoke continued.

"We have to do something," Vicki said. She rushed upstairs and onto the balcony.

Lenore stood holding Tolan close to her chest. "They're huge," she whispered, "just like you said."

A ring of horses had circled the house. The rider in front of Vicki was right at eye level. She stared into the horseman's face. The being seemed angry and determined. He wore a brightly colored breastplate that gleamed in the sun. This small detachment of the demon army was there to destroy another unbeliever.

Vicki mustered her courage and spoke. "Leave this place now! In the name of Jesus Christ, the almighty God, I command you to leave."

The horseman's face was dark, like a bottomless pit. He turned and looked at Vicki, and she saw the monstrous, evil face with sharp teeth and a look that defied description.

Vicki turned away and closed her eyes. *Father, I ask you to send these things away. If they stay, there's no way Janie will ever become a believer. Please, have mercy on her and make these things leave.*

Suddenly, the horse reared and waved its hooves in the air. Fire shot from its nostrils and soared over the roof of the schoolhouse. The fire fell like molten lava on the ground, burning trees and bushes. The schoolhouse was unharmed.

The horseman controlled the demon animal and glared at Vicki. He didn't say anything, but he seemed to communicate with the others that it was time to leave. They turned from the house and followed the river until they were out of sight.

Janie had inhaled some of the foul-smelling smoke, but she was still alive when Vicki reached her. They brought her upstairs and tried to help her breathe. When she stopped coughing and gagging, she asked, "What happened?"

Melinda began to answer, but Vicki held up a hand. "Just rest and we'll talk about it later."

Downstairs, Melinda looked confused. "Don't you want her to believe?"

"I do," Vicki said, "but her heart is hard. I don't know what else God could do to soften it, but I know if we go in there and try to tell her some cosmic horsemen made her cough, she's going to laugh and say we're making it up."

"It took me a while to realize the truth," Melinda said. "Maybe she just needs a little more time."

"Which is what we don't have," Mark said. He called everyone together in the computer room. "I just got a message from Carl in Florida. He says the GC is going ahead with their plans for the satellite schools. A special order was sent out yesterday to the directors of the project to have their centers ready for students within the week."

"All this death and devastation and they're starting a school?" Lenore said.

"Carl said they want to put their own spin on what's going on."

Shelly shook her head. "A third of their classes are going to be gone before the horsemen get done."

"We need to figure out a plan about the school nearest us," Conrad said.

Mark scratched his chin. "Yeah, but there's something else Carl said that worries me."

Vicki looked over Mark's shoulder as he read the e-mail out loud. "*I told you that part of the reason the GC is starting these schools is to identify possible recruits for their Morale Monitors. Now they have something new brewing. I*

81

haven't been able to find out exactly what it is, but I'm positive it won't be good for believers."

Vicki wondered what new things the GC could dream up to hurt believers. If Tsion Ben-Judah was right, the next few years were going to be anything but easy for those who followed Christ.

Judd slowly came out of his shell over the next few days. He went to Sam and sat with him for a few hours, not saying a word.

Finally, the boy opened up and talked about his father. "It feels like my prayers were wasted," Sam said. "I prayed so hard for him. What went wrong?"

"God wants people to know him, but he gives us a choice. You and I chose to accept God's gift. Your dad rejected it."

"I picture my father suffering now. I wish I could take his place."

Judd knelt by Sam. "This is going to hurt for a long time, but you're not responsible for your dad's choice. The only person God holds you responsible for is you. You can pray and plead with others, but it's their decision."

Sam nodded and thanked Judd. "You're right about it taking a long time. I can't imagine not feeling this ache in my heart."

"Yeah, me too."

Judd watched the news reports about the horsemen. Lionel, Sam, and the others gathered around when the ceremony was held in honor of Captain Montgomery

(Mac) McCullum and Mr. Abdullah Smith. Leon Fortunato took the stage in front of thousands and explained that the attempt on his life was actually a planned assassination of Nicolae Carpathia.

"However, while the gunmen succeeded in destroying the plane and killing four staff personnel, heroic measures by both the pilot and first officer saved my life. The assassins died as a result of the immediate response by Global Community Peacekeeping Forces."

Judd noticed a slight smile on Mac's face as Leon talked.

"Is Abdullah a believer as well?" Mr. Stein asked.

"I think Mac mentioned that he was," Judd said.

Fortunato introduced Nicolae Carpathia. "We honor these brave men today. In the face of overwhelming odds and much firepower, these two put their lives on the line for the good of the Global Community. On behalf of the loyal citizens of the Global Community, I thank you."

The crowd went wild as Mac and Abdullah stepped forward and shook hands with the potentate. "I present you now with the Golden Circle, the prize for valor, with thanks." Carpathia stood back, beaming.

As they watched the coverage, Judd scanned through other news he had missed. He sat up straight when he came upon information about a plane crash. It had been reported some time ago, but it still made him nearly sick to his stomach as he read it aloud.

" 'A large private aircraft has crashed off the coast of Portugal. The plane's lone passenger was Hattie Durham, former personal assistant to Global Community Potentate Nicolae Carpathia. The pilot, Samuel Hanson of Baton Rouge, Louisiana, United States of North America, is also presumed dead.' "

"That's the Hattie we know, right?" Lionel said.

Judd nodded. "I have to talk to Mac about this."

9

JUDD dialed Mac's secure phone later that night.

Mac answered and said, "Is that you, Rayford?"

"It's Judd Thompson, Mr. McCullum."

"Hey, what a surprise! You guys finally make it to Israel?"

Mac grew silent as Judd explained what had happened to Nada and her family. Judd choked up twice as he recounted the events, but he finally got through it. Telling it to Mac was difficult, but it felt good for someone on the adult Trib Force to know what was going on.

"Well, I'm sure sorry to hear about Nada. She was a good kid. I admired her courage. We need more people like her. I'll ask Rayford and the others to pray for you and her family."

"I'd appreciate that, sir."

"It must be doubly tough after what happened to that Rudja guy."

"Pavel's dad?" Judd said. "What happened?"

"I'm sorry. I thought you knew. Something must have gone haywire at the funeral for his son. The GC kept it quiet, but they were hunting him for a couple of days afterward. They finally got a tip from one of his friends. Seems the guy was trying to tell him the truth about God and his friend ratted him out."

"Where is Mr. Rudja now?"

"They arrested him and charged him with rebellious acts against the Global Community. He's in prison with a life sentence."

Judd shook his head. He told Mac about Pavel's funeral. "You can bet he's leading even more people to faith inside that prison."

"You got that right," Mac said.

"I called because I have a couple questions. The first is about Hattie Durham. Is it true she died in a plane crash?"

Mac sighed. "That was a big GC ruse. We think she's alive. Rayford said Hattie was ticked when she left the States. She's after Carpathia."

"She wants to kill him?"

"Rayford's trying to find her before she blows their cover or gets herself killed."

"Where is she?" Judd said.

"Europe somewhere, we think. Biding her time until she can get close to the big guy. What else you want to know?"

"We all watched the ceremony with you, Carpathia, and Fortunato."

Mac chuckled. "Yeah, the chance of a lifetime."

"What really happened in Johannesburg?"

"Well, it wasn't like Leon said. To hear him tell it, the GC was on the scene and took care of the assassins immediately."

"If the GC didn't kill them, who did?"

"The horses and riders. We were on our way to a meeting in Africa when my copilot thought he saw horses in the air."

"Did you see them too?"

"I thought he was dreaming or something, but a split second later I saw them. They filled the sky. Abdullah jerked the plane around until we figured out we could go right through them. But Leon and the crew in the back were coughing and sputtering because of the smoke. We landed in Khartoum with two dead and four gasping for air."

"I had no idea the horses could be that high."

"Me either. But we heard an awful lot of Mayday calls from pilots who were going down."

"So you flew from there to Johannesburg?"

"Yeah, Leon was hot to meet with the former head of the United Nations. But when his limo pulled up to the plane, Leon crashed into the cockpit and told us to take off."

"The assassins," Judd said.

"Yeah. I blasted them with some jet exhaust, but they got their guns and caught up. They blew out the tires of the Condor, and we were stuck.

"That's when I noticed there wasn't another plane in sight. No emergency vehicles. Nothing."

"It was a setup."

"Exactly. I didn't think we were going to survive. We

had two pistols in the cargo hold, but by then they'd opened up on us and ripped holes in the fuselage. We were pinned down on the floor of the plane."

"How *did* you survive?"

"I got on the radio and called in a Mayday. That's when they threw in the concussion bomb and the plane filled with smoke. We were on fire with nowhere to go. Abdullah and I opened the main cabin door, and we all tumbled out before the fire caught up to us."

"Weren't the assassins waiting for you?" Judd said.

"Tell you the truth, I shut my eyes so tight I thought my cheekbones were in my forehead. I figured I'd open my eyes in heaven. There was smoke and fire, gunshots, Leon screaming for God to help him . . . I thought we were dead. I fell on top of Leon as we hit the ground, and a bullet ripped open my right shoulder. Another hit my right hand, and I was waiting for a shot to the head.

"Then everything got real still. I thought maybe the gunmen knew they had us and were walking up to finish the job. When I looked up, the smoke was so heavy I could hardly see past my nose. Then I caught sight of them."

"The gunmen?"

"The cavalry," Mac said. "I don't know if you've seen them, but these things were hovering off the ground, galloping and trotting around. They looked even worse than the locusts. They swished their snake tails and snorted fire and smoke. They were only about a hundred feet away. Two of the assassins were near the plane, dead. They had been close enough to kill us all with their next shots. The other one ran down the runway."

"So that's why I saw that little smile on your face when Fortunato said the GC had killed the assassins."

Mac laughed. "I couldn't help it."

"So you saved Fortunato's life?"

"Not on purpose, but it worked out that way."

"Spend much time in the hospital?"

"Yeah, I had some major work done on my shoulder and hand. They saved all the fingers, but I can't do much with them. My thumb won't bend. Best thing that came out of that ordeal is that we met two believers who work with the International Commodity Co-op. A couple from Oklahoma saved our hides with Leon. It's a long story, but a happy ending."

"What happens now?"

"For the next few weeks we'll be off on a tour. The ten regional potentates are supposed to roll out the red carpet for Leon so he can personally invite them to the Gala in September."

Judd thanked Mac for the information and asked his opinion on getting back to the States.

"Travel is still difficult with the plague. There's no telling how long that will last. The GC estimates about 10 percent of the population has died since the start of the smoke and fire and sulfur. That means about three times that will eventually die. If you can find a commercial flight, take it."

It took Vicki a few days to recover from their trip. She had lived out of a suitcase for so long that she had a hard time adjusting to her own room. Each morning as she awakened, she thanked God for their travels, the people she had met, and the believers who had been encouraged.

The kids met and decided who would and would not attend the nearest GC satellite school when it opened. Conrad volunteered to scout out the site and the best way to get there from the schoolhouse.

Early one Friday afternoon Mark called for Vicki from the computer room. "I think you'll want to see this."

Vicki looked at the screen. It was a message from the pastor in Arizona.

"It was sent to our address, so I read it. I hope that's okay."

The message read:

> Dear Vicki, Conrad, and Shelly,
>
> First, I can't thank you enough for the computer. It has really come in handy. I think you'll be pleased to know that your efforts here have paid off. The underground church is growing in Tucson. Many unbelievers who survived the horsemen's rampage have come to us with questions. The young believers you taught were able to clearly explain how to have a relationship with God, and many have become believers. I suspect the other areas you visited can say the same. You were truly a gift of God to us.
>
> The other exciting news concerns Jeff Williams. He has become a believer!

Vicki gasped and put her hand over her mouth. For a moment she couldn't read.

"Is he related to Buck?" Mark said.
Vicki nodded and looked at the screen.

Jeff stayed away from the church for a few days, then came back. We had a great talk. He went home without praying but knocked on my door at 3 A.M. He couldn't wait to tell me he had accepted Christ, and he wanted to be sure he had done it right. I could tell by the sign on his forehead that he had.

Jeff talked to his father the next day. He's not a believer yet, but they're both attending our church, and I have great hopes for Mr. Williams.

"I can't wait to tell Buck," Vicki said.
"Better read the last part," Mark said.

Jeff has asked that you not tell his brother any of this. He fears for Buck's life and thinks any contact with him will somehow endanger him. Please don't give him this information.

The pastor signed off, and Vicki quickly clicked the reply button. *Thank you for letting us know this wonderful news. We're excited about the new addition to the kingdom! We'll be praying for Jeff's father. Let us know if anything in that situation changes, and don't worry about us telling anyone. We'll keep the information to ourselves.*

Judd found Mr. Stein excitedly talking with other witnesses one day and asked what was going on.

Mr. Stein gathered Lionel, Sam, and Judd together. "The Lord spoke to me last night and told me there will be more opportunities for people to become believers in Christ. And God will do it right here in Jerusalem, under the nose of the most evil man on the face of the earth."

"What's the plan?" Lionel said.

"God showed me the faces of people who will come here from every part of the globe. Of course they will be here to celebrate Nicolae Carpathia's Gala, but God will meet them here, and he will use many of the witnesses who have been staying with Yitzhak."

"You mean, you'll just preach in the streets?" Sam said. "Eli and Moishe do that."

"True. But God revealed that something will happen during those events that will cause some to turn to him. When that happens, we will be there and I want you with me."

Lionel looked at Judd. "We've stayed this long, might as well stick it out and see what happens."

"I'm in too," Sam said.

"Let's get Jamal and Kasim in here," Judd said. "I want them to hear this."

Judd went to the family's room in the basement and found Jamal and Lina. "Where's Kasim?"

"Out," Jamal said.

Judd explained Mr. Stein's plan and asked the two to join them.

"No need," Jamal said. "I can assure you, we will stay until the week of the Gala."

Lina looked away. Something didn't feel right. As

Judd passed the back door, he noticed Kasim walking in the alley. He held something under his arm. Judd opened the door, and Kasim looked startled.

"Where've you been?" Judd said.

"I didn't know I had to check with you when I went out."

Judd squinted. "I didn't mean anything by it. I just wondered."

"Fine. Now if you'll excuse me." Kasim brushed by Judd and headed downstairs.

Judd called after him. "Mr. Stein has a plan to reach people during the Gala."

Kasim stopped and turned. "Whatever the plan is, I'm sure my family will be pleased to help. Excuse me."

Judd shook his head. Had he said something to offend Kasim and his father? Judd waited a moment, then followed him to the family's room.

"Did you get it?" Jamal said.

Kasim unzipped his jacket and paper rattled. "This is the best they had. It will reach the target from a great distance."

Lina interrupted, clearly upset. "I told you I do not like this. Nada is dead. Now you two want to join her."

"Don't worry," Jamal said. "In the crowd, no one will notice until it is too late."

Judd peeked around the curtain. Jamal inspected something. Judd realized the man was holding a high-powered pistol.

"Perfect. Nicolae Carpathia will pay for the pain he has caused us and the rest of the world."

JUDD walked back upstairs, reeling from what he had seen and heard. First Hattie Durham, and now Jamal and Kasim planned to kill Nicolae Carpathia. And who could blame them? After all they had been through, who wouldn't be angry enough to want to kill Nicolae?

Now what do I do? Judd thought.

"Did you find them?" Lionel said when Judd returned.

"They're busy."

Mr. Stein talked more about spreading the gospel during the Gala. Lionel suggested they print pamphlets in different languages. Sam thought of renting a huge hall and holding special meetings.

"Why not speak from one of the Global Community stages?" Mr. Stein said.

Judd laughed.

Mr. Stein stared at him. "I'm serious. If it's what God wants, perhaps he would make a way for someone to preach from the enemy's stage."

"I guess it could happen if God wants it to," Judd said, "but won't the GC crack down as soon as you get up there?"

Mr. Stein nodded. "Perhaps. But there must be a way."

Judd waited for a lull in the conversation. "I have another question. Would it be wrong for a believer to kill Nicolae?"

"Whoa," Lionel said. "Where'd you come up with that?"

"I'm just wondering. The guy's going to be killed anyway. Is it wrong?"

The kids looked at each other. Lionel shrugged. "He's supposed to come back to life, so it's not really going to be murder."

"What?" Sam said. "You mean, like some kind of vampire?"

"The Bible says the Antichrist will be killed and then wake up."

Mr. Stein sighed. "I haven't considered this. God does not permit murder. It is one of his commandments. But there are certain circumstances, in warfare for instance, where God tells his people to kill those who are against him. I would assume the Antichrist fits into this."

"Back up," Sam said. "How do you know this is supposed to happen?"

Mr. Stein grabbed a Bible and flipped to the book of Revelation. "In chapter 13 it talks about the beast that is Antichrist." He found the passage and read it aloud.

"'I saw that one of the heads of the beast seemed wounded beyond recovery—but the fatal wound was

healed! All the world marveled at this miracle and
followed the beast in awe.' "

"So, how's he supposed to be killed?" Sam said.
"Does it say?"

"In the following verses it talks about another person
who is able to deceive the world. This person requires
everyone to worship the one who was wounded. A later
verse refers to 'the beast who was fatally wounded and
then came back to life.' I take that to mean that Antichrist is to be wounded in the head by a sword. The
language there could be figurative, but I believe Tsion
Ben-Judah thinks the same, and he hasn't been wrong
yet."

"There's one thing for sure," Lionel said. "Whoever
does the killing will probably be put to death on the
spot."

"And Carpathia will come out looking more of a hero
than ever," Sam said.

Judd swallowed hard. Jamal and Kasim were in big
trouble. If they went through with their plan, the GC
could come after the entire group.

"Why does God even allow somebody like Carpathia
to live?" Sam said. "It doesn't make sense."

"God's plan has been in place since the beginning of
time," Mr. Stein said. "Satan and his evil angels and all
who follow them are merely part of God's divine design.
Satan is God's devil, and he only gets away with what
God allows him to."

"But if God knew all this bad stuff was going to
happen . . ." Sam paused and looked at Mr. Stein. His lip

quivered. "God knew my dad wouldn't respond to
the message, but he made him anyway. I don't understand."

Mr. Stein put a hand on Sam's shoulder. "And neither
do I. How can we understand someone whose wisdom
and knowledge are so far above our own? But I do know
this. If your father had never existed, neither would you.
And you would not have had the opportunity to follow
Christ."

Sam nodded. "I'm thankful I came to know God. I
guess there are some things I'll never understand."

"Know this," Mr. Stein said. "Satan and his followers
will be punished for their evil deeds. But the next few
months and years will be very dark for those who believe
in the one true God."

Judd looked up as someone walked into the room. It
was Kasim.

"So who do you think will actually kill Nicolae?"
Lionel said.

Kasim glanced at Judd.

"I would think the person who kills Nicolae will be
filled with anger," Mr. Stein said. "He will no doubt be
desperate, willing to sacrifice his life for something he
feels is right."

"Will the person be insane?" Lionel said.

"Perhaps," Mr. Stein said. "But he may believe it to be
the most sane thing he's ever done in his life. He will be
desperate but cunning. To get close enough to the potentate to inflict this kind of wound will be an impressive
accomplishment."

When they had finished talking among themselves, Kasim came to Judd. "We need to talk."

"Later."

"Tonight."

Over the next few days, Vicki taught Melinda as much as she could about the Bible, prophecy, and what they would experience in the Great Tribulation. Melinda soaked up the information. She asked good questions and took notes in a small, red notebook she kept with her at all times.

After their studies one afternoon, Vicki took Lenore's baby, Tolan, so Lenore could take a break. Vicki had always loved kids and figured that one day she would get married and have some of her own. She enjoyed baby-sitting, except for the wild kids in the trailer park where she used to live.

As she played with Tolan in front of the schoolhouse, she thought about the kids she used to run with and where they were. Most of them had probably died in one of the plagues.

Shelly brought Tolan's food and sat beside her. Vicki told her what she was thinking, and Shelly nodded. "Sometimes I play the what-if? game. You know, what if the Rapture hadn't happened? What if the Young Trib Force had never gotten together? What if I hadn't become a believer?"

"What are the answers?"

"For all the bad stuff that's happened to the world, I wouldn't change anything because now I know the truth."

Vicki nodded. "I was just thinking about who I might have married if things had stayed like they were."

"Did you have a steady boyfriend?"

"There were a bunch of guys I used to party with. I'm not proud of it, but it's the truth. If I'd stayed mixed up with them, I'd be an alcoholic or in jail or both."

"What about now? Where do you see yourself in a couple of years?"

"I don't know," Vicki said. She took Tolan by both hands and pulled him to a sitting position. "This is probably the most eligible bachelor among us."

"And the cutest," Shelly laughed.

Conrad drove the sports car up the long driveway. Vicki elbowed Shelly. "Did something happen between you and Conrad during the trip?"

"We did have a lot of time to talk." Shelly smiled. "Conrad's a nice guy. He sure cares a lot about you and the others."

Conrad sat down and asked to hold Tolan. Vicki handed the boy to him, and Conrad lay back and put him on his chest. Tolan giggled and tried to grab Conrad's nose.

"He's good with kids too," Vicki whispered.

Shelly rolled her eyes.

"What did you find out about the satellite school?" Vicki said.

Conrad handed Vicki a pamphlet. "Plenty. First session is a week from today. Kids are actually lining up to register."

Vicki studied the pamphlet. On the front was the

insignia of the Global Community. Nicolae Carpathia's face was at the top. Pictures of teenagers from around the world were shown underneath.

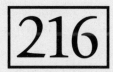

ANNOUNCING THE OPENING OF GLOBAL
COMMUNITY SATELLITE SCHOOL #1134.

The date of the opening sessions was given as well as registration times.

ALL STUDENTS TWENTY YEARS OF AGE
AND YOUNGER MUST SIGN UP. COME PREPARED
WITH AT LEAST TWO PIECES OF IDENTIFICATION.

"Are they fingerprinting?" Shelly said.

Conrad shook his head. "I don't think so. But they were unloading some big machines as I left. One of the workers said a new ID system is in the works."

Vicki felt a chill. "You know what that means. Pretty soon Carpathia will unveil his plans for making everyone take his identification."

"The mark of the beast?" Shelly said.

Vicki nodded and flipped the pamphlet open.

The world we see today is very different from the one
we knew a few years ago. People of all ages are looking

for answers. For young people, this is a stressful time. You've lost family and friends. You want to know what will happen in the future.

That's why Potentate Nicolae Carpathia and the leaders in education around the world have teamed to bring you Global Community Satellite Schools. You don't need math and science right now. You don't need tests in English composition. You need to know how to survive.

Potentate Carpathia wants every young person to fulfill his or her destiny. He says, "If you want to make a difference for the good of humankind, attend the opening session of the new satellite school in your area. You are the future of the Global Community. We need you."

The pamphlet gave more specific information about times and locations. "What about the plague of the horsemen?" Vicki said.

"The building they're using used to be some kind of civic center. They're claiming that it's airtight and smoke-proof."

"How can they claim that when the smoke even gets into airplanes?" Shelly said.

"They seem pretty confident," Conrad said.

The kids met later to finalize plans on who would attend. Vicki and Darrion already had fake IDs that Zeke Jr. had made for them. They all felt it too risky for Conrad to go, since he had been a Morale Monitor.

"I've decided I'm going," Melinda said.

"What?" Vicki said. "No way."

"I've been praying about it, and I think God wants me to get in the game again."

"You're in the game," Mark said, "but you have to be smart about how you play. The GC wanted you and Felicia dead."

"I know that. But it's been so long, they've probably forgotten about me. If not, I can get a phony ID just like you guys."

Mark shook his head. "I think you'd be more valuable to us here than in some GC prison."

"I appreciate your concern, but—"

"Let's let the group decide," Vicki said.

Everyone voted that Melinda should stay away from the satellite school.

Melinda sighed. "If that's what everybody thinks . . ."

"What's the plan once we're inside?" Darrion said.

"Spread out and see if we can find other believers. Our main job is to figure out the GC's agenda. If we get a chance to share God with somebody, we'll do it. But we have to be careful."

Janie walked in holding one of the GC pamphlets. "Did you guys see this? I want to go."

Vicki looked at the others. "I wouldn't recommend it."

Janie slammed the paper down on a table. "You guys think you know everything. You think Nicolae's the problem. Well, I think he's the answer. And if you're too stubborn—"

Vicki put up a hand. "Janie, you broke out of jail. You're a fugitive. That's why I don't think you should go. The GC will nab you. You don't want that."

Janie looked stunned. "Right. Well, I was going to put on a disguise. I'll do anything to get out of this place."

When Janie left, Mark said, "Maybe Janie going would be the best thing. The GC would catch her, and she becomes their problem."

"I've been praying for that girl ever since I became a believer," Lenore said. "I'd hate to see anything happen to her."

"How long do you keep praying for somebody?" Vicki said.

The room fell silent. Vicki wondered if there was any chance that Janie would ever believe.

11

JUDD was able to avoid Kasim that evening and the next morning, but Kasim cornered him the next night. Judd agreed to talk with him alone in a secluded room downstairs. Kasim's face had healed from the abuse he had taken at the GC jail, but he seemed in pain.

Before Kasim spoke Judd said, "I've been meaning to talk with you about Nada."

"This is not about her—"

"Please. It would help me."

Kasim crossed his legs and sat back. "What do you want to know?"

"We didn't have much contact in the final few weeks. Did she talk about me?"

"We couldn't get her to shut up about you. It was Judd this and Judd that." Kasim looked away. "I hurt her feelings."

"How?"

"She told us some story about the two of you meeting in a garden in New Babylon."

"I remember that."

"She went on and on about her feelings for you. I'd finally had it and said something like, 'Why don't you get married?' "

"Ouch."

"Yeah. I tried to apologize, but she wouldn't talk. My mother said not to bother her. We weren't together again until the GC cornered us."

"What happened?"

"Nada heard something suspicious, and my father went to check it out. We heard the commotion and ran for the fire escape.

"We were on the ground when they burst into the apartment. The squad cars found us with their lights. At the end of the street was a chain-link fence. Nada climbed it, but my pant leg caught at the top." Kasim shook his fists and closed his eyes. "It was such a stupid thing."

"It wasn't your fault."

"She came back to help. I yelled at her to go, but she was determined."

Judd looked at the floor. *That was Nada.*

"If she hadn't come back for me, she probably would have gotten away. And if she had gotten away . . ."

"Don't do this. I blamed myself for what happened, and it almost ate me up."

"Maybe you are to blame," Kasim said softly. "If you had loved my sister the way she loved you, she wouldn't be dead."

Judd stared at Kasim, his heart beating faster. He stood and said, "I'm not taking that."

Kasim grabbed Judd's arm and pulled him down. "Sit!"

Judd leaned close. "I loved your sister. I'd give anything to have her back. I'd take her place if I could. But you have no right to blame me for what happened."

"If you loved her, why didn't you get more serious? That's why she was so hurt by what I said. She knew you would never marry her."

Judd looked away. "Your sister knew me better than I know myself."

Kasim lowered his voice. "I'm sorry. I know you didn't want anything bad to happen to her." Kasim was quiet for a while. He rubbed his arms as if he were cold. Finally, he looked at Judd. "We have to talk about what you heard."

Judd raised an eyebrow.

"Don't play dumb. You saw something or heard something after I came in the other night."

"The GC will kill you if you go through with this."

"Who else knows about our plan?"

"No one. I brought up the question with Mr. Stein and the others. My biggest fear isn't that you'll go through with this. It's that you might succeed, and then the GC will be all over this place and anyone who had anything to do with you."

"The time for fear is past. Now is the time for action."

"Why? You're talking about killing the—"

Kasim put a finger to his lips. "From now on, refer to

this as Operation Gala. As to why, I had followed Carpathia as a god. I hung on every word. Now I see how evil he is and where he is leading the world. I don't want anyone to make the same mistake I did. I want to be the one to stop him."

"But you know from reading the Bible that it's not going to last."

Kasim leaned forward. "I don't care. We will do this thing. And whether you like it or not, you are part of our plan."

Judd put up his hands. "No way. If you want—"

Kasim interrupted. "We will leave you and your friends out of it and make sure there is no possible connection, but you must not tell anyone, not even your closest friend. Do you promise?"

"I can't promise that."

Kasim gripped Judd's arm again. "In memory of my sister, for the love you had for her, I beg you to keep our secret. Tell no one."

Judd took a breath and nodded. "All right. I promise."

Vicki inspected her photo ID as she waited in line at the satellite school. Her hair had grown since Zeke had dyed it, so Lenore and Shelly helped match the color in the picture. Once again she was Jackie Browne. Vicki wondered about the real Jackie. Who was she and how had she died?

Vicki handed the license to a woman at the front of the line and looked around for her friends. They had parked the car and split up, hoping to meet each other inside.

"Did you register ahead?" the woman said.

"No, I just found out about the school the other day."

The woman shook her head and clicked a computer keyboard. "I need two pieces of ID."

"The license is all I have left," Vicki said.

The woman frowned and handed her a form. "Fill this out and get back in line. I can't promise you'll get inside."

As Conrad had suggested, Vicki gave her address as an apartment building in a nearby town. In the space for the phone number she wrote "doesn't work." She finished and got back in line. After what seemed like days, she made it to the front again and saw a young woman who looked familiar. Her badge said Marjorie Amherst.

"These are the meeting times," Marjorie said. "Make sure you get to the first one. Someone very special is going to speak. If you have any language requirements, you can go to the back of the arena. We have radios for translations in just about any language."

Marjorie handed Vicki a wrist badge that had just come through a special printer. "This is a little warm. You'll need to wear it at all times. You won't be able to get in or out without it."

Finally, Vicki recognized the girl. She had been the valedictorian at Nicolae High when Judd graduated. Judd had said she worshiped Leon Fortunato. Judd had taken her place at the podium when she became too nervous to speak.

"Didn't you go to Nicolae High?" Vicki said.

"Yes, how did you know?"

"I was at your commencement ceremony."

Marjorie put out a hand, and Vicki shook it. "That was such a wonderful meeting until . . . well, you remember what happened."

"Right, that Judd guy got up and ruined everything."

Marjorie leaned forward. "There may be more of his kind around, but don't worry. We'll take care of them."

Vicki winked and smiled. "I'm glad."

Vicki walked through what looked like a huge metal detector. Global Community Morale Monitors stood nearby. Above the machine were two computer screens. The first flashed each person's name as he or she walked through. The second screen scanned each person for weapons.

Vicki wandered through the concrete hallways looking for any sign of Darrion, Mark, or Shelly. She looked for others who had the mark of the true believer as well but didn't find any. Vicki stopped in her tracks when she noticed a small booth set up near a side entrance. The sign above read Tsion Ben-Judah Material.

Vicki shook her head. *Who would be stupid enough to fall for that?* Since the meeting was about to begin, she went inside to find a seat.

The arena was packed. Some kids threw paper airplanes and even tried bodysurfing through the crowd. Finally, the lights dimmed, and the crowd cheered as the gigantic theater screen flickered to life.

The first image on-screen was a candle flame. A low

note sounded and rumbled throughout the darkened arena. As faces from across the country flashed on the screen, a deep-voiced announcer slowly said, "We have come from different places. From different backgrounds. All of us have lost much. Family. Friends. Homes. But we are not without hope."

Nicolae Carpathia's face appeared on the screen, and immediately the crowd rose and applauded. Some whistled. Others screamed. The music rose and drowned out the cheers. The announcer's voice eclipsed the noise. "One man. One mission. To bring peace to all people on earth. He is Potentate Nicolae Carpathia."

Vicki plugged her ears. A girl beside her punched her in the arm and shouted, "Stand up. It's really him!"

Vicki stood. Nicolae walked toward a podium in New Babylon. *Is this live?* she thought. Though he was thousands of miles away, Carpathia seemed to sense the worship. He held up both hands, smiled, then began.

"I greet you in the name of peace," Nicolae said, and again the audience went wild. Carpathia smiled again and raised his hands for quiet. "I welcome participants in this great movement of young people around the globe. In spite of the mysterious deaths we have seen in the last few weeks, you have chosen to gather and learn about the great mission before us.

"Never in the history of the world have we needed our young people more. In the words of a former president of the United States, I charge you to ask not what the Global Community can do for you—ask what you can do for the Global Community."

Again the crowd rose and cheered. The girl beside Vicki turned. "Isn't he great?"

"Yeah," Vicki said.

"If we are to make this world better," Carpathia continued, "if we are to succeed in our pursuit of world-wide peace, we will do so with your help."

The camera pulled in tight to Carpathia's face. The man was handsome; there was no question. He was blond, trim, and looked like a movie star. Vicki remembered what Buck Williams had said about Carpathia's ability to use mind control. Was he doing this now? And if so, would believers be affected?

As the potentate continued, his face positioned in the middle of the screen, video clips appeared around him. The scenes showed Carpathia holding babies, speaking at the United Nations, walking through cheering crowds, and consulting with other world leaders.

"The Global Community has brought a new ideal to all. Tolerance. We seek to get along with each other, to appreciate differences instead of fight about them. We embrace each other and accept these differences, for in the end they can make us stronger."

The music switched to a minor key, and Carpathia seemed to get more intense. "However, there are those who would oppose our peaceful objectives. People such as the two who inflict plague after deadly plague on the world."

The screen showed Eli and Moishe, the two witnesses at the Wailing Wall. The arena filled with boos and hisses.

"These evil men and those who follow their teaching must be stopped. And I guarantee you, they will be. I will deal with them at the upcoming celebration in Israel. There will be an end to the plagues, drought, famine, and bloody water. When I have dealt with them, we will see the end of rebellion and revolt against the most powerful and loving government that has ever existed."

"So much for tolerance," Vicki muttered.

But no one heard her. The music grew with Nicolae's speech and built to a screaming climax. Kids stood, fists raised in the air.

"I invite you all to join us, either in person or by way of these meetings, for a spectacle unparalleled in human history. The Gala in Jerusalem will be a supreme celebration of peace and tolerance."

Nicolae raised his hands, and the crowd stood as one. Vicki wondered if every arena where this was being seen had done the same.

"I give you my blessing and my full devotion. I will not stop in my quest, for I have been given complete authority. And I now give you this sacred duty. Go into all nations and tell everyone that the true path to peace and understanding lies with the Global Community. Obey what I have told you, and you can be sure I will be with you always. Even unto the end."

12

VICKI searched for Darrion, Mark, and Shelly after the morning session. She found them at the prearranged meeting place by a food court.

"Can you believe that guy used the words of Jesus?" Shelly whispered.

"Those are some of the most sacred words to every believer," Mark said. "He twisted them to make it sound like he's god."

"If there was any doubt as to who he really is," Darrion said, "there's no doubt now."

Vicki told them about meeting Marjorie and what she had said about taking care of believers.

"What's she talking about?" Darrion said.

Mark shrugged. His phone rang and he answered. "Hey, Conrad, what's up? . . . You're kidding. When did you notice? . . . I can't believe it. All right, we'll keep our eyes open."

"What is it?" Vicki said.

"Conrad's been up since we left. He says they can't find Melinda."

"Oh no," Vicki said, "you don't think . . ."

"Let's spread out and see if we can find her."

———————————————

Judd and the others heard about the start of the satellite school but didn't dare go near the local gathering at Teddy Kollek Stadium. They tried to find a feed of the broadcast on the Internet but couldn't.

"That must be one of the ways to get people to come," Sam said. "They can't see it any other way."

"They want to get them in the door so they can count how many potential Morale Monitors they can sign up," Lionel said.

Judd felt torn about the situation with Kasim and Jamal. When he saw them, he felt like leaving the room. He had promised not to talk with anyone about their plan, but he felt he had to tell someone.

Lionel, Sam, and Judd helped Yitzhak and Mr. Stein with the daily duties. On any given day there might be as many as twenty witnesses staying in the house or as few as five. Preparing meals, changing beds, and cleaning kept the three busy.

In his spare time, particularly late at night, Judd searched the Internet for the latest news and Tsion Ben-Judah's postings. He tried to keep up to date with what was going on at the schoolhouse, but the e-mails had been few since the coming of the horsemen. Judd read

Tsion's latest message, then clicked on the kids' Web site, www.theunderground-online.com. Mark had done another good job of taking Tsion's words and making them understandable for people of any age.

Judd watched the news about travel and was shocked at how hard it was to find flights. Smoke and fire and sulfur continued to affect every aspect of life.

Judd also checked the Global Community Web site based in New Babylon. Clearly, many workers had been killed by the latest plague, and by the looks of the Web site, many of them were in the technical area.

Though Nicolae Carpathia rarely talked about anyone but himself, he wasn't afraid to blame Tsion Ben-Judah for the deaths around the world. Judd found one newscast fascinating. Carpathia was in rare form.

There is probably no one more dangerous on the face of the planet as this religious zealot, Tsion Ben-Judah. The man tried to kill me before thousands of witnesses at Teddy Kollek Stadium in Jerusalem more than a year ago. He is in league with the two old radicals who spit their hatred from the Wailing Wall and boast that they have poisoned the drinking water. Is it so much of a stretch to believe that this cult would wage germ warfare on the rest of the world? They themselves clearly have developed some antidote, because you do not hear of one of them falling victim. Rather, they have invented a myth no thinking man or woman can be expected to swallow. They would have us believe that our loved ones and

friends are being killed by roving bands of giant
horsemen riding half horses/half lions, which
breathe fire like dragons. Of course, the believers,
the saints, can see these monstrous beasts.

Carpathia went on to mock believers and accuse them
of murder.

The Ben-Judah-ites cannot persuade us with their
intolerant, hateful attacks, so they choose to kill us!

Judd shook his head. Anyone who knew the truth
could see through the man's lies, but most people
followed Carpathia like a god. Judd could see what was
coming. If Nicolae said it enough times, he could turn the
whole world against believers in Christ. It was hard
enough to stay away from the Global Community as it
was. What would happen when the Morale Monitors and
every citizen kept watch for followers of Christ?

Vicki looked for Melinda in front of the arena. The next
session was about to begin, but Vicki didn't want to stop.

The hallway cleared as speakers inside boomed with
music and voices. A Morale Monitor walked up to Vicki
and said, "Can I help you?" Vicki could tell the girl
meant, "Why aren't you inside where you belong?"

"I'm looking for a friend of mine. I really wanted her
to hear the first session with Nicolae, but—"

"You mean Potentate Carpathia," the girl corrected.

"Right, Potentate Carpathia. Anyway, I don't see her, so I'll head back inside."

"What does your friend look like?"

As Vicki described Melinda, the Morale Monitor inched closer. "What's your friend's name?"

Vicki hesitated. Melinda surely wouldn't have used her own name. But she didn't have a fake ID. "Uh, why? Have you seen someone who looks like her?"

"Come with me," the Morale Monitor said.

Vicki followed a few paces, but when they headed for an identification machine, Vicki ran.

"Stop! In the name of the Global Community, I order you to stop!"

The girl pressed a button on her radio that alerted other Morale Monitors. Vicki ran down the concrete hallway. She reached for a door that led to the arena. Before she could open it, two Morale Monitors burst through.

Mark scanned the crowd, looking for Melinda. There were thousands of faces. He moved to an upper tier and sat next to a boy with binoculars. "Mind if I borrow those for a minute?"

"Sure," the boy said, handing them over. "Did you see Carpathia?"

"Yeah, that was something, wasn't it?"

"The guy that's on right now is their top education man."

"Quiet!" someone in front of them whispered.

Mark scanned the crowd as Dr. Neal Damosa talked about the new world kids were facing. The man paced the stage at a huge arena in Atlanta. His hair was neatly cut, and he wore an expensive suit.

"Probably everyone here and everybody watching by satellite believes that Potentate Carpathia is right when he says there has never been a time in history when we need our young people more."

The audience applauded politely. *Carpathia's a tough act to follow*, Mark thought.

"If *you* don't step up at this critical time, who will? If *you* don't learn to embrace the truths taught by the Global Community and begin to spread them to others, who will? If not *you*, who? If not now, when?"

A murmur spread through the auditorium as Dr. Damosa went into the audience. Kids turned and watched him. Lighting men fumbled, trying to keep a spotlight on him.

"What's this guy doing?" Mark said to the boy beside him.

"I think he's looking for somebody."

Dr. Damosa placed a hand against his earpiece, nodded, and walked a little farther.

"Is there a Stan Barber in this section?" Dr. Damosa put his hand to his ear again and nodded. "Stanley? Are you here, Stanley Barber? Come out, come out, wherever you are!"

Kids giggled and laughed as Dr. Damosa called the name again and again.

Finally, in another section, a young man of about seventeen stood. He had the unmistakable mark of the believer on his forehead. "I'm Stan Barber."

Dr. Damosa ran forward with a wireless microphone. He asked Stan a few questions, and Stan answered with one- and two-word answers. He was clearly nervous.

"I don't like this," Mark muttered.

"This doctor guy's cool," the boy beside Mark said.

"Stan, let me ask you something. What did you think of Potentate Carpathia's message today?"

Stan took a deep breath. "Well, I suppose it was about like any other message by him."

"Do you think it was good, bad, somewhere in between?"

Stan squirmed. He folded his arms in front of him and looked away from Dr. Damosa.

"You don't want to answer that because you're a follower of Dr. Ben-Judah, aren't you?"

The crowd gasped. Mark closed his eyes and prayed, *God, help this brother get through this situation right now. Give him the right words.*

"The truth is," Dr. Damosa continued, "you hate everything about the Global Community, and you've been working with other teenagers in different areas to fight everything we stand for."

The camera pulled in close to Stan's face. The boy was sweating. Dr. Damosa read Stan's address, gave his phone number and e-mail address, and gave information about the secret church he attended each week. "We've had our eye on you and your friends down here for some time. Nice of you to drop in on our party."

Kids in the audience began to boo.

"Let's keep Stan right here and go to our site near

Cleveland. I understand we have someone there who agrees with Stan."

The satellite feed clicked and crackled until a woman appeared with a microphone in front of an equally full arena. "I'm looking for a Deborah Mardy? Deborah?"

One by one believers were called out from different locations. Mark wondered how the GC could have found them all.

"Throw them out!" someone yelled.

"Get rid of the bums!" another said.

The rest of the crowd picked up the chant, and the noise was almost deafening.

Finally, the arena settled when Dr. Damosa came back on camera. "Now, on to a location near Chicago."

Mark stood and looked for the person with the microphone. He saw an older man coming down the steps toward him. No microphone.

His heart beating wildly, Mark looked at the screen. A Morale Monitor was outside the arena. "Dr. D., we have someone here who not only follows the teaching of Tsion Ben-Judah, but is also on the wanted list of the Morale Monitors."

Mark gasped. *Melinda.*

Vicki was nearly knocked down by the Morale Monitors who came through the door. One caught her by the arm and helped her stay on her feet.

"Boy, am I glad you guys are here," Vicki said, out of breath. "That girl over there needs some help."

"Come on!" one boy said to the other.

"Are you sure you're all right?" the other said.

"Yeah, go ahead and see if you can help her." Vicki rushed into the darkened arena and let her eyes focus. She looked at the screen and couldn't believe her eyes. It was Melinda.

A woman with a microphone was beaming. "We set up a booth and offered free material from the rebel Ben-Judah. When this girl stopped, one of the other Monitors recognized her. She's going to have some explaining to do back at headquarters."

Applause broke out in the arena. Vicki turned to find a seat and was met by three men in uniform.

The late spring sun had just set on the horizon over Jerusalem when Judd sat down to write an e-mail to Tsion Ben-Judah. He knew the man was busy and probably didn't have time to write back, but he wanted to explain what had happened in the last few weeks.

Lionel shouted from the back of the house, "Come here, quick!"

Judd ran to the patio and stood next to Sam. Mr. Stein was there with Yitzhak, crowded onto the small space.

Lionel pointed in the direction of some dark clouds. Judd looked closer and realized they weren't clouds. In the glint of the setting sun were millions of horses and riders. Smoke and fire swirled in black and yellow plumes. As they approached the ancient city, Judd shuddered. The massive horsemen looked angry and ready for death. The horses galloped faster and faster, rumbling toward the city. Their due time had come. All the other deaths by sulfur and fire were a prelude to this stampede. The breastplates of the riders flashed.

"Have mercy on us, O God," Mr. Stein prayed softly. "You have permitted us to see this cavalry of demons on their final attack. Let this assault turn many from the evil one to you. May you be glorified forever."

As Mr. Stein finished, the riders swept past the patio in a frightening display of power. Judd rushed to the computer and found the latest news. Fire and smoke and sulfur enveloped the globe. The 200 million horsemen were loose for a final attack.

AS THE crowd in the arena wildly applauded, three uniformed men approached Vicki Byrne. One said something into a radio as Vicki concentrated on the screen. She had hoped she was wrong, but it was true. The Morale Monitor outside the arena had nabbed her friend Melinda Bentley.

"We believe there are more Ben-Judah followers inside," the Morale Monitor on the screen said, "and we're going to conduct a thorough search before this session is over. Right now, let's go to Houston, Texas, and find out what's going on there."

The scene switched to a domed stadium, where it appeared other believers were about to be exposed by the GC plot.

Vicki wanted to help Melinda, but she feared the men beside her. One was a GC Peacekeeper. The other two were younger and wore Morale Monitor uniforms.

Vicki scanned the crowd for a familiar face or someone with the mark of the believer. The auditorium was
built in a circle and used for everything from sporting
events to rock concerts. She saw no one she recognized.
Suddenly, the Peacekeeper grabbed Vicki's arm. "Come
with us."

"What did I do?"

Kids nearby turned and shushed them, then stopped
when they saw the Peacekeeper.

The man leaned close. "You were running from one
of our Morale Monitors. You know the girl we have in
custody. Now come quietly or we'll disable you." The
man flashed a stun gun.

"Let me get my purse," she said.

The man let go of her for an instant, just long enough
for Vicki to break free. She rushed down the row, climb-
ing over legs, stumbling as she stepped on people's
shoes.

"We've got a runner!" the man yelled into his
radio.

Someone in the crowd shouted, "She's one of the
Judah-ites!"

Vicki made it to the end of the row and headed down
the steps. Another Morale Monitor came toward her so
she turned and headed for the top. Seconds later, another
boy in uniform descended toward her.

Vicki spotted a railing and darted into the crowd.
Some scooted out of her way while others tried to grab
her. She fought to the railing and looked over the side.
Too far down. As the men converged on her, she swung

her legs over the side and eased down. She took a deep breath and closed her eyes as she prepared to let go.

But a boy grabbed her arm. His T-shirt sported the face of Nicolae Carpathia and the words *The Hope of the World.* "I got her! Help!" he yelled.

Vicki let go of the railing and lunged at the boy with her free hand. She missed, but the boy let go and Vicki fell toward the concrete.

Judd Thompson Jr. knew from reading Tsion Ben-Judah's letters to other believers that the horsemen would kill many more people. Tsion had written that as the world came closer to the forty-second month into the Tribulation, the death toll from the 200 million horsemen would reach a third of the population.

Judd ran back to the patio and joined his friends. He had seen the angry horses before, but never this many. Hundreds and hundreds of thousands stampeded the old city of Jerusalem. The horses had the heads of lions, and fire and smoke poured from their nostrils and mouths. The riders wore gleaming breastplates. Flashes of color nearly blinded Judd, and he had to turn away.

The enormous beasts made no sound as they galloped. It was like a horror movie with the sound muted, but this was scarier than anything Judd had ever seen.

He counted nine people on the street, all unaware of the angels of death ready to strike down anyone God would let them. The people coughed and choked as the smoke billowed around them. All nine fell to their knees and grabbed their throats. One man pulled his shirt over his head in an attempt to block the suffocating smoke. Three collapsed into the gutter and lay motionless.

Mr. Stein knelt and closed his eyes. "I have never seen anything so horrible."

The army of horsemen and their animals kept coming, storming the city in search of more victims. Judd shook his head.

Lionel leaned close. "This makes all the other attacks look like picnics."

"You think this is happening to the kids back in Illinois?"

Lionel frowned. "From what I'm reading off the Internet, this is happening everywhere."

Vicki tried to land on her feet, but she fell backward and smacked the concrete floor, stunning her. When her head hit, it almost knocked her out, but she some-how managed to struggle to her feet. Her legs weren't cooperating, but she realized she hadn't broken or sprained anything. Kids leaned over the railing, pointing and shouting. Two Morale Monitors sprinted down the steps.

Vicki lurched into another hallway and staggered around a corner. She rammed into someone full force, and they both went down.

It was Mark. "Keep going," he said, helping her back up. "I'll stall them."

Vicki raced on, hearing him yell something at the Morale Monitors. As she neared a concession area, she heard footsteps and ducked into a rest room.

Mark Eisman waited until the Morale Monitors were nearly through the tunnel when he stepped out and collided with one of them. "Are you looking for that girl?"

"Yeah, which way?" the Morale Monitor said.

Mark pointed away from Vicki. They turned down the hall, talking into their radios as they ran. Mark looked for Vicki, but she was gone.

He went back inside the arena and noticed a flurry of activity in the stands. Morale Monitors and GC Peacekeepers were searching the stands. A local announcer interrupted the live GC feed on the screen and asked for the cooperation of the crowd. The man described Vicki and asked anyone who saw her to report to the nearest Morale Monitor.

"This girl is a Judah-ite," the man said, "and is dangerous. There is a reward for anyone who helps us arrest her or any other Judah-ite."

The crowd seemed energized. Many looked around while others got up and moved toward the nearest exits.

Suddenly, Mark noticed something strange on the huge video screen. People in Texas were panicking, many running from the domed stadium. The picture switched to a civic center in Memphis, where kids were also running from their seats in terror.

Mark shook his head. Only one thing could scare people that bad.

———————————

Vicki found the last stall in the bathroom empty. She quickly swung the door shut behind her and locked it. She took a moment to catch her breath, then looked underneath the stalls. She was alone.

Vicki had to get out of the building without the GC seeing her, but how? Mark or Darrion or Shelly could help, but with thousands of kids in the arena, finding them seemed impossible.

The rest-room door burst open. Vicki held her breath, her heart beating furiously. She sat and raised her feet off the floor. Someone kicked in the first stall door, then the next.

The intruder kicked Vicki's stall door, and when it didn't open jiggled the lock. Vicki saw the standard GC-issue black boots under the door.

She scooted as far back as she could but soon heard what she dreaded. "Global Community Morale Monitor! Unlock this door!"

Vicki opened the stall and a female Morale Monitor stepped inside, closed the door, and locked it.

"You're a Judah-ite," the girl said, "the one we're looking for?"

Vicki studied the girl's face under her uniform cap as footsteps sounded outside.

"Natalie?" someone shouted from the hall.

"In the bathroom!" the girl said.

"Find anything?"

"Nobody," Natalie said. "Had to make a pit stop."

"Get out here. We need your help."

"Why did you do that?" Vicki whispered.

Natalie pushed back her hat, and Vicki saw the mark of the believer. Vicki shuddered. "I thought I was caught."

"You will be if you don't get out of here fast," Natalie said.

"Wait. How did you become a believer?"

"Long story," Natalie said. "No time now."

"The girl being held outside is my friend. We need to help her."

"They've probably already put her in the van. There's no way . . ."

Natalie's voice trailed as screams came from the hallway. Now panicked voices, shouting, and hundreds of kids running.

"Stay here," Natalie said and left.

Moments later she returned. "You're not going to believe this. Come on."

"But they'll see—"

Natalie shook her head. "You're the least of their worries now."

The two made their way through the frightened crowd to the outer ring of the arena. There, Vicki looked through huge windows at a sight she would never forget. Bearing down on them were thousands upon thousands of horses and riders. Hundreds of kids streamed through the smoke- and sulfur-filled hallways, knocking each other down, trampling, coughing, gasping for air, and covering their mouths.

"This is the first I've seen of these things," Natalie whispered. "I read Dr. Ben-Judah's descriptions, but this is worse than I imagined."

Vicki quickly told of her encounter with the horsemen at the schoolhouse. "Remember, the Spirit who lives in you is greater than the spirit who lives in the world."

Natalie nodded. "But what's going to happen to all these people?"

Kids were desperately trying to get outside, but those already out were scrambling to get back inside. "A lot of people are going to die today."

A Morale Monitor raced through the crowd toward Natalie. He raised his gun and fired at the huge window behind them. Glass crashed in the hallway, spreading everywhere. Before Natalie could stop him, the boy jumped through the window and fell to certain death.

Natalie handed Vicki a small key. "Find your friend. This will open the handcuffs."

Vicki gave the girl the address of the kid's Web site, www.theunderground-online.com. "If they discover you or if you want a safe place to stay, write us."

Vicki pushed through the crowd. Kids huddled in corners, screaming and crying. Others had already been trampled to death, their crumpled bodies strewn in the hall like rag dolls. Vicki stepped over bodies, stopping to check for a pulse here and there, soon realizing there was no point.

She spotted the GC truck that had been used for the satellite uplink. A microphone lay on the pavement. The Morale Monitor who had caught Melinda was gone. Mark and Shelly ran up and hugged Vicki. Darrion followed a few moments later.

"I thought they had you," Shelly said.

"Let's get Melinda," Vicki said.

As they walked across the plaza toward the truck, Vicki had to focus. Horses with lions' heads galloped overhead and angry riders bore down on the frightened crowds. Vicki knew she wasn't in danger, but walking close to the thundering herd of demonic beasts was still scary.

Vicki picked up the dented microphone. The truck door was closed, but through a small window she saw an incredible display of video monitors and a huge mixing console. Shelly gave a whoop from the front of the truck, and Vicki and Mark came running.

In the driver's seat sat the Morale Monitor who had shown Melinda on the worldwide satellite feed. Her eyes were open, but she had stopped breathing. Beside her sat Melinda, handcuffed to the passenger-side door handle.

Vicki used the key and quickly freed Melinda. "Let's get out of here."

A huge explosion rocked the plaza. The kids huddled behind the truck and watched the arena fill with flames. Kids scrambled to get out of the way. Some were caught in the blast and killed instantly. Others were trapped inside.

"We have to help them!" Mark yelled over the noise. He ran to the front of the building. Kids screamed and pounded on a huge window, trying to get out. Vicki picked up a heavy rock and threw it as hard as she could, but it didn't even crack the glass.

"Too thick!" Mark said. "I'll be right back." He ran from the area, fumbling in his pocket for something.

Vicki and the others helped as many kids as they could. Some coughed and wheezed, trying to breathe. Others lay motionless.

Moments later Mark raced up in their car. He honked the horn and yelled, "Tell them to move back from the window!"

Vicki motioned for the kids to move back as Mark revved the engine and hurtled toward the building. The crash sent glass flying as kids streamed out, pushing and shoving.

When they had done all they could do, Mark inspected the car. "Flat tire. I'll change it before we head back."

Vicki looked at Melinda. "How did you get here from the schoolhouse?"

"Walked to the main road and hitched a ride."

Vicki frowned. "No way all five of us are getting in this little car."

Mark touched Vicki's shoulder. "I have an idea."

14

"**YOU** can't be serious," Vicki said, pulling Mark away from the others.

"I'm dead serious. I've had this idea for a long time. This truck could help people learn the truth about God."

"But that thing costs hundreds of thousands of Nicks! It's not right to steal it, even if it's for a good cause."

"We wouldn't be stealing it; we'd borrow it."

Darrion approached and asked what was wrong. Vicki told her.

"I'm with Vick," Darrion said. "The GC will come looking for this."

Mark pointed at the arena. "The GC is reeling from this judgment. They won't be back in operation for at least a couple of days. We can work on my idea in the meantime."

"Tell us," Darrion said.

"I want to break into the GC satellite feed. We wouldn't have much time, but if Carl helped us from Florida, it might work."

Vicki squinted. "You mean, go live to the arena?"

"Not just here, but to every country taking the feed. Think of it! Everybody twenty and under will be at these meetings. If we come up with a creative way to tell the truth, something slick the GC will think is supposed to be there, it could be huge. And with the equipment in the truck, we can record a drop-in and they wouldn't know it's anti-Carpathia until it's too late."

"Didn't you guys do this with a newspaper at your school?" Darrion said.

"Exactly," Mark said. "It'll be the *Underground* by satellite. What do you think?"

Vicki hesitated. "I like the idea. I *don't* like stealing."

"How else are we going to do it?"

"He's got a point," Darrion said. "It's a shame to waste the opportunity."

Vicki pursed her lips. She knew once Mark got an idea, it was difficult to talk him out of it. Vicki recalled the discussions they had had about the militia movement. Judd and Mark's cousin John had advised Mark not to get involved, but he hadn't listened. Vicki wished Judd could help make the decision about the truck.

"I don't feel good about it," Vicki said. "If God wants us to do this, he'll provide—"

"He *is* providing a way!" Mark shouted. "Don't you see? He's put this truck right in front of us, and you're letting it slip through our fingers."

Vicki tried to talk, but Mark cut her off. "Every time Buck Williams writes an article for his Internet magazine, *The Truth*, he's breaking the law. Every time Tsion Ben-

Judah writes a letter about Carpathia to believers, he's breaking the law."

"That's different. They're telling the truth, not stealing from the GC."

"Dr. Ben-Judah was a wanted man, and Buck smuggled him out of Israel. Was that right?"

"Of course! Buck saved Tsion's life."

"A lot of people lost their lives today," Mark said. "I want to tell those who are still alive the truth before it's too late."

"I agree. I just don't think God would want us to break one of his commandments so we—"

"Fine," Mark interrupted. "I won't argue theology with the great Vicki Byrne!"

"That's a cheap shot!"

Mark turned and stomped toward the car. He opened the trunk and pulled out the spare tire.

Darrion put a hand on Vicki's shoulder. "Don't let Mark change your mind. Stick with what you know is right."

Lionel watched the final assault of the horsemen with terror and fascination. He knew these were demonic beings, the same as the locusts. But how did they know which people would die? How did the smoke and sulfur and fire kill only people who weren't believers?

Lionel's friend Sam Goldberg logged onto the official Global Community Web site to get the latest official information. "They don't want to admit it, but these horsemen have to be killing a lot of GC personnel."

As the horsemen continued their rampage, Lionel walked alone through the streets near Yitzhak's house. People who had been overcome by the smoke and fumes lay dead in the street. Those who had survived coughed and wandered about, looking for family members. Men and women cried like children. It was a scene his parents wouldn't have let him watch on TV, but now he was living it.

He stood on a corner and watched several Peacekeepers load bodies into a truck. *Where will the GC put all the bodies?* He shuddered and kept walking.

Lionel wanted to be home with the others in the Young Tribulation Force. They had been here in Israel so long. But Mr. Stein's plan of reaching people at Carpathia's Gala interested him. He could wait the three months until that was over to get back to his friends.

As he walked past abandoned cafés and street vendors' booths, he thought about the changes in the nearly three and a half years since the disappearances. He missed his brother and sisters more than he wanted to admit. He had trouble remembering their faces. He had one worn photo of his family left, and he took it from his wallet now and studied it. Clarice had been sixteen when the Rapture happened, the same age as he was now. A wave of guilt swept over him. He had pulled so many pranks on Clarice, everything from messing up her room to lying to boys who called her on the phone. He had once been so mad that he threw her favorite hairbrush in the toilet.

Lionel hadn't treated his little brother and sister,

Ronnie and Talia, that bad. In fact, he had hardly paid attention to them. He called them "munchkins." When Ronnie asked him to play basketball or ride bikes, Lionel made up some lame excuse.

Lionel's dad, Charles, had been a heavy-equipment operator in Chicago. He worked long days and was usually exhausted when he got home. Weekends were spent at church, but a few times he'd taken Lionel to a White Sox game.

Thoughts of his family came back at different times. Sunday mornings were hard. Lionel remembered the drive into the city, the stop at the donut shop where the kids would pick out their favorites. Birthdays at his house had been a huge deal, with cakes and presents, parties, and friends. His mom had always organized the fun. She had a way of knowing exactly what Lionel wanted, even without asking him. It was almost like she could crawl inside his mind. He would come home from a bad day at school and try to keep it inside.

But when his mom got home from her job at *Global Weekly*, all it took was one look. "What's wrong?" she would say, and he would spill it all. Of all the people on earth, he missed his mother the most.

On the morning of the disappearances, Lionel had been with his uncle André. It didn't take Lionel long to figure out what had happened. Unlike others who didn't have a clue, he knew exactly where his family was. Sitting next to his father's bedclothes, watching the horrifying news on television, he had felt so alone. Why couldn't he have been taken to heaven? But he knew the answer. He had never begun a relationship with God. He had played the good Christian, and everyone bought it. Everyone but God.

Now, as Lionel walked through the burning streets of Jerusalem, he knew there were many others just like him. They had either played at church, or they believed there was some way to God other than through Jesus.

Lionel found himself quite a distance from Yitzhak's house. He turned to retrace his steps, but stopped when he saw part of the city with no smoke or fire. He was near the Wailing Wall. A few steps farther and he saw Eli and Moishe, the two prophets of God.

Vicki and the others waited while Mark changed the tire. They could barely see through the smoke and fire near the arena. It billowed black and yellow.

"Will these things disappear like the locusts?" Shelly said.

Vicki shrugged. "I guess they'll leave when they're supposed to."

Melinda watched for any sign of GC Peacekeepers. Most had run away or had been killed. A few walked through the crowds, coughing and sputtering.

Vicki took Melinda aside. "I thought we made it clear you would stay at the schoolhouse."

"I know," Melinda said, "but I was so excited—"

"I understand, but you're not just living for yourself now. You're part of a group. What you do or don't do affects everyone."

"I didn't think about getting you guys into trouble."

140

Mark finished with the tire and handed Shelly the keys. "There's not enough room for all of us. You guys head back."

"We're not leaving without you," Vicki said.

"Yes, you are. I'll find another way."

"No!" Melinda said. "This is my fault."

Mark held up a hand. "I've made up my mind. I'll see you guys back at the schoolhouse."

Vicki nodded and all four girls climbed inside the little car. As Shelly drove away, Vicki noticed Mark walking into a thick cloud of smoke.

"How's he getting back?" Darrion said.

"He'll find a way."

Lionel walked slowly toward the two witnesses. They still wore sackcloth robes and looked like the picture of John the Baptist in Lionel's first Bible. They had dark, leathery skin, and their feet were dirty. Their bony hands stuck out of their clothes like sticks, and their long gray hair and beards floated in the breeze.

Each time Lionel had seen the two witnesses in televised reports, there were crowds of curious onlookers and GC guards nearby. Now there were only dead bodies near them.

Lionel wondered if the two would notice him. If they did, would they speak to him?

Eli turned his head slightly and said, "Oh, taste and see that the Lord is good; blessed is the man who trusts in him!"

Moishe, without moving his lips, raised his voice. "The eyes of the Lord are on the righteous, and his ears are

141

open to their cry. The face of the Lord is against those who do evil, to cut off the remembrance of them from the earth."

Eli stood and motioned for Lionel to come further. "'The righteous cry out, and the Lord hears, and delivers them out of all their troubles. The Lord is near to those who have a broken heart.' "

Lionel thought of Judd and Nada's family. Could these two prophets of God be giving him a message for them?

"Comfort one another with these words," Moishe said.

Lionel sighed and inched closer. "If you'll permit me to ask a question?"

The two stared past Lionel. Finally, Eli moved his head a few inches.

"I know the Bible says you're going to prophesy for a set time. What happens after that?"

Eli and Moishe spoke together. "As it is written, 'And I will give power to my two witnesses, and they will prophesy one thousand two hundred and sixty days.' "

" 'When they finish their testimony,' " Eli said alone, "'the beast that ascends out of the bottomless pit will make war against them, overcome them, and kill them.' "

The two witnesses fell silent, with sad looks on their faces. Finally, Moishe said, "Take heed. The god of this world seeks the death of those who follow the true and living God. Be wise as serpents and harmless as doves."

"The beginning and ending are written in the book," Eli said. "Be diligent to present yourself approved to God, a worker who does not need to be ashamed, rightly divining the word of truth."

Eli and Moishe sat. Lionel could tell his time was up. He didn't know what to do, so he bowed, said thank you, and left.

As Lionel walked to Yitzhak's house, he thought about Eli's and Moishe's faithfulness to God. He slipped inside the house unnoticed and looked up the first news report about the witnesses. Carefully counting the number of days, Lionel calculated when the 1,260th day would be. He studied a calendar and gasped.

———

Mark Eisman watched Vicki and the others drive away. He climbed a brick wall near the arena to survey the area. Bodies littered the plaza and fire licked at buildings. A gas station a few blocks away was nothing but a hole in the ground.

Mark walked back into the arena. The screen was blank and the auditorium empty, except for dead bodies. Through a window he noticed the satellite truck. He ran outside, keeping watch for Peacekeepers or Morale Monitors, and climbed behind the wheel.

He picked up a cell phone on the seat and punched a few numbers. After several rings a man answered and said, "Satcom headquarters."

"Carl Meninger, stat!" Mark said.

———

Vicki and the others were exhausted when they pulled up to the schoolhouse. Lenore made them all sit and tell what had happened while she made dinner.

Charlie stood. "What's that rumbling?"

Vicki went to the window. A cloud of dust rose from the secret entrance to the hideout.

Janie rushed into the kitchen. "Is it the smoke and fire again?"

"I don't think so," Vicki said. She ran outside and gasped as a satellite truck pulled in front of the schoolhouse.

Conrad gave a low whistle. "Cool."

Vicki shook her head. "Not cool."

Mark jumped out. "I know what you're thinking. Just hear me out."

Vicki crossed her arms. "We agreed we weren't going to steal GC property."

"That's the good news. This truck doesn't even exist. Carl got into the computer at headquarters. This thing was destroyed in the attack."

"How could it be destroyed if we have it?" Charlie said.

"They'll never look for it," Mark said.

Conrad ran to the back of the truck and opened the door. "Hey, guys, come see this!"

"We know," Vicki said. "The latest technology and—"

"No," Conrad said, glancing at Mark. "Didn't you inspect this?"

"Inspect it for what?"

Conrad opened both doors. The truck was filled with video monitors and complex electronic equipment. On the floor lay someone dressed in a Morale Monitor's uniform.

Conrad looked at Vicki. "She's still alive."

VICKI stared at the girl and shook her head. She couldn't believe Mark had endangered them this way.

Mark put his hands in the air. "I didn't know she was here. Honestly, I'd never—"

"Doesn't matter now," Vicki said. "Let's get her inside."

Conrad and Mark carried the girl upstairs and gently placed her on a cot. Lenore brought medical supplies.

"I know this girl," Vicki said. "She's Marjorie something, the one who checked me into the arena."

Lenore turned her name tag over. "Her last name is Amherst."

Vicki nodded. "She was the valedictorian at Judd's graduation."

"She's in bad shape," Lenore said. "I'll work on her while you decide what to do if she wakes up."

Vicki went downstairs and found Mark explaining his idea. Their friend Carl was preparing to uplink the kids on the GC satellite.

"How's Marjorie?" Melinda said.

Vicki gave them an update and told them who she was. Mark remembered her and said they had taken a couple of classes together. "She was always blowing the grading curve because she got such high scores. Everybody hated and admired her at the same time."

"How could somebody so smart fall for Carpathia's lies?" Charlie said.

"The Bible says people will never find God through human wisdom," Vicki said. "When we talk about Jesus dying for them, they think it's foolish."

"You mean, you can't be smart and believe in God?" Charlie said.

"No. Look at Tsion Ben-Judah or Buck Williams. They're really smart." Vicki picked up a Bible and turned to 1 Corinthians. "God picks things we wouldn't pick to show how great he is. He chose David even though he was a shepherd. He chose Jesus to be born in a stable to very poor parents."

"So God does things backwards to the way we'd do them?" Charlie said.

"Yeah, in a lot of ways. Listen to this: 'God deliberately chose things the world considers foolish in order to shame those who think they are wise. And he chose those who are powerless to shame those who are powerful. God chose things despised by the world, things counted as nothing at all, and used them to bring to nothing what the world considers important, so that no one can ever boast in the presence of God.' "

"I get it," Charlie said. "People with a lot of brains can

follow God as long as they understand God is smarter than their smartest ideas."

The kids smiled and Vicki chuckled. "And it also means you can use all kinds of arguments, but people have to realize they have a problem only God can fix."

"Sin," Mark said.

"I thought I was pretty smart," Darrion said. "When Ryan talked about God, I thought he was nuts. Somehow, God showed me I needed forgiveness."

"Which brings us to Marjorie," Vicki said.

Melinda frowned. "Sounds like she's really into the GC."

"This is my fault," Mark said. "If she recovers, we'll blindfold her and I'll drive her back in the satellite truck."

"The one that doesn't exist?" Vicki said. "That'll tip off the GC, and we'll get Carl in trouble."

"All right, I'll take her in the car."

"Wait," Melinda said. "Is that all we're going to do with her, just ship her back? You didn't do that with me. You guys were straight with me from the start."

"That's because you were holding a gun," Mark said.

"I think you would have told me the truth even if I hadn't been."

"She's right," Vicki said. "I don't want to pretend. We shoot straight with Marjorie, and if she wants to go back to the GC, we'll take her."

"She might still be able to lead them to us," Mark said.

"True, but she might also believe what we tell her," Vicki said.

Lionel couldn't wait to tell about his meeting with Eli and Moishe, but he especially wanted to talk with Judd. He found everyone downstairs in Yitzhak's house with a new group of witnesses. Lionel described the meeting with Eli and Moishe, then pulled out a piece of paper.

"I've counted up the 1,260 days since Eli and Moishe first appeared. If I'm right, their final day will come during Carpathia's big celebration."

"That's in less than three months," Judd said.

Mr. Stein shook his head. "Perhaps that is the reason for the party. Carpathia will snuff out these precious lives, and everyone will praise him for ending the judgments."

"They're really just beginning," Lionel said.

A tall man with huge shoulders stood. He wore tattered clothing like Eli and Moishe, and spoke with a thick European accent.

"God has given us a wonderful tool in the Scriptures," the man said. "We can read history ahead of time if we look to the Bible."

"What's going to happen to the two prophets?" Sam said.

"Tsion Ben-Judah has written much about our friends at the Wailing Wall. If you examine the Bible, you see that God has given them power to pronounce judgment on his behalf."

The man continued. "But their mission will end. The Bible says that one day they will complete their testimony, and the beast of this world will kill them. And their bodies will lie in the main street of Jerusalem."

"I don't want those guys to die," Sam said. "We have to save them."

"Everything has a purpose in the plan of God. After they die, no one will be allowed to bury them. People from all over the world will come to look at their bodies and celebrate. The people will even give presents to each other as they rejoice in the deaths of these two prophets."

"How will Carpathia kill them?" Judd said.

"I'm not sure, but our friends will not stay dead. God will raise them to life."

"I want to see that," Sam said. "And I want to see the look on Carpathia's face when it happens."

Lionel motioned for Judd and called Nada's family together. "I think Eli and Moishe gave me a message for you."

"What do you mean?" Kasim said.

"Both of them quoted verses from the Psalms. They talked about God hearing the cries of the righteous. They said God's against those who do evil. And then they called me closer. The way Eli looked at me . . ." Lionel felt the tears coming as he looked at Nada's mother.

"What did he say?" Lina said.

"I printed it. It's from Psalm 34." Lionel's hands trembled as he read. "'The righteous cry out, and the Lord hears, and delivers them out of all their troubles. The Lord is near to those who have a broken heart; he rescues those who are crushed in spirit.'"

When Lionel looked up, Nada's parents were crying.

Kasim looked at the floor. "One of the last things Moishe said was 'Comfort one another with these words.'"

Jamal wiped his eyes. "We've known God cares about our loss, but these words help more than you can know. Thank you."

Vicki took turns with the others watching Marjorie. Lenore had taken the girl's pulse and blood pressure every hour, but there was no change. Vicki volunteered to stay with her through the night.

Lenore gave Marjorie's walkie-talkie to Mark. Her empty gun was on the nightstand alongside a radio. Vicki tuned in a GC station to get the latest news.

The announcer seemed shaken by the numbers of dead or missing. "Experts fear fatalities may go higher. Global Community officials have no further word on the cause of the plague of fire and smoke. Potentate Nicolae Carpathia will address the world from New Babylon tomorrow."

Mark laid the walkie-talkie on the nightstand. "It doesn't have a homing device. I removed the solar cell so she can't communicate with headquarters."

Vicki followed Mark into the hall and told him about the Carpathia address. Mark turned. "I'm really sorry about bringing her here."

Vicki smiled. "I've made a lot of bad decisions since I became a believer. But I do believe God even uses our mistakes."

"What do you want to do with the truck?"

"Let's see what happens with Marjorie. I like your idea

about breaking into the satellite school signal, but I don't have any idea how you would do it."

"I talked with Carl for a long time tonight. We're getting a plan together. You know the believers who were singled out in the meetings?"

"I can't get them out of my head."

"Carl says only a few were taken into custody. Most got away when the horses attacked. He told me what it was like watching those horses come in over the Atlantic."

"Scary, I'll bet."

"Yeah. The GC picked up a cloud on radar that stretched from Florida to Maine. Carl got into one of the observation towers and said he could see millions of horses coming over the water."

Vicki shuddered. "And it happened all over the world at about the same time."

"Yeah. Carl said the horses killed a lot of the GC communications team. He's one of the higher ranking officers now."

"Tough way to get a promotion."

"The interesting thing is what happened when the horses left. Carl saw them from the observation deck running toward the water. Millions of horses passed him and instead of running on top of the water, the horses and riders dove straight down and disappeared."

"So it's over?" Vicki said.

"Sounds like it to me."

"What's the next judgment?"

Mark squinted and looked past Vicki.

"What?"

"I thought I saw something move."

Vicki turned and walked into the room. Marjorie lay still, her eyes closed. Vicki took the girl's wrist to check her pulse.

Marjorie opened her eyes and grabbed Vicki's arm. With her other hand she snatched the gun from the nightstand and pointed it at Vicki. The girl sneered at Mark. "Come inside and close the door, Judah-ite!"

VICKI backed away as Marjorie released her arm and rolled out of bed. When the girl's feet hit the floor, she wobbled and nearly fell. She tried to keep the gun steady. "Get inside and close the door. I don't want to have to kill anyone else."

Vicki looked at Mark. He stepped inside and closed the door. "How long have you been awake?" Vicki said.

Marjorie coughed. "Long enough to know you guys aren't followers of Potentate Carpathia. How did I get here?"

"We found you in the back of the satellite truck outside the arena," Mark said.

Marjorie put a hand on the wall to steady herself. "I remember the smoke and that awful smell. I ran for the truck because . . ." She looked up. "You kidnapped me!"

"We didn't know you were inside."

Marjorie moved gingerly to the window and glanced outside. "You stole it?"

"It's a long story, but—"

"Where are we?"

Vicki stepped forward. "Sit down. You look woozy."

"Stand back. I don't need your help." Marjorie grabbed the walkie-talkie and clicked the microphone. "Morale Monitor Marjorie Amherst. I'm being held hostage. Over."

Marjorie clicked the radio again but there was no answer. She threw it in the corner. "Smoke probably ruined it. Tell me where I am."

Vicki decided there was no reason to make up a complicated story Marjorie wouldn't believe. "You're right. We're followers of Jesus Christ."

"Ben-Judah, you mean."

"He's one of our teachers, yes."

Marjorie studied the moonlit woods surrounding the schoolhouse. "What is this place, a Ben-Judah training camp?"

Vicki smiled. "Not a bad guess. We moved into this abandoned building after I had a dream about it."

Marjorie squinted. "You *are* crazy."

"I know it sounds weird, but it's true. There are a bunch of us living here. When the locusts came, we took in a lot of people and tried to help. We did the same when the horses and riders started—"

Marjorie shook her head. "I'm not buying the horse story. It's a trick. Somebody's been releasing poisonous gas and setting fires. You Judah-ites are the main suspects."

"Why?" Vicki said.

"Have you seen any Judah-ites getting sick or dying? You know exactly when and where things are going to happen, like at the arena yesterday."

Mark rolled his eyes. "You were there. Did you see anyone setting fires or releasing poison? God's the one letting this happen."

"Right. It was God who let my parents and most of my friends get killed. It was God who killed our principal at Nicolae High. Mrs. Jenness was one of my best friends. . . ."

Marjorie sat on the bed. Vicki stepped closer, but the girl looked up and waved the gun again. "Stay away."

"We want to help you. If you'll let us explain, I think it'll all make sense," Vicki said.

Before Marjorie could speak, the door opened and Lenore peeked inside. She gasped when she saw Marjorie.

"Get in here! Now!" Marjorie shouted.

Vicki waved Lenore inside. "It's okay. She can't hurt us."

"What do you mean? I'll shoot all of you."

"How long has she been awake?" Lenore said.

"Not long," Vicki said as she stepped closer to Marjorie and reached for the gun.

Marjorie scampered back onto the bed, her hands shaking. "I swear I'll shoot."

Vicki held up her hands. "We don't want to hurt you. We just want you to know the truth."

"Don't say I didn't warn you." Marjorie pointed the gun at Vicki's knee and pulled the trigger. *Click. Click. Click.* "You tricked me!"

Judd watched the reports of death on the Global Community News Network. Reports from around the world were grim. The GC braced for yet another mysterious "attack," as they called it, but Judd and the others at Yitzhak's house believed the horsemen were gone.

Judd decided to come up with a creative way to publicize Mr. Stein's meetings during the GC Gala. Judd was glad to get his mind off Nada's death and Jamal and Kasim's plan to kill Nicolae. He went to Mr. Stein and suggested they print pamphlets and let witnesses pass them out in Jerusalem.

"Wonderful," Mr. Stein said. "Now I have news. I have met with Yitzhak and some of the other believers, and we believe we should not wait. We want to begin these meetings now."

"Why now?"

"People are struggling with the deaths of loved ones. They need the hope we can offer."

"What about during the Gala?"

"We're still planning it, but we think God wants us to get the message out now."

Yitzhak gave Judd directions to a print shop owned by a believer. As Judd walked, he felt he was being followed. He quickly ducked into an alley. Moments later, Kasim ran past and Judd grabbed him. "Why are you following me?"

Kasim pulled Judd deeper into the alley. He caught his breath and said, "I didn't want to talk to you at the house. I've made up my mind to assassinate Carpathia on the first night of the Gala."

"That'll put a cloud over the celebration," Judd smirked.

"Yes, but it also means Eli and Moishe might have more time."

Judd shook his head. "You know it doesn't work that way. The Bible says—"

"Your interpretation is different from mine. If I can get to Carpathia, it could change everything."

"It's clear that Eli and Moishe—"

"What happens in the future happens. I can only do my part and rid the world of this evil man."

Judd sighed. "Okay. I don't agree with you, but I made a promise not to tell anyone about this."

"I don't want you just to keep quiet. You must help. I have a diagram of the buildings near where the stage will be built."

"No way! This idea belongs to you and your dad."

Kasim looked away. "My father is not willing to help any longer. That's why I need you."

"What changed his mind?"

"It may have been the words of Eli and Moishe that Lionel shared. Or perhaps my mother persuaded him to give up the idea."

"Has he tried to talk you out of it?"

Kasim looked away.

Judd grabbed Kasim's arm. "Listen to him. Forget your revenge on Carpathia. Use your energy for something more important. There are people who might come

to know God if we can reach them with the message."
Judd pulled out the file he had worked on for Mr. Stein.
"We can reach so many people if you'll help. That's the
real way to get back at God's enemy. Steal people who
would otherwise choose Carpathia."

Kasim leaned against the brick wall and slid to the
ground. "You don't understand. I wake up at night sweating, planning Carpathia's demise. It's all I can think about.
I pledged my life to this monster before I understood the
truth. I don't want anyone to make that same mistake."

"I understand that, and I know how much you loved
Nada and how bad you feel about what happened. But
the truth is, even with Carpathia dead, his evil will
continue. The prophecy is clear—"

"Nothing you say will keep me from this. The only
question is whether or not you will help me."

Vicki didn't want to lock Marjorie in the basement hideout, but the kids couldn't let her get away. Vicki made sure
Marjorie didn't see the door to the underground tunnel
and that there was enough food and water for the night.

The next day, Mark brought Marjorie to the computer
room, where Lenore and Vicki were waiting. Everyone else
stayed out of sight so they couldn't be identified later.

"The GC are probably looking for me right now,"
Marjorie said.

"We want to do the right thing," Vicki said. "We'll take
you back if that's what you want, but we need a little time."

"I can't stay here. The satellite schools—"

158

"It'll take a few days to get everything running," Mark said. "I've been watching the news." Mark turned on the monitor in time to see the introduction to the live broadcast of Nicolae Carpathia.

Vicki leaned close to Marjorie. "What we'd like you to do—"

"Wait. I want to hear this. Turn it up."

Mark turned up the audio as Nicolae began. He expressed his sorrow for the families of victims who had died in the past few months.

"My advisors inform me that more people have died in this most recent wave of deaths than those who disappeared nearly three and a half years ago. That means there will be perhaps as many as a billion who have passed away since the beginning of the smoke, sulfur, and fire.

"There is no one on the planet who has not been touched in some way by this destruction. And it is my goal to end the suffering."

The camera zoomed in on Carpathia. He looked down, bit his lip, and gave a slight nod. "My advisors also inform me there is reason to believe this disaster was not a natural phenomenon. The earthquake and the fiery meteors were clearly explainable events, but this chemical warfare and arson are part of a calculated plot by the enemies of peace."

"That's what you guys are!" Marjorie yelled.

"This guy has never wanted peace," Mark said.

"Just wait, he'll show you."

"I am asking anyone who has knowledge of those responsible for these deaths to go to your local Global

Community authorities. Any tip or lead that exposes those responsible will be rewarded."

Nicolae outlined a plan to dispose of the bodies. "Of course, many have already been destroyed by fire, but in order to keep our world healthy and free of disease, I have ordered our ministers of health to arrange mass burnings throughout the world. This will not be a pleasant task for loved ones or for the officials charged with this duty, but it is something that must occur."

Vicki thought of the grisly job of burning the dead. Who would they hire to do such a thing? Vicki shuddered and tried to concentrate on Carpathia.

"I have plans for at least two of our enemies, and those plans will be carried out at the Gala in Jerusalem. It is time for us to put the death and grieving aside. And so I invite you, wherever you are, to this grand party. Even those who are against our ideals should come. To show how accepting and tolerant I am, I extend a personal invitation to Rabbi Tsion Ben-Judah. He may attend our celebration as an international statesman."

"That shows you what kind of man the potentate is," Marjorie said. "He even invites his enemies."

The camera pulled back as Carpathia walked to the front of his massive desk. "We have every reason to want revenge, but as your leader and a man committed to peace, I offer one more opportunity to our enemies. Let us put aside our differences and strive together for a new world of love and unity. Join the faith of your brothers and sisters across the planet, the Enigma Babylon One World Faith."

Mark shook his head as Carpathia finished. "That doesn't make sense. Those people at the satellite school were determined to catch followers of Ben-Judah. Now Nicolae's giving us a free ticket to his party?"

Vicki faced Marjorie. "There's one condition to taking you back. You have to listen to the truth."

"I just heard the truth. Potentate Carpathia *is* the truth."

Janie opened the door and walked in. "I didn't know you guys were in here. I heard there was a Morale Monitor in the house, but—"

Marjorie studied Janie's face. "Do I know you? You look familiar."

"I'm sure we haven't met." Janie asked if she could stay, and Vicki said it was okay.

Vicki turned to Marjorie. "Let me explain what we believe before you leave. After you hear me out, if you still want to go back, we'll work it out."

Janie sat down, rolled her eyes, and muttered, "Don't waste your breath."

Marjorie sat up. "Now I remember. I saw a poster with your picture. You were in a reeducation facility downstate."

Janie shifted in her chair. "That's crazy. I don't know what you're talking about."

Marjorie looked at Vicki. "I'll listen on one condition."

"What's that?"

"If I listen to you, you have to listen to what I think about the Global Community."

"Deal."

VICKI asked Marjorie what she thought had happened to those who had disappeared three years earlier. Marjorie gave the same answer as Global Community scientists. Their theory didn't make much sense, but Vicki didn't challenge it.

"And what do *you* think happened?" Marjorie said.

"I think the Bible came true before our eyes."

Marjorie rolled her eyes. "Oh yeah, God came back and took all the good people to heaven and left the bad ones. What does that say about you?"

"The people who disappeared weren't perfect. They had a relationship with God."

"Which means that my mom and dad, who were really good people, came up on the short end?"

"I'm not criticizing your parents or you. I'm telling you what happened. Did you have any brothers or sisters?"

"I'm an only child."

"Figures," Janie muttered.

Vicki gave Janie a look, then explained what had happened to her family. "The same thing happened to most of us here. One girl actually saw her mom disappear, and right before she did, her mom told her exactly what I'm about to tell you."

"I can hardly wait."

Vicki told the truth as simply and clearly as she could. Marjorie smirked when Vicki quoted Bible verses, but Vicki knew God's word had the power to change a person's heart.

"In Romans it says, 'For all have sinned; all fall short of God's glorious standard.' But it doesn't stop there. God loved us enough to give himself and pay the penalty for our sin. Then it says, 'Yet now God in his gracious kindness declares us not guilty. He has done this through Christ Jesus, who has freed us by taking away our sins. For God sent Jesus to take the punishment for our sins and to satisfy God's anger against us. We are made right with God when we believe that Jesus shed his blood, sacrificing his life for us.'"

Marjorie yawned.

"Another verse says that the punishment for sin is death, which means we'll be separated from God forever."

"That doesn't seem fair. I only do one bad thing and I get the death penalty?"

Vicki explained God's holiness. "Say you have a gorgeous new Morale Monitor uniform. You've just shined all the buttons, you have a pair of bright white gloves on, and then you find out somebody has worn your boots and walked through mud."

"I'd be ticked."

"Would you wear the boots?"

"Of course not. I'd shine 'em up."

"Right," Vicki said. "Now think about God. Every part of him is perfect. Would you expect him to allow anything in his presence that's not perfect?"

"I guess not. But that would mean we're all doomed."

"Exactly, but stick with me. God knew we were all imperfect. He knew we'd do bad stuff, and that even one sin is enough to separate us from him forever."

Marjorie made a face. "I still say it's not fair. Why couldn't we have one more chance?"

"God did better than give us another chance. He took the sentence himself."

Vicki showed Marjorie different parts of the Gospels. She quoted John the Baptist, who looked at Jesus and said, "Look! There is the Lamb of God who takes away the sin of the world!" She told her about the miracles Jesus performed, that he lived a perfect life, and was finally crucified.

"If he didn't do anything wrong, why was he put to death?"

"Most of the religious leaders of the day hated Jesus because he said he was God. They handed him over to the secular leaders to kill him. But the truth is, Jesus let himself be killed. That's what the Bible means when it says God sent Jesus to take our punishment."

Marjorie hesitated. "I guess some of it makes sense, but if I have to choose between your religion and Potentate Carpathia, I'm going with the GC."

"Jesus said anybody who isn't for him is against him."

"Carpathia thinks Jesus was a great man."

Vicki shook her head. "That's not an option. Jesus said he was the only way to God. He claimed to *be* God. If that's not true, he's either a fake or he's crazy. Would you call someone who's lying or loony a great moral teacher?"

"I guess not."

"Then there's only one other option. Jesus is God."

Marjorie walked to the window. "I'm confused."

Vicki came close. "You know Carpathia is out to get believers in Christ. Can you really trust him?"

"Of course. I look up to him. He's like a god. You saw what he said, how much he loves people and cares about them. He's always here for us. He always helps us get through the hard times."

Vicki wanted to tell Marjorie what Buck Williams saw at the United Nations building. Carpathia had killed two men with one bullet, then convinced everyone except Buck that he hadn't done it. Vicki knew Marjorie wouldn't believe the story. She had to convince Marjorie another way. But how?

Judd made copies of the flyers and hurried back to Yitzhak's house. Everyone seemed excited as Mr. Stein passed out samples to the witnesses.

Mr. Stein asked everyone to write in the time of the first meeting in a blank space on the pamphlet. "We begin inviting people tomorrow. God has given us a small meeting room a few blocks from one of the government buildings."

Lionel took a stack of flyers and wrote down the information. "This is going to be great."

Nada's father, Jamal, came into the room. He touched Judd on the shoulder. "May I speak with you downstairs?"

Judd followed him to a secluded spot.

"I see now that my anger fueled my desire for revenge. God can handle Nicolae Carpathia without my help. My main concern now is Kasim," Jamal said.

"He says he's going through with his plan. He wants me to help."

"We had a disagreement. When I told him my feelings, he ran from the house. He says he's not coming back."

"What do you want me to do?"

"Stay close to him. Tell him you'll help. Then, when the time comes, we will stop him and hopefully save his life."

"I don't want to lie," Judd said.

"You're not. You *are* helping him. Do this for Lina and me. I cannot bear to lose my son again."

Vicki was still thinking when Janie spoke up. "I've got something to say."

Mark moved toward her but Vicki stopped him. "It's okay. Go ahead."

Janie leaned against the wall and nodded toward Vicki. "I met her in an awful place. It was a detention center. Wouldn't send a dog to it, but that's where we wound up. Because of her, I got out and had a chance at a new life."

Vicki said, "Janie came to live with me and my adopted dad for a while."

"What's this got to do with—"

"Just hear me out," Janie said. "I got in trouble at the high school, and they sent me away. I blamed everybody else, including Vicki, but it was my own fault. After I escaped the GC, I got lucky and found this place."

Janie rubbed her neck and looked away. "Only, I honestly don't think it was luck. I think there was somebody watching out for me. Somebody caring for me."

"So that proves there's a God?" Marjorie said.

"I've royally messed up my life. I've been into drugs. I've lied to people who were my friends." Janie faced Marjorie. "When those locusts came, these people warned me, but I wouldn't listen. When the fire and all that stinking smoke came, Vicki stuck with me."

Marjorie turned. "Vicki? You're not Vicki Byrne, are you?"

Janie said, "Sorry, Vick."

"That's okay. Yes, I'm wanted by the GC."

Marjorie sat and ran a hand through her hair.

Janie knelt before her. "What I'm saying is, these people care about you. It doesn't matter to them if you've been into drugs or if you lie or steal. They don't care if you're the most loyal follower of Carpathia there ever was. They care about you because God cares about them. They want you to know him."

"Why are you saying this?" Marjorie said.

"I've caused them no end of trouble. I used to think Enigma Babylon was the way to go, but after being here and seeing them in action, I know what they're saying's true. And you'd best believe before the next judgment hits."

Vicki stared at Janie. She couldn't believe what the girl was saying.

Janie walked back to her chair and sat. "That's all I've got to say."

The room fell silent. Vicki didn't know whether to talk with Marjorie or Janie. Mark looked stunned and sat on the floor.

Finally Marjorie said, "I know you people are sincere, and I believe you care. You could've taken my gun and shot me with it, but you didn't."

"We want you to know the truth," Vicki said. "It can change you forever." Vicki turned to Janie. "But I don't understand. If you believe what we say and that God cares about you, why don't you follow through?"

Janie smiled and looked away. "I've heard you guys say God doesn't make mistakes. Well, I think you're wrong. I'm the biggest mistake he ever made."

Vicki put a hand on the girl's shoulder. "Janie, I've prayed for you almost every day since I've known you. I've asked God to soften your heart. Don't tell me you understand and you've walked this far but you won't take the last step."

Janie put a hand to her forehead. "I don't deserve . . ."

"Don't give me that," Vicki said. "None of us deserve—"

"You don't know the stuff I've done! If you did, you'd have never taken me into your house."

"You just said it yourself—it doesn't matter. I don't care what you've done. God loves you. He wants to call you his daughter."

Janie wrapped her arms around her chest and sobbed.

Lionel sat up in bed and listened for sounds in the house. Sam and Judd slept soundly in bunks nearby. Something was wrong, but Lionel didn't know what it was.

He remembered that hot summer night when he was ten. He was sleeping at a friend's house in Chicago. A burglar had tried to crawl through a window on the other side of the room. Lionel had screamed and woken everyone up. His friend's father had caught the guy and held him until the police came.

Lionel crept into Yitzhak's living room. Nothing. He opened the door to the basement and heard snoring. He went back to bed but couldn't sleep.

"God," Lionel whispered, "maybe you woke me up for a reason. Is there something you want me to do?"

Chills went through Lionel's body. He didn't hear a voice or see a vision, but he had a strong feeling he should pray. "Okay, pray for what?"

Silence.

"God, I'll pray for anything or anyone you want me to, but tell me who."

Silence.

Lionel shook Judd awake and told him what had happened. Judd woke Sam and scampered out of the room. A few minutes later, he returned with Mr. Stein.

"God is at work with someone you know," Mr. Stein said. "Perhaps they need safety. Perhaps they need wisdom. Many times I have felt the prayers of other believers."

"Let's start," Lionel said.

All four knelt and buried their heads in their hands. The first person Lionel prayed for was Vicki.

Vicki hadn't seen Janie cry like this since the GC took her away from Nicolae High.

"I've listened in on some of your meetings," Janie said. "I'd give anything to be part of your group, but somehow I always wind up treating you like dirt."

"God can change all that," Vicki said.

"And what if you guys take a chance on me and I let you down? I'd feel even worse after all you've done for me."

Vicki felt a tug on her shoulder. It was Marjorie. "Okay. I understand now. I want to become one of you guys. What do I do?"

Vicki looked from Janie to Marjorie and back again. "Uh, I can lead you in a prayer if you really want to do this."

"I do."

"Okay, you can say this out loud or just say it to yourself."

Marjorie clasped her hands and bowed her head. "I'm ready."

Vicki prayed. "God, I believe you're there and that you care for me. I'm sorry for the bad things I've done. Forgive me. I believe Jesus died in my place on the cross, and right now I want to receive the gift you're offering me. Change my life from the inside out. Save me from my sin and help me to follow you every day of my life. In Jesus' name, amen."

Vicki turned to Janie. "Would you like to pray too?"

Janie lifted her head and Vicki gasped. On Janie's forehead was the mark of the true believer.

Vicki hugged the girl and they both cried.

"I feel like a new person," Marjorie said.

Vicki looked at Marjorie and gasped. She had no mark.

18

VICKI tried to act cool and hugged Marjorie. Janie pointed at Vicki's forehead. "I thought you guys were making that up."

"Making what up?" Marjorie said.

Vicki turned. "Things will become clear as we go along. We'd like to get you into a class first thing in the morning."

"Great," Marjorie said, "but I really want to go back to the GC and work as a secret agent. That would help the cause, right?"

Mark stepped forward. "Sure. We could use all the information about the GC that we can get."

Janie looked puzzled. "But she doesn't have—"

Vicki held up a hand. "People who are new to the faith usually go through a few classes to learn the basics. Marjorie, why don't you room with me for the first few nights?"

"Fine."

Vicki showed Marjorie their room, then asked Mark to explain things to Janie and call an emergency meeting of the Young Trib Force.

Judd sent an e-mail to the kids at the schoolhouse and noticed an e-mail from Tsion Ben-Judah. Judd had told the rabbi all that had happened in the past few months.

Tsion wrote:

> *I am very sad to hear of the death of your friend Nada. We have all lost so many loved ones. I think about my wife and children every day, and I'm sure you will think of Nada often.*
>
> *Judd, it is important for you to grieve this loss. I find great comfort in the Psalms as the writers pour out their hearts to God. Don't pretend this didn't happen or that it's not painful. Keep a journal to write down your thoughts and feelings. I hear many people saying they need to "move on," and they miss the work God could do in them through this grief.*

Judd thought of Kasim. Instead of grieving for his sister, Kasim had immediately decided to kill Carpathia. Judd continued reading.

> *The way you described the horsemen was exactly what I saw. Rayford Steele and others had told me about them, but I had never seen them myself. I was praying for my*

*friend Chaim Rosenzweig when I saw them. I thought it
was a dream. An army of angry horsemen filled my
window. I can't imagine what it was like to see them in
the middle of Jerusalem.*

Tsion spoke of the Tribulation Force's hiding place
and how the summer heat was getting to them.

*Pray for us as we work together. The bright spot in our
world is baby Kenny, but he gets cranky at times and is
difficult. I pray God will enable us to accomplish whatever task he gives in his power and in his timing.*

The computer beeped. A video message was coming
from the schoolhouse. Judd quickly adjusted the equipment and was surprised to see Mark and Vicki.

"We have a situation here," Mark said. "We thought
you might want to have some input."

Mark explained what had happened with the satellite
truck and Marjorie Amherst. Judd remembered the girl
from his graduation ceremony. "If I'm right, she was the
head of the drama club."

"That makes sense," Vicki said. "She's putting on an
acting job."

"What do you mean?"

Vicki told Judd about Marjorie's prayer. "The good
news is that Janie is now a believer. She's understood a lot
more than we thought. But Marjorie doesn't have the mark."

"You think she's faking it?"

Vicki nodded. "Everyone who asks God to forgive

them receives the mark. She seemed to change her attitude right after she found out my name."

"I get it," Judd said. "She's acting like a believer until she gets back to the GC. Where is she now?"

"Janie's keeping an eye on her."

"Has she seen any of the others?"

"Only a few of us," Vicki said. "We're keeping everyone else out of sight until we figure out what to do."

"Get her away from there as fast as you can. If she gets in touch with the GC, that hideout is cooked."

"I agree," Mark said.

"But what if she really changes her mind about God?" Vicki said. "It happened to Janie."

"That's your call," Judd said. "Some people are always going to be blinded to the truth. I'd say she's a huge risk."

Mark excused himself to check on Janie and Marjorie. Vicki scooted closer to the monitor. "I heard something about your friend in New Babylon dying."

Judd told Vicki about Pavel's death and how his father had helped the kids get out of New Babylon.

"What about Sam?" Vicki said. "Last I heard, you guys were looking for him."

Judd nodded. "The GC questioned him. He was released, but his father died in the last stampede of the horsemen. Sam will probably travel with us."

"I'd like to meet him. When do you think you'll come back?"

Judd told Vicki about Mr. Stein's plan to give the message of truth at the Gala.

"Sounds risky. I like it."

Judd bit his lip. "Vicki, I've got something awful to tell you." Judd explained his friendship with Nada and how it had grown. "I think you would have really liked her."

"Would have?"

Judd told Vicki what had happened the day of the final attack. When he told her how Nada had died, Vicki put a hand to her mouth. "I'm so sorry. I had no idea."

Vicki recalled a phone conversation with Mark while she was on her cross-country trip. Lionel had written briefly about Judd's girlfriend. Vicki had made fun of Nada's name. Now she felt guilty.

"I got an e-mail from Tsion that really helped," Judd said. "I'm going to look up a bunch of psalms he suggested."

Vicki moved closer to the screen. "I can't tell you how sorry I am. I wish I could be there."

Judd nodded. "When I get back, I'd like to talk. I know we've had our good and bad times. If it's okay with you, I'd like to patch things up."

"I'll look forward to talking face-to-face. And I'll be praying for you."

"Thanks. If there's anything we can do from this end about the satellite feed, let us know."

Vicki closed the connection and sat back. She felt bad for Judd's loss. She couldn't imagine what Nada's family was going through. But there was something else to her sadness, something she couldn't explain. Was it jealousy? fear? She had to admit that the news about Judd's romance had affected her. Usually she could push her thoughts aside until she went to bed. It was then that her feelings about Judd, the past, and the next judgment came to the surface.

Vicki checked with Mark to make sure their plan for Marjorie was in place. She found Marjorie talking with Janie. Within an hour, Marjorie had begun speaking about God and Jesus and saying nothing about Nicolae Carpathia.

"It'll be such a blessing to meet the rest of the group," Marjorie said. "When can I see them?"

"I'm sure we'll work it out," Vicki said. She handed Marjorie her gun and walkie-talkie. "No need to keep these from you anymore."

Marjorie tossed her gun on the bed and looked at the GC radio. "I was going to ask God to help me figure out what's wrong with this. Does he answer prayers like that?"

"What do you want to do with it?" Janie said.

"If I can reach my superiors, I'll tell them I'm all right and I'll be back soon. Then I can report to you guys." She opened the back and gasped. "Somebody took out the solar cell."

Vicki asked Mark to come in. He brought glasses of lemonade on a tray. "Lenore thought you guys would like something to drink before bed." He handed Marjorie a glass, then let Janie and Vicki choose theirs.

Marjorie downed hers in two gulps. "Do you know anything about the solar cell?"

"Yeah, I took it out when you got here," Mark said.

"Well, go get it so I can radio headquarters. Then we'll all praise the Lord!"

Mark looked at Vicki. "Okay. I'll be right back."

"The GC is going to come looking for that truck," Marjorie said. "When I get back, I'll tell them it was destroyed."

Vicki thought about Carl. If Marjorie told the GC about the truck, Carl would be in danger. "We already took care of that. We hacked into the GC database and listed it as destroyed."

"You can do that?" Marjorie said.

Vicki yawned. "It's getting late. Maybe you should radio them in the morning."

Marjorie sat on the bed and put a hand to her head. "No, I want to call them tonight, if it's okay." She closed her eyes and opened them wide. "Is it me, or is something wrong in here?"

"Lie back," Vicki said. "You need to rest."

"Yeah, maybe a little snooze will help."

Marjorie turned her head and drifted to sleep. Janie squinted. "What's the matter with her?"

Vicki motioned Janie into the hallway and closed the door softly. "Lenore found something in the medical supplies that helps you sleep. We put it in her lemonade."

Mark ran up the stairs. "Is she out?"

Vicki nodded. "But Lenore said it won't last long."

"All right. Let's go."

Conrad joined them and helped Mark carry Marjorie to the car. Vicki got in the back to steady Marjorie during the bumpy ride to town.

"This looks good," Mark said as they approached a

GC headquarters building. "I don't want to get too close and have them spot us with a surveillance camera."

Conrad stopped, and the three carefully placed Marjorie on the ground. Mark hooked up the solar cell to the walkie-talkie and handed it to Vicki. "You've always wanted to be a Morale Monitor, right?"

Vicki smiled and clicked the radio. "Headquarters, this is Morale Monitor Marjorie Amherst. I'm in trouble. Need help. I'm just a couple of blocks from headquarters on the side of the road."

Vicki slurred her speech and said, "I'm passing out. Help me. Please."

Vicki fastened the radio to the holder on Marjorie's shoulder and jumped in the car. Conrad drove into a nearby alley. Moments later a GC patrol car pulled up to the curb and two uniformed officers got out.

"She's okay," Mark said. "Let's go."

"You think the GC will believe her story?" Vicki said.

"They will when she tells them about the satellite truck," Mark said.

Vicki slept late the next morning. Janie was waiting for her when she came into the kitchen. A Bible and a notebook were open on the table. "I'm ready to learn. I promise I'll listen and take notes this time."

Judd helped Mr. Stein and the others prepare for their first meeting. Everyone was excited at the response from people on the street. Some had thrown the pamphlets down, but others eagerly read the information. Many had said they would attend.

Judd found a note on his bed the afternoon of the first meeting. "Meet me at 5:00 P.M. Tell no one." Underneath was an address. Judd stuffed the paper in his pocket and told Lionel he was going out.

"What about the meeting?"

"I'll be back."

The Global Community had tried to make things seem normal, but how could anything be normal with a third of the world's population dead? Bodies had been removed from the streets, but there was still the smell of charred buildings in the air.

He found the address and buzzed the correct apartment. The door to the entrance clicked, and Judd walked inside and up two flights of stairs. A single bare bulb lighted the hallway. Judd had to squint to read the apartment numbers.

Kasim opened the door and let Judd inside. There was a table and a couple of chairs but not much more. The refrigerator was old and smelled funny. "Love what you've done with the place."

Kasim motioned Judd to the window and opened a curtain. "I'm not here to decorate. I'm here for the view. Look."

The window looked out on a huge plaza. There were shops to the right and left, then an open area. "What is it?"

"I broke into the main GC computer in New Babylon. "That's where they'll build the stage. This window will give me a clear shot."

Judd closed his eyes. "You mean at Carpathia?"

Kasim nodded and pulled out his handgun. "But I have a problem. I need to find some kind of rifle with a scope. This won't reach that far with any accuracy."

"Why are you telling me this?"

"You have to help me find one. The people I bought this from are upset. You can travel freely. I can't."

"No thanks."

Kasim opened a nearby Bible to Revelation 13. "It says in here that one of the heads of the beast will be fatally wounded. I think that's Nicolae, and I'm going to be the one to wound him."

19

VICKI and the others worried that Marjorie's return to the GC would trigger a search for the satellite truck, so the kids pulled the truck into the woods below the schoolhouse. Conrad showed them an old logging road that ran by the river, and the kids parked the truck near it. Charlie and Shelly scoured the surrounding woods for branches and limbs to cover the truck. When they were finished, it was completely hidden.

"The best chance they have of spotting it is from the air," Mark said.

"You can't see it from above," Conrad said. "The satellite dish is out in the open, but it's pretty small."

Over the next few days the kids monitored GC satellite transmissions. The head of the Global Community Department of Education, Dr. Neal Damosa, outlined his future plans at a press conference. Before the transmission, Damosa talked with an aide as they clipped on a microphone. A huge mural of New Babylon was placed behind him.

"Here are the notes you requested, sir," the aide said.

Someone tipped the painting and it nearly fell on Damosa. The man cursed and screamed at the work crew. "That happens again and I'll have you all fired."

Conrad looked at Vicki. "I wonder if that's how Carpathia acts off the air?"

"He's probably worse," Vicki said.

Damosa scanned the notes. "I asked for numbers of dead in the age range—"

The aide quickly turned the pages and said, "Page three, sir."

Damosa studied the numbers. "We have lost a third of those eligible for attendance. But it has just become easier to keep track of all our students. That is our goal, you know. We want to track every person alive. Have the security measures been stepped up?"

"Yes, sir. In addition to the Morale Monitors, we will have Peacekeeping presence as well."

"Good. The Morale Monitors can ferret out our enemies, but they are helpless when the attacks occur."

"The Monitors now wear stun guns. If they suspect a Judah-ite in attendance, they have been instructed to stun the individual and ask questions later."

Damosa smiled. "I doubt there will be many Judah-ites at our next lessons."

"We'll be ready if they come."

Mark wrote something on a scrap of paper. "I want

everybody to know about the stun guns. I'll put it on the Web site pronto."

The aide fussed with Damosa's collar as someone shouted cues. Reporters took their places in front of the podium. Finally, Damosa went on the air. When the cameras were on, his scowl turned to a warm smile.

"This guy is almost as good as Carpathia," Conrad said.

"Before I take questions, I have a brief statement," Damosa said. "I come to you with a heavy heart, knowing that many who were with us at our first meeting are no longer alive. Now more than ever, we need those of the younger generation to understand the importance of their contribution. In spite of the danger of possible attack, we will send a message to our enemies that we will not be intimidated by their terrorist tactics."

Vicki shook her head. "I don't know how they can blame believers for this and get away with it."

Damosa continued. "This is a time of great fear. It would be easy to panic or simply stay in the safety of your homes. By attending the satellite schools, we show that we will not cower. Just as Potentate Carpathia has led us in the pathway of peace, so our young people will strive toward that same goal.

"Therefore, I urge everyone up to and including the age of twenty to attend our next session. We have many surprises in store, and your safety is our utmost priority."

Vicki noticed Charlie in the back of the truck drawing something. When she asked to see it, Charlie turned the page around. It was a replica of the picture behind Damosa.

"That's pretty good," Shelly said.

Vicki took the paper. "It's better than pretty good. It's perfect. Where did you learn to do this?"

"I've been able to draw since I was little. I'm better at buildings than people."

Vicki handed the drawing back to Charlie. "Do you think you could do that on a big sheet of paper? or maybe on a wall?"

"Sure. Why?"

"If we're going to break into a GC telecast, I want them to think it's something coming from New Babylon."

Vicki heard a strange noise. "Is that coming from the satellite feed?"

Mark turned down the volume, but the sound was still there.

Conrad opened the door. The droning grew louder. "It's a plane or maybe a chopper."

"Quick! Hide the dish!" Mark said.

Conrad leaped from the truck and threw a sheet over the satellite dish. When he was safely inside, Vicki shut the door.

"That's definitely a chopper," Conrad said. "Probably GC."

The kids listened as the helicopter drew close. Vicki's heart beat faster and faster. What would the kids do if the GC spotted their hideout?

Judd walked to the meeting in a daze. Now that Kasim had his own apartment, he would be harder to stop. It wasn't that Judd cared for Carpathia. The man was the enemy of their souls. Judd didn't want Kasim to get hurt or bring the GC down on their group.

When Judd entered the small meeting room, he saw his friends surrounded by forty to fifty people. Some were young, others old. A few were Orthodox Jews and stood to the side. People sat in metal folding chairs arranged in a semicircle.

Mr. Stein got everyone's attention. "We have prayed for you," he began. "As we passed out the flyers, we asked God to draw those open to truth. We praise him for your presence tonight."

A few of the Orthodox Jews headed for the door. Mr. Stein took a step forward. "Please, my friends, don't go until you have heard our message."

One man turned. "We are not your friend and we do not serve the same God as you."

Holding out his hands, Mr. Stein approached the man. "We agree about many things. There is one God. Nicolae Carpathia is not who he claims to be. He is not our ruler and king."

The man nodded. "You are right. We have watched Carpathia closely and do not believe he is truly a man of peace."

"God above has given you this wisdom. But many will turn from the true and living God to serve this man of sin."

"We may agree about this, but we cannot follow your teaching about the one you call the Christ."

Mr. Stein smiled. "I was once like you. I did not

accept the claims of Jesus as the Messiah. When my daughter told me she had turned from my faith, I counted her as dead. I turned my back on her."

"As well you should," the man said. Others agreed.

Mr. Stein asked for his Bible. Lionel brought it to him. "I admire your faith and your zeal. But as the Bible predicts, our society will become more and more sinful. Soon, even to this holy city, there will be such great evil and wickedness. And one day in the future, the temple you now worship God in shall be defiled by the Antichrist."

"How could you know such things?" the man said. "Are you a prophet?"

"I am a humble follower of the King of kings and Lord of lords. He has given me and others the ability to speak in different languages so that everyone may hear the truth."

The group grumbled and urged the man to leave. Mr. Stein pleaded, but one by one the Orthodox Jews filed out of the room. Mr. Stein bowed his head. He returned to the front of the room, weeping.

Vicki and the others listened to the chopper pass. Mark peeked out the back window. "It's GC all right, but I don't think they slowed down as they went over the schoolhouse."

"That was way too close," Vicki said. "We have to be ready to get out of here fast."

"Already got that covered," Conrad said. He took a

sheet of paper from Charlie and marked the escape route. Vicki couldn't believe the detail of the plan.

"This is only if the GC find us, right?" Charlie said.

Conrad nodded. "I'd like to remove some equipment from the truck and set it up downstairs. Then we can pull the truck a little farther onto the logging road."

Vicki nodded. "Let's get the equipment out of here. Charlie, you start on the painting. Choose a room downstairs and make one of the walls as much like the picture we saw on TV as you can."

"Got it," Charlie said.

The kids stopped when they heard the *thwock thwock thwock* of the chopper again.

Judd prayed as Mr. Stein composed himself and stood before the group. People turned to each other and talked, many in different languages.

"We want to tell you the best news you could ever hear. We want to tell you how you can have true peace with God and live with him forever."

The people stopped talking as Mr. Stein read or recited several Bible verses. Something shuffled outside in the shadows, but Judd couldn't make out what or who it was.

Suddenly the door burst open and three Global Community Peacekeepers charged in with rifles drawn. "Hands up! Everyone!"

Everyone obeyed except Mr. Stein. He stepped toward the men. "What is this about? We have no quarrel with you."

"Hands in the air!" the Peacekeeper shouted. "This is an unlawful assembly. You will all be arrested and questioned."

Several in the audience started crying. Lionel got Judd's attention and nodded toward a back door. Judd shook his head. He didn't want to risk getting shot by running.

Mr. Stein knelt. "Our Father, we have been faithful to the task you have given. If you desire us to speak about you to those in authority, we will gladly do so. But we ask your divine protection on these who have not yet been able to respond—"

The lead Peacekeeper kicked Mr. Stein in the side. "On your feet, old man!"

Mr. Stein slumped to the ground as Judd rushed to help him. A woman nearby leaned down and whispered, "If we believe what you are saying, what are we to do?"

Mr. Stein closed his eyes. "Lord, give us enough time to show these people how to respond to you."

Someone gasped and another man cried out. Judd looked up as all three Peacekeepers fell backward. Two darted outside and ran away. The third landed on the floor, his gun clattering against a metal chair. The man pulled his knees to his chest and shook with fear. "Please, don't hurt me!"

Judd picked up the gun and walked to the man. "I'm not going to hurt you."

"Not you." The man's eyes were as big as saucers as he pointed toward Mr. Stein. "Them."

Judd turned. The room looked the same as it had all night. "Who are you talking about?"

"Those two beside the guy with the beard."

Judd looked again. The Peacekeeper was clearly pointing toward Mr. Stein, but there was no one beside him.

"What do they look like?" Judd said.

"Big. Shiny. It hurts to look at them. And they have weapons! Please, tell them not to hurt me."

"It's okay," Judd said, trying to figure out what the man had seen. "Leave now and you won't be hurt."

The Peacekeeper stood and ran out the door.

Judd turned to Mr. Stein. "What was that all about?"

Mr. Stein smiled. "God has protected us again. We asked for his help and he has given it."

20

WHEN the helicopter was gone, Vicki and the others helped Conrad remove equipment from the satellite truck. Though some of the gear was permanently attached, Conrad took enough inside for the kids to watch the satellite school transmissions and make their own recording.

Mark called Carl to find out how they could uplink Vicki's video. Since Janie was the newest believer, Vicki asked her to help craft an explanation of the truth.

"Carl says you'll probably have about five minutes, tops, before the GC figure out how to jam the signal," Mark said. "We'll record ten to fifteen minutes just in case, but make sure you get the important stuff up front."

"How do we get the video to Carl?"

"Still working on it," Mark said. "Hopefully we can align the dish and let Carl take care of the rest."

Vicki scribbled notes of things she wanted to say. Janie and Melinda told her what had helped most in changing their minds about God. Vicki had written several pages when Conrad asked them to come into the new control room.

The basement had been transformed into a television studio. Conrad had the camera set up near the wall Charlie was painting. A huge monitor sat in the corner.

"It'll take some time to figure out how to link up with Carl," Conrad said, "but we can record as soon as you guys are ready."

Charlie had draped a sheet over two ladders to keep his painting private. Vicki asked if she could come in, but Charlie said he wanted to wait until he was finished.

"How much longer?"

"I'll work through the night. Should be ready by tomorrow afternoon."

Vicki typed her notes into the computer so she could read them from the monitor. She wanted everything about the recording to be perfect. "Can we put any kinds of graphics or messages across the bottom?"

Conrad smiled. "Just tell me what you want me to put on the screen."

After the Peacekeepers had run from the room, many people stood to leave. Mr. Stein tried to stop them.

"We don't want them to come back and shoot us!" one man said.

"Stay and hear the message!" Mr. Stein said.

"If we leave, will you kill us?" another asked.

"Of course not."

Mr. Stein talked about Jesus to the few who remained. When he was through, several prayed. One man who had just prayed approached Judd. He was older with a square jaw and piercing eyes. He had a powerful handshake and towered over Judd. "You are American. Do you have a place to stay?"

"Yes, but there are others passing through who might need somewhere to sleep."

The man handed Judd a card. "I have many rooms in my house. One as big as this. Tell your friends. I will be back tomorrow night with my neighbors."

When they returned to Yitzhak's house, Judd asked Mr. Stein why the Peacekeepers had run.

"This also happened during my trip to Africa. The Bible shows many examples of angels helping people. I fear tonight we were in very serious trouble, but the Almighty protected us."

Lionel nodded. "If that's true, maybe we shouldn't go back to the same place two nights in a row. The GC could be waiting for us."

Mr. Stein scratched his beard. "You're right. But where do we go? And how do we let people know we've moved the meeting?"

Judd pulled out the man's card from earlier that night. "This man said he has a lot of room at his house."

Yitzhak squinted as he read the man's name.

"What is it?" Lionel said.

"This man is one of Israel's leading military planners. They call him the General. He lives near Chaim Rosen-zweig's estate."

One of the witnesses said, "Who is Chaim Rosenzweig?"

Sam stood. "Only one of the most famous men in all of Israel. He discovered a formula that makes the desert bloom like a garden."

Judd said, "Some in the Tribulation Force are talking to him about God."

Mr. Stein took the paper. "General Solomon Zimmerman. We must go and see this man."

Vicki gasped when she saw the detail of Charlie's work. The painting had intricate details of the New Babylon skyline. The kids and Lenore clapped when they saw it. Little Tolan giggled and laughed as Charlie held him in his arms.

"Almost looks like you could walk right into it," Darrion said.

Vicki winked at Conrad. "Let's get started."

Since Mark had the deepest voice, Vicki had him read a brief introduction. Mark tried to sound like a GC announcer, but laughed when Conrad made a face. After a few tries he got through the introduction, and Conrad played it back.

"In cooperation with the Global Community Department of Education, we proudly present the new ambassador to the next generation, Connie Goodwill."

Conrad found an instrumental fanfare and mixed it under Mark's voice. The kids were amazed. "This is where we fade up on Vicki—"

"You mean, Connie," Shelly said.

"Right," Conrad said. "We'll start with Connie sitting in front of Charlie's painting."

Lenore slipped out and returned with something on a hanger. "Charlie's not the only one with talent. Z sent some material in his last supply shipment, and I tried to match that Damosa character's suit. Here's what I came up with."

Lenore unveiled a new outfit for Vicki that looked almost exactly like Dr. Damosa's suit. On the shoulder was the insignia of the Global Community.

"Where did you get the insignia?" Vicki said.

Lenore smiled. "Just get dressed and record your message, Ambassador."

Judd shook his head as he walked into the courtyard of Solomon Zimmerman's home. When he had seen the man the night before, the General looked like any other person off the street. Now, standing in the midst of what seemed like a tropical garden, Judd saw that he was a man of great wealth and stature.

A man in uniform led Judd and the others inside. They waited in a foyer until General Zimmerman met them and showed them into his massive library. While Mr. Stein talked about using the house for the next meeting, Judd studied the volumes that lined the man's bookshelves. There were biographies of great military leaders, works of fiction about warfare, volumes of reference material, and even different translations of the Bible.

The General said he would be delighted to have them meet in his home. Before they left, Mr. Stein asked how the General had heard of their meeting.

"One of my aides found a flyer on the street. I have seen much death and bloodshed in my career, but these last few years have been extraordinary. I was curious to hear your explanation last night, and in the process, I discovered the truth."

"Weren't you in command when the nuclear attack against Israel began?" Yitzhak said.

General Zimmerman closed his eyes and nodded. "I remember it like it was yesterday. I suppose that's when I first began to think there might be a God." The General looked at Judd. "I saw you looking at my books. Are you surprised I have copies of the Bible?"

Judd nodded. "If you didn't believe in God, why would you have them?"

"I studied the Bible because to me it was a book of warfare. In my military history classes I learned, and later taught, about the many battles described in what you call the Old Testament. There is great wisdom in the way Gideon divided his men, the way King David attacked the Philistines, and of course, God's soldier Joshua, and the way he took Jericho. In all the time I studied those battles, I never considered them of any spiritual importance. They were simply stories. Now that I know the truth, they are much more than stories."

"What happened when the Russians attacked?" Lionel said. "We studied this in school, but I'd like to hear your version."

General Zimmerman smiled. "I suppose we have my neighbor to blame." He pointed out the window. "If Dr. Rosenzweig had not created the formula that literally changed the landscape of our country, perhaps we would not have been attacked."

"The Russians wanted the formula?" Lionel said.

"Russia's economy had been devastated. All they had was military might. When Israel prospered, they were determined to occupy the Holy Land. We had an inkling something bad was coming, but we had no idea it would be an all-out attack."

"Didn't it come in the middle of the night?" Judd said.

General Zimmerman nodded. "I was awakened and told missiles were heading toward our largest cities. Fighter-bombers with nuclear weapons flew overhead as I reached our defense headquarters. We had no time to ask for help. We were outnumbered one hundred to one. But we had to act.

"We launched surface-to-air missiles toward the enemy, and the first ones hit their targets. But the number of missiles attacking us was overwhelming. Our radar screens were filled with targets we could not possibly destroy.

"Then the explosions began. Planes slammed to earth. We knew the end was near. But we discovered the planes were falling from the sky without us shooting them down. The Russians' nuclear weapons exploded high above the earth. The sky was on fire and night turned to the brightest daylight. You cannot imagine the heat."

General Zimmerman ran a hand through his hair. "I went outside the bunker. I figured we were all dead anyway. Then came the hail, which turned to freezing rain. After a few minutes, the fire in the sky went out and darkness settled in, along with deathly silence. The entire Russian air attack was consumed in fire that night."

"What did you think happened?" Lionel said.

"Some believed it was a meteor shower, but how could such a thing happen and not harm one living soul on the ground? How could so many planes crash and burn without killing anyone except the pilots? I have asked that question many times, but I have not come up with a believable answer until now. Now I know that God protected Israel like he protected us last night."

The General explained what had happened since the rise of the Global Community. Zimmerman said he had never fully trusted Nicolae Carpathia, and now that he knew the truth about God, he cringed at what would happen during the Gala.

"We have other plans while that celebration occurs," Mr. Stein said.

"Tell me," General Zimmerman said. "I want to help tell others the truth."

It took Vicki a number of takes to get through her message. She felt nervous with others watching her and asked them to leave the room.

"Hundreds of thousands are going to see this," Conrad said.

"I know it's silly, but I'd feel better if it was just you and me in here."

200

When she finished, Conrad began editing. "Shouldn't take me more than a couple days to have the final product."

"How did you learn how to do this?"

"My brother had a pretty sophisticated computer with a lot of video and editing software. He used to let me play around on it."

Conrad's voice trailed off. It had been a while since Vicki had asked about Taylor Graham. She said, "I bet you miss him."

Conrad nodded. "When we're in the middle of a project like this, I stay focused. But at other times, like when we were driving cross-country, I think about him a lot. I wish I'd had more time to talk with him."

Vicki put a hand on Conrad's shoulder. "Maybe what you're doing here will help a lot of kids know the truth."

For the next few days the kids watched the news and the countdown to the return of the satellite schools. Conrad finished Vicki's recording and played it for the entire Young Trib Force. Charlie beamed when he saw his painting. Everyone was impressed with Vicki and for fun called her "the Ambassador."

Finally the day arrived when Dr. Neal Damosa appeared before cheering crowds around the world. The kids watched closely and took notes on the latest teaching from the Global Community.

Mark tapped Vicki on the shoulder and asked her to come upstairs. His face was grim.

"The helicopter's not back, is it?" Vicki said.

Mark shook his head. "When we brought the stuff in

from the truck we must have damaged the satellite. We can't get the signal to Carl."

"What does that mean?"

"Unless we come up with another plan, no one will see your recording but us."

21

OVER the next few weeks, Judd and the others held meetings nightly at General Zimmerman's home. Some nights there were only ten or fifteen people, but as time went on and more heard about Mr. Stein's teaching, General Zimmerman's house began to look like a convention center. People hungry for the truth returned with neighbors and friends. Mr. Stein was elated.

Judd spent little time at Yitzhak's house and hoped Kasim would forget his assassination plan. But a conversation with Jamal changed that.

"Kasim came here late last night looking for you," Jamal said.

"Did you tell him where we're meeting?"

"I mentioned the General's house, and his eyes lit up for some reason. I wouldn't be surprised if he shows up for a meeting there."

That night Mr. Stein asked Judd to tell his story. As the meeting began, Kasim walked in. He smiled at Judd.

"You thought you could avoid me, Judd? Aren't you going to help me with the plan?"

"No," Judd said. "I'm sorry. And I think you should—"

Kasim interrupted. "But you led me here, right? You're helping me without even knowing it."

"What are you talking about?"

"General Zimmerman is known for his collection of military weapons. Where does he keep them?"

General Zimmerman had given Judd and the others a tour of his home and had shown them guns dating back to the American Civil War. There were swords and shields from the Roman Empire. And, as Kasim believed, the collection upstairs also contained some of the most recent weaponry.

"Come to the front and tell your story," Mr. Stein said. People turned and looked at Judd.

"Don't do this," Judd whispered to Kasim.

Judd was almost finished with his story when Kasim walked down the steps with something under his arm. He caught Judd's attention and held out a rifle. Seconds later Kasim was out the door and gone.

Vicki wished she could help Mark and Conrad with the satellite feed, but the maze of wires and electronic equipment overwhelmed her. The kids worked frantically to link up, but nothing worked. The next satellite school transmission was hours away, and the Gala was fast approaching.

"Can't we mail the recording to Carl?" Vicki said.

"The GC inspects all the packages," Mark said. "We should have taken it to him."

Conrad talked with Carl in Florida and tried different switches. "Let me put you on the speaker."

"Isn't this dangerous for you, Carl?" Vicki said.

"I'm off duty in a truck parked next to our main studio," Carl said. "I'm okay as long as they don't catch me."

"What do we do now?" Conrad said.

"Try it again. If we can get this to work, I'll record here and then figure out how to put it on the main feed to the stadiums."

Tolan crawled into the room and bumped against the door. He wailed. Conrad yelled, "Get that kid out of here!"

Vicki picked Tolan up and comforted him. Lenore came and took him upstairs. Vicki knew the pressure of the uplink and the summer heat had everyone frazzled.

The satellite schools attracted record crowds of kids around the world. More were attending and seemed to buy what was being taught by the speakers. It was the perfect time to break in with their message, but Vicki worried that their plan was going to fail.

The satellite school was popular because of the top-notch celebrities and entertainment. Each broadcast featured a film star, a sports celebrity, or a musical artist who would praise the work of the Global Community. On the Friday before the GC Gala, the kids were surprised to see a stage in the shape of a dove.

"What are they going to do with that?" Shelly said.

Vicki shook her head. "Whatever it is, it's part of the GC's brainwashing."

Lionel convinced Judd and the others to let him go to Teddy Kollek Stadium to observe the latest satellite presentation. Mr. Stein reluctantly agreed when Lionel promised he would stay outside and watch on the huge monitors. Lionel grabbed a stack of flyers and headed out the door.

The sun was setting orange and yellow as Lionel neared the stadium. Someone tapped him on the shoulder. It was Sam.

"You can't be here," Lionel said. "The GC could recognize—"

"Stop. We're both taking a chance."

Lionel pointed to a small, box-shaped shack outside Teddy Kollek Stadium. Around the structure were free handouts. A sign above said "Read the Latest from Tsion Ben-Judah!"

"They must think we're stupid," Lionel said.

A few kids in black clothes passed the shack and jeered. One grabbed a few pamphlets and tore them up. Another tried to set fire to the canopy that hung over the racks. Soon a crowd had gathered and kids chanted, "Death to Ben-Judah! Death to Ben-Judah!"

Sam frowned. "Looks like the GC's training is working."

A husky boy ran at the structure and hit it full force, like a linebacker tackling a running back. Boards cracked and pamphlets flew into the air. A window opened and two uniformed Peacekeepers with video equipment shooed the kids away.

While the Peacekeepers tried to repair the damage,

Lionel spotted a GC motorcade. They drove straight into the stadium and onto the field near the dove-shaped stage.

The cars were greeted with a deafening roar. First out of a long, black limo was the head of GC education, Dr. Neal Damosa. He ran onstage like a rock star.

Sam tapped Lionel on the shoulder and pointed behind them, where a huge transport plane approached. Lionel shrugged and moved closer to the monitor.

"Fellow citizens of the Global Community, I welcome you in the name of peace!"

The stadium roared again as people inside and outside came to their feet. Lionel noticed there was a delay between what happened inside the stadium and what he was seeing on the monitor.

The plane passed directly over the stadium and banked left. Several objects fell out a side door. Lionel counted ten specks falling toward earth.

Damosa quieted the crowd and took control. "We come in peace, in a place of peace—Jerusalem. This city and its people were made a promise by Potentate Carpathia more than three years ago, a promise that has been kept. And so we gather on this stage and stand on this symbol of unity and peace, where in a few short days there will be a celebration like no other in the history of the world."

Again the crowd cheered. Damosa invited young people from every continent to join them in Jerusalem. He pointed to the sky. "Watch and see the precision of the Global Community, as members of the Peacekeeping Paratroopers descend to this very stage!"

The parachutes opened, and the ten slowly fell to earth. An announcer read the names of each Peacekeeper, one from each of Nicolae Carpathia's ten regions. Smoke trailed from the paratroopers as one by one they landed on different points of the dove. At each landing, the crowd screamed and yelled. When only one paratrooper was left, Damosa ran to a small platform in the center of the stage.

"The final member of the team will attempt to land right where I'm standing, carrying a flag with the insignia of the Global Community."

"He's going to try and land on that little square?" Sam said.

Lionel nodded. "These people are good."

The announcer called the name of the last jumper, a female from the United Carpathian States. The crowd hushed as she floated over the stadium, spinning in a circle. When she fell quickly, the crowd gasped and Lionel thought she was out of control. Suddenly, she pushed the toggles she held and landed perfectly on the small X in the middle of the platform.

The crowd went wild. A searchlight flashed in the sky, and thousands of doves flew through the light. Drums beat while cameras followed the flight of the birds. A screaming electric guitar pierced the air, and the cameras focused on the stage, which was completely enveloped by fog.

"It's that smoke and fire again!" someone next to Lionel said.

The crowd panicked. Dr. Damosa walked forward calmly. "We told you to expect something special, and here they are, live, The Four Horsemen!"

Lionel shook his head as the most popular band in the world launched into their wild and frenzied music. They had risen to fame a few months earlier with their song "Hoofbeats." They bashed Tsion Ben-Judah, Christianity, Jesus, and anything to do with the underground church. Lionel wasn't surprised that the Global Community embraced the group, but to link them with the satellite schools was a stroke of genius on their part.

Kids clapped, screamed, and sang along with lead singer Z-Van. He wore wraparound sunglasses and a skintight outfit that made Lionel wonder how he could possibly dance around the edge of the stage without falling off. GC security allowed kids to stream onto the infield and surround the huge dove.

Z-Van screamed his lyrics and the audience screamed back. When the first song was over, he stood on the edge of the dove, spread his arms wide, and fell backward into the crowd. The music rose, and the singer belted out more hateful lyrics as he rode the crowd like a surfboard.

Vicki peeked into the makeshift control room. Carl was on the phone going over their connections from the room to the satellite truck again with Conrad. "What happens when you try the auto-alignment?"

"It still reads *Error*," Conrad said. "I've tried it a million times."

"Shut the whole system down. We'll start over," Carl said.

Mark flipped switches, and the monitors went dead.

The kids in the other room, still watching the Four Horsemen on TV, asked what had happened. Vicki explained.

"I used to really like these guys," Janie said. "Now I think they're sick. I wish they knew the truth."

Vicki asked everyone to pray. One by one, the kids asked God to do something miraculous.

Conrad motioned Vicki inside the control room. "I'm sorry about yelling at Tolan. I'm just—"

"It's okay," Vicki said. "You can give Lenore some free babysitting when this is over."

Conrad smiled. "It's a deal."

"Powering up!" Mark said as he flipped switches throughout the room. A few moments later the band was back on the monitors. Z-Van was now wearing a horse costume. As he sang, flames shot into the air.

Shelly put a hand on Vicki's shoulder. "Their music is bad, but you have to admit they're kind of cute."

Vicki shook her head. "All of their songs are just twisted lyrics from Dr. Ben-Judah's e-mail messages. I can't get past that."

"Okay, I have a green light on the controller," Conrad said. "I think the auto-alignment's working."

Mark turned on the camera and pointed it toward Charlie's painting. "Carl, if this is working right you should be—"

"I'm getting something from New Babylon."

Mark walked in front of the camera and waved. "How about now?"

"Wow!" Carl said. "I thought that was real. Great job on the painting."

"So you have us?" Conrad said.

"Picture's perfect. Let me get ready to record." Carl tapped at his keyboard and his computer blipped. "Okay. Go ahead and upload the drop-in."

Conrad searched the hard drive and inserted a different disk in the computer.

"What's wrong?" Vicki said.

"It's not here. When we powered down, we must have lost it."

The noise from the concert rose as The Four Horsemen ended a song. Z-Van threw the microphone into the air and caught it behind his back. "This will be our last tune before we take a break. Then Dr. Damosa has a few words. Put your hands together and help us out on this one!" The crowd went wild as drums beat and fireworks shot from all sides of the stage.

Vicki shook her head. "This would be the perfect time to play the message."

"You're right," Carl said, "and after the band finishes, you'll be on."

"What do you mean?" Vicki said. "We can't find the recording."

"Forget the recording. We're going live!"

22

VICKI stared at the phone, then looked at Mark and Conrad. "Is he serious?"

Mark nodded. "Can you get back into your GC getup? This song won't last long."

"But how—"

"I'll put your script on the monitor," Conrad said. "You'll be even better live than on the recording."

Janie ran upstairs. "I'll get the outfit for you."

Conrad pulled up the text of Vicki's message as Mark checked in with Carl. "How are you going to jam this onto the main GC signal?"

"I checked the wiring a few days ago and rigged the truck just for this. The guys inside think they have control, but I routed the main signal through here."

"What if they figure it out?"

"I've got a tiny camera in the GC control room," Carl said. "I'll monitor them and switch back to the main feed if they get close."

"Are you sure you'll be safe?"

"They don't know I'm here. If Vicki plays it cool and takes direction, we'll be fine. Remember, we'll only have four or five minutes."

Janie returned with the clothes and Vicki changed in the downstairs bathroom. When she came out, the band finished their song and the crowd went wild. The Four Horsemen waved and hurried offstage.

"Get in position!" Conrad said.

Mark picked up the phone. "I'll relay any directions. We don't want the GC hearing Carl's voice in the background."

Vicki grabbed Janie's arm. "Get the others and pray."

The sound was deafening as Lionel stood outside the arena. Thousands cheered and fireworks exploded overhead. Cameras panned the stadium, showing kids screaming and waving cigarette lighters in the dark.

Finally the audience settled, and the camera focused on Dr. Damosa. Before he could speak, the picture switched to a scene in New Babylon. A girl in a suit walked in front of the camera.

"Pretty cool concert, brought to you by your friends at the Global Community Department of Education. We'll get back to The Four Horsemen and Dr. Neal Damosa in just a moment, but first an information time-out."

"I don't believe it!" Lionel said.

"What's wrong?" Sam said.

"That's a friend of mine. Vicki. This is going to really be cool."

Vicki felt the heat of the overhead light as she continued. What she had written for the recorded version didn't seem appropriate now, so Vicki improvised.

"My name is Vicki B. I'm the new ambassador to youth for the Global Community. On behalf of Dr. Damosa, the Peacekeepers, Morale Monitors, and our potentate, Nicolae Carpathia, I want to thank you all for making this satellite school program a huge success."

Carl Meninger's hands trembled inside the satellite truck in Florida. As he listened to Vicki, he studied the control room inside the GC Communications Compound. When Carl had first switched to Vicki, several people jumped. The engineer held his hands over the console and said, "I didn't do that. What's going on?"

Carl heard them through a tiny speaker near his monitor. Just as Carl was about to switch back to the regular feed, someone said, "Oh, this must be one of those drop-in segments."

"Yeah," another said. "They're probably feeding this from Israel."

"I can see why they picked this girl. She's cute."

Vicki wanted to be calm and just read the script, but something told her to wing it. Be creative. She knew she had to connect with viewers. If they sensed she was nervous, they would tune out.

Vicki ran a hand through her hair and said, "You know, it's a good idea to analyze the lyrics of songs. I used to listen to whatever was on the radio, and I told myself the words didn't really matter. But as a peace-loving follower of Nicolae Carpathia, you need to understand what people are saying.

"A good place to start tonight is Z-Van's lyrics. The latest Four Horsemen recording is 'Praying to Air.' I don't know all the words, but in the chorus Z-Van sings, 'You're praying to air, you're talking to sky, your mind's full of mush, 'cause you're willing to die . . . for a book.'

"What Z-Van is talking about there, of course, are the followers of Rabbi Tsion Ben-Judah. Some call them Judah-ites. Others say they're followers of Jesus. Whatever you want to call them, you have to admit there's a lot of them out there.

"The book Z-Van refers to is the Bible. As a matter of fact, I have one right here."

Lionel listened closely as Vicki read different verses. Some in the stadium booed when she pulled out the Bible, but most who were outside watched and listened with their arms folded. They seemed a little skeptical, but Vicki had their interest.

"I wonder how they're pulling this off," Sam said.

"I don't know, but this is the best thing I've seen in a long time."

Carl watched Vicki and smiled. He checked the clock. Three minutes into the broadcast.

A phone rang in the GC control room. Carl turned Vicki down as he watched the engineer sit up straight in his chair. "No, sir. We thought it was coming from you." A long pause. "Yes, sir. Right on it, sir."

The engineer slammed the phone down. "The feed's not coming from them."

"Then where—"

"I don't know. Just figure out a way to cut this girl off. Now!"

Carl grabbed the phone. "I'm going to have to cut Vicki off. Give her thirty seconds."

Vicki watched Mark type "30 seconds" on the screen. Vicki nodded.

"So, while many people call the followers of Ben-Judah crazy, weirdos, and even dangerous, we all have to admit that what this rabbi has been saying has come true.

"Think about that. Potentate Carpathia says we should be tolerant of other beliefs and religions. Maybe it would be helpful to talk more about what these Judah-ites think in our next segment.

"I'm Vicki B. Let's get back to the fun."

The feed switched to Teddy Kollek Stadium. The audience sat in silence until a frazzled Dr. Damosa came on the screen.

"Perfect, Vicki," Mark said. "Carl says congratulations. Your timing's flawless."

"Yeah, but why did you use your real name?" Conrad said.

Vicki shrugged. "It just kind of happened. I think it sounds better than Connie Goodwill. When can I go on again?"

"Stand by," Mark said.

Carl watched the GC control room settle. The engineer had hit every switch and turned every knob possible. Just as Vicki had finished, they hit a power switch and Carl switched back to Jerusalem.

"Leave that off," the engineer yelled. "It must have something to do with it."

Carl asked to be put on the schoolhouse speaker-phone. He praised Vicki for her poise. "You're a natural at this. Ought to have your own show."

"But I didn't get to what I really wanted to say."

"You will," Carl said. "When you come back on, you'll have the whole place in the palm of your hand. Damosa's supposed to speak for about twenty minutes and then bring the band back. Listen to what he says, and we'll cut to you before he introduces the band."

"I'll be ready," Vicki said.

Lionel was stunned at what the kids back home had accomplished. How they had tapped into the interna-tional satellite feed, he couldn't tell. But they had done it.

Dr. Damosa cleared his throat and gave a nervous smile. "Well, that was an interesting perspective. I'm not sure who Vicki B. is, but we'll have to have a talk with her."

Lionel whispered to Sam, "Sounds like the GC have no idea what's up."

Carl watched the control room on his monitor and listened closely for anyone moving outside his own satellite truck. He wanted to give Vicki one more chance on the air.

A phone rang in the control room. "We didn't put her on!" the engineer yelled. When he hung up, he said, "Here's the scoop. Headquarters says a Morale Monitor in Illinois recognized this Vicki B. character. She's one of those Ben-Judah followers."

"How could she hack into our satellite?"

"She stole a sat truck in Illinois."

"But that still doesn't explain—"

"Look, I don't know!" the engineer said as he checked connections and wires. "That's what we have to figure out."

"Maybe she really is in Israel and they're tapping in from there."

The engineer shook his head. "She stole the thing in Illinois. You think they floated to Israel?"

"Better call Meninger."

"Yeah, Carl will trace it."

Carl's cell phone beeped. He let the engineer leave a message. "Things are getting hot down here," Carl said to the kids. "We've got one more chance. Let's roll."

"Now?" Mark said. "In the middle of Damosa's speech?"

"Right now."

Vicki took her place and watched Dr. Damosa walk back and forth on the dove stage. "Peace comes with a price, and that price must be paid by those who enjoy it. There are some of you who think what I'm saying doesn't apply to you. You just want the band to come back. That's okay. I want to hear them again too."

Damosa paused for dramatic effect, and the camera zoomed out. It panned the crowd and got tight shots of those in attendance.

"If you want peace, you must commit to it. You can't *say* you follow the Global Community or that you *like* Potentate Carpathia. You must join us."

Conrad held up a hand, then pointed to Vicki. The screen switched from the stadium to Vicki. "Go!"

"Hi, it's Vicki B. again. Sorry to have to break into Dr. Damosa's speech, but he's making a good point. If you want to be part of something, you've got to do more than just talk about it. That's what I want to challenge you to do right now."

Conrad hit a button, and on the bottom of the screen flashed the kids' Web site, "www.theunderground-online.com."

"I told you earlier how many of the Bible's predictions have come true. If you read Tsion Ben-Judah's words on our Web site, you'll see this isn't some loony guy looking for attention. If you're skeptical, read it."

Vicki stood and leaned against a table. Mark zoomed in tight on Vicki's face. "But many of you know the stuff the Global Community is throwing at you is hollow. You don't have peace with God. Every time something terrible happens—an earthquake, stinging locusts, meteors, whatever—you're scared. You're afraid you might be the next one whose name shows up on the death list.

"I want you to know you don't have to be scared. You don't have to be afraid that God's going to zap you. You can have real peace with him today.

"Dr. Damosa was right about there being a cost to peace. It cost God the death of his Son, Jesus Christ. Jesus gave his life as a sacrifice for you and me, so that we could be forgiven and made right with God. If you want to commit your life to a peace that will be in your heart and will last not only a lifetime, but even after you die, you should pray with me right now."

Lionel watched people outside the stadium talking and calling for the return of The Four Horsemen. But when Vicki started her message, they became quiet.

"I think this girl is one of the Judah-ites," someone nearby said.

"Shut up," someone else said. "I want to hear this."

Carl watched the control room closely as Vicki continued her prayer. The engineer and others frantically searched the room.

"Where's Meninger?" the engineer screamed.

Carl turned down his monitors and dialed the control room. "I got your message. What's up?"

"Get in here now! Somebody's pirated our signal, and we can't find the source."

"What!?"

"It's the Judah-ites. Instead of the live feed from Jerusalem, we've got some girl praying."

Another phone rang. "It's Damosa!" someone screamed.

"How soon can you get here, Carl?"

Carl noticed Vicki was about to end her prayer. She looked at the camera, smiled, then gave the Web site address again.

"There's no time," Carl said. "Cut the main power grid for the entire facility. That'll cut out the satellite feed, but it'll also cut off the girl. I'll be there as soon as I can." Lionel heard Vicki's last words before the screen went blank. Sam looked at him and said, "Incredible."

A boy about Sam's age walked up and stared. "Why do you guys have that funny looking thing on your foreheads?"

23

VICKI collapsed in a chair and sighed. Conrad smiled and nodded at her. "Told you."

"What?" Vicki said.

"That you'd be even better live."

Janie ran in. "You were awesome!"

Lenore carried Tolan in and hugged Vicki. "God used you today, young lady. He was bringing people to himself through you."

Vicki wiped sweat from her forehead. "I was really nervous when I thought of all those people watching. Then I remembered my speech teacher. She said I should focus on one person and talk to him. So I pictured somebody sitting there by the camera."

"Who?" Lenore said.

"You don't know him. His name was Ryan Daley. He was one of the original members of the Young Trib Force who died in the wrath of the Lamb earthquake."

After Vicki's transmission had been cut, Lionel and
Sam wandered into the stadium to see if they could find
any more new believers. When they reached the top
of the runway, the lights went out and The Four Horsemen came back onstage. As fire flashed behind the
group, Lionel scanned the crowd. Every few rows he
saw kids with the mark of the believer. As the music
began, many of them made their way out of the
stadium.

"Come on," Lionel said. As new believers filed out,
Lionel and Sam handed them invitations to General
Zimmerman's home. Sam and Lionel split up as more
believers left the concert.

"How did you know I'd prayed that prayer?" one girl
asked Lionel.

He pointed to his forehead and explained the mark.
The girl said she was going right home to look up the
Web site of the Young Tribulation Force.

When Sam and Lionel finally got back together, they
had both run out of flyers. Sam said he had written the
General's address on scraps of paper and even on people's
hands. "I lost count at about seventy."

"I talked to around a hundred," Lionel said.

The music still rocked the stadium. Lionel and Sam
headed back to give the others the good news.

Vicki wanted to thank Carl for his work, but he didn't
answer his phone. The kids gathered to watch a recording

of Vicki's message, but Mark interrupted and called every-one upstairs.

Lionel and his friend Sam were on the computer screen when Vicki walked into the room. When they spot-ted her, they clapped. Judd was in the background giving her a thumbs-up.

"I don't know how you did that, but it was beautiful!" Lionel said. He explained what had happened outside the stadium after her broadcast. "We didn't see any believers beforehand, but we counted almost two hundred coming out of the stadium."

"And think of all the other locations that aired you," Sam said.

"You'd better get ready for a lot of hits on the Web site," Lionel said.

"I'm behind on one of Tsion's letters," Mark said. "If somebody else can handle that, I'll write something for people who prayed today."

"Call it the Vicki B. File," Lionel said.

Vicki smiled. "I'll take a shot at Tsion's letter, if that's okay."

Mark agreed, and Lionel and Sam said good-bye. Judd stepped closer to the camera. "Wish I could have seen you tonight, Vick. Sounds like a pretty good show."

"It was a team effort. What's up with you?"

Judd gave the kids an update on General Zimmerman and Mr. Stein's meetings. "Hopefully a lot of kids who saw the broadcast will come."

"Anything we can pray about?" Conrad said.

Judd hesitated. "There is something. A believer I know is about to get into trouble."

"With the GC?" Conrad said.

"Yeah. And it could put the rest of us in a tight spot. Pray that I'll know what to do when the time comes."

All the kids said they would pray. Tolan toddled into the room and waved at Judd on the camera. Everyone laughed.

Vicki went to her room to read the letter from Tsion Ben-Judah. Vicki loved everything Tsion wrote. This letter dealt with the Global Gala that was coming up quickly. Vicki shook her head. With all the death and grief in the world, Nicolae Carpathia wanted to throw a party.

Tsion said he would not attend the Global Gala, even though he had been invited as an international states- man. *An earthquake is prophesied that will wipe out a tenth of that city,* Tsion had written.

Vicki thought of Judd, Lionel, and the others. Would they be safe from the earthquake? Would other believers be hurt?

Vicki read the rest of the letter and tried to rewrite it in a way anyone could understand. At first it felt weird to change any of the letter. But she knew some kids wouldn't be able to understand all the words.

She wrote:

> *Because death will be in the air in Jerusalem next month, I will not attend this outrage. This festival is an excuse to bring about the evil plans of Satan himself.*
>
> *I will follow the Gala on the Internet or television, like the rest of the world. But I believe this event will*

*begin the second half of the Tribulation, called the Great
Tribulation, which will make these days seem relaxing.*

*If you watch the GC newscasts, you know how bad
things have become. Crime and sin are beyond control.
The food and supplies we need to live on are in short
supply because many workers who make and distribute
them have died. Life is cheap, and our neighbors die
every day at the hand of criminals who steal things from
them. Many Peacekeepers have died, and the ones left
are either overwhelmed with their jobs or are crooks
themselves.*

Vicki moved through the rest of the letter, highlighting Tsion's belief that evil would become worse and worse.

*I urge you to prepare for the day when it is illegal not
just to read this Web site or call yourself a believer. One
day you will be required to take the terrible mark of the
beast on your forehead or your hand in order to buy or
sell anything.*

*Don't make the fatal mistake of thinking you can
take that mark and privately believe in Christ. Jesus has
made it plain that those who deny him before men, he
will deny before God. I will talk more later about why
anyone who takes the mark of the beast will not be able
to change their minds.*

Vicki thought of Lionel and Judd. They had called themselves Christians before the Rapture. Playing church wasn't an option now.

If you have asked God to forgive your sins and have trusted Christ for your salvation, you have the seal of God on your forehead. This mark is also not reversible, so you don't have to be afraid of God turning away from you.

Tsion quoted a verse from Romans and Vicki opened her own Bible. She had read the passage before, but thinking about the current world situation brought tears to her eyes. She read: *If God is for us, who can ever be against us?* Vicki smiled. That verse said it all.

Tsion's letter continued to quote Scripture.

Can anything ever separate us from Christ's love? Does it mean he no longer loves us if we have trouble or calamity, or are persecuted, or are hungry or cold or in danger or threatened with death? No, despite all these things, overwhelming victory is ours through Christ, who loved us.

With the apostle Paul, I am persuaded that neither death, nor life, nor angels, nor principalities, nor powers, nor things present, nor things to come, nor height, nor depth, nor any other creature shall be able to separate us from the love of God, which is in Christ Jesus our Lord.

Vicki closed her eyes. She didn't know whether any of the new believers would understand the word *principalities*, so she cut it, but left the rest in. Tsion closed by urging every believer to give thanks to God for every victory he gives. He ended with *Steadfast in love for you all, your friend, Tsion Ben-Judah.*

Vicki thanked God for those around the world who had watched the satellite broadcast and had become believers. She thanked him for Janie and Melinda, whose lives had radically changed. She prayed for Judd and the situation with his friend, and for Carl in Florida.

When she had finished praying, Vicki felt troubled but couldn't figure out why. A few rooms away Tolan whimpered and cried, and Vicki realized why she felt so uneasy. If the kids had to run, there wouldn't be enough room for everyone in the satellite truck.

Carl Meninger sat in his office in Florida waiting for a call he didn't want to take, and hating himself. He had screamed at the people in the control room and blamed them for something he was secretly responsible for—Vicki's satellite broadcast.

"Don't you realize this could mean my job?" Carl had yelled.

The engineer and the others had looked at the floor while Carl ranted and raved. When Carl was finished, the engineer said, "There's no way they could have done what they did unless they had help on the inside. It could be in New Babylon or Jerusalem or it could be here."

"And who do you suppose it is?" Carl said. "Look around. Who's the mole who helped the Judah-ites?"

No one in the room spoke. Carl finally told them to search "every inch of the compound" to make sure the problem wasn't in-house.

Carl felt isolated from the rest of the Young Trib

Force. It had been his decision to go back to the Global Community and work from the inside, but he had had no idea how alone he would feel. There wasn't another believer in the entire compound, and Carl missed talking to Vicki, Mark, and the others.

He read Tsion Ben-Judah's e-mails religiously in his apartment. The rabbi's Web site, along with www.theunderground-online.com, was his lifeline to other believers.

The phone startled Carl. He checked the readout and sighed. His supervisor was a foulmouthed man who could make anyone feel worthless. He picked up the phone, and the man screamed at him. Carl held the phone away from his ear as his boss cursed and threatened Carl if Vicki ever got on the air again.

"I understand, sir," Carl said. "We're working to find out how it happened."

"Work faster," the supervisor said. "I've got Damosa and his people, and even Fortunato, busting my chops."

"I heard Fortunato was traveling," Carl said.

"He is. Called me from Africa or wherever he is this week and said if we didn't find this nest of Judah-ites, he would personally see there would be GC personnel executed."

"Executed?"

"Yeah, so make sure no one's working on the inside. We think we know where this girl and her cohorts are."

"Where?" Carl said.

"Illinois. A Morale Monitor got kidnapped by these crazies. Choppers are looking for a stolen satellite truck."

"Any luck?"

"Not yet, but we'll find them."

"I'm sure you will, sir."

"I want a full report on anything suspicious. Oh, and one more thing."

"Yes?"

"Dr. Damosa has called another satellite school uplink for this Saturday to make up for this fiasco. The Global Gala starts Monday. I don't have to tell you how important it is that this goes as planned."

"Yes, sir," Carl said.

Carl hung up and turned on his cell phone. He had turned it off to make sure no one from the Young Trib Force called him while he was talking to the others. Now he couldn't wait to talk with Vicki and Mark. It was time for an encore.

24

WHEN Mark told her what Carl had said, Vicki called a meeting of the Young Trib Force. Everyone crowded into the computer room. Conrad held Tolan to give Lenore a break.

"Marjorie told the GC everything she knows," Vicki said. "We need a twenty-four-hour lookout in the bell tower."

Darrion volunteered for the first shift.

Shelly raised a hand. "Why don't we all just leave? Wouldn't that be safer?"

Mark stood. "Because Damosa's called another satellite meeting for this Saturday."

Vicki nodded. "The reports from around the country and a couple of sites overseas tell us we've had incredible results. The truth is changing these pro-Carpathia kids. We estimate there were one to two hundred decisions made at each site."

"That means there are thousands who are now believers," Charlie said.

Vicki nodded. "We think a lot more might pray at the next meeting. We can't throw away this opportunity."

"What about Carl?" Darrion said. "He's going to get caught."

"They've asked him to head up the transmission this time," Mark said, "so he's wiring a button underneath the control board that will let him switch back and forth without anyone knowing."

"But they'll eventually find it," Darrion said. "And even if they don't, they'll punish him for letting Vicki get on the air again."

Vicki took a deep breath. "You're right. He's in trouble if I go on again, but he wants to take the chance. He thinks this may be our last shot."

"If everything goes as planned," Mark said, "he'll get out after the broadcast."

"What about us?" Janie said. "Where are we going?"

Vicki had thought about that question for weeks. The truth was, she didn't want to leave the schoolhouse. It was the perfect hideout. There was space for the kids to spread out and not bother each other, and they had been able to take in unbelievers.

"There are a few of you who came here during the locust attack," Vicki said. "We'd love to be able to stay together, but we can't. We'd like you to go back to your homes and tell others what you've learned. Help them know God."

Tolan squirmed in Conrad's arms and got down. He went to his mother and hugged her. "Mommy cry?"

Lenore picked him up, tears streaming down her cheeks. "I'd like to say something." She handed Tolan to Shelly. "You kids saved my life. Literally. And you saved my son's life. But that's not the best thing you did for me. You gave me a reason to go on. You showed me how I could know God. For that, I'll be forever thankful.

"I knew this day would come. I didn't want it to, but I figured eventually the GC would find this place and you'd have to run. My house is not big, but I'm willing to open it up to any of you who want to stay with me."

Charlie raised a hand. "Do I get to go, or do you want me to stay here?"

Vicki smiled. "You're with us."

Charlie smiled and slapped Conrad a high five.

When the others had left the room after the meeting, Darrion shared an idea, and the kids agreed it was a good plan. They helped the others pack and said good-bye. Vicki held Tolan a long time and wiped away a tear. "I wanted to watch you grow up."

Conrad loaded the small car and handed Lenore the keys. "We won't be needing this."

Lenore strapped Tolan in the back and waved. "We'll be praying for you every day."

With the Global Community Gala approaching fast, Judd, Lionel, Sam, and Mr. Stein moved to General Zimmerman's home to be closer to the city.

"I talked with my neighbor today," the General said.

"Chaim Rosenzweig is excited about being invited to the Gala as an honored guest."

Judd shook his head. "He still thinks Carpathia is a good guy?"

"Apparently so. I tried to talk with him, but he seemed tired. His speech was somewhat slurred."

"Did you tell him about the earthquake prophecy?"

General Zimmerman nodded. "He wouldn't listen. I tried to explain what happened to me at the meeting, but he said he has many Judah-ites trying to convince him to become one of them."

"I hope he does before it's too late," Judd said.

Late Friday afternoon Vicki climbed into the bell tower to relieve Janie. Janie gave her a pair of binoculars, scooted to the other side of the small enclosure, and pointed. "They'll come from that direction."

Vicki wiped away a bead of sweat. The intense heat of July and August had given way to a sweltering September. She closed her eyes and thought of her home in Mount Prospect. Her family had lived in a trailer that had only one air conditioner. On hot nights, the family crowded into the cool room or sought refuge in a screened-in porch her father had built. The constant hum of the air conditioner would put the others to sleep, but not Vicki.

"What are you thinking?" Janie said.

Vicki told her and Janie smiled. "At Northside we used to put wet towels over us on nights like this. We only had one fan per floor."

Vicki told Janie she could go, but Janie said she wanted to stay. "I've got a bad feeling I'm going to mess things up."

"What do you mean?" Vicki said.

"I've done a lot of bad stuff. From booze to drugs, stealing to, well, you name it. What happens if I go back to any of that?"

"Do you want to go back?"

Janie cringed. "Never."

Vicki sat back and smiled. "God's working on you."

"What?"

"I know you think I'm some kind of saint, but the truth is, I was pretty messed up myself. I did bad stuff and didn't care, because it was fun. After I came to know God, I wondered if I'd ever go back."

"Did you?"

Vicki shook her head. "I'm not perfect, by any stretch. But after I understood how much God loves me, I didn't want to do any of that. It's like God opened a door. When I saw what was on the other side, I didn't need the booze or hooch or anything else to make me happy."

"Sometimes the stuff I did comes back on me and I think maybe God made a mistake. He couldn't love somebody like me."

"But he does. All I have to do is look at your forehead, Janie. That mark is God's seal that says you're his child."

Janie sat with Vicki and talked until dark. When Mark relieved Vicki a few hours later, Janie was still there.

———————

Carl Meninger made sure no one was in the control room
very early Saturday morning when he checked the system
a final time. He had asked Conrad and Mark to leave the
camera on at the schoolhouse. He punched up the satellite feed and saw a volleyball with a face drawn on it.
Underneath someone had written, "Hail, Potentate
Nicolae Carpathia."

Carl grinned and tried the button below the console.
He raised his knee a few inches and pushed it. No one
would be able to tell he was the one allowing the kids to
have their say.

———————

It was still dark when Vicki awoke and checked her notes
for the broadcast. She couldn't wait to tell more people
the truth.

Dr. Damosa walked swiftly to center stage of Teddy
Kollek Stadium, beaming in the late-morning sun in Jerusalem. When he spoke, Conrad punched a button on his
watch. "We're on in exactly seven minutes."

"How do you know that?" Shelly said.

"Carl's instructions," Conrad said. "He can't communicate by phone, so we're supposed to go on exactly seven
minutes after Damosa begins."

Vicki took her place in front of the camera. Dr. Damosa
welcomed everyone around the world and in Jerusalem
and explained that some would be watching by tape delay.
"Only two days from now we will experience the most
exciting event in the history of the world. Already more

than a million people are here to enjoy Potentate Carpathia's Gala. We will celebrate without limits. Young and old alike are gathering. But you don't have to be here to enjoy the party. You can participate wherever you are."

Damosa paused. "I need to mention something that happened at our last gathering. Someone illegally broke into our satellite signal. This is a criminal offense and will be treated accordingly. We believe the young Judah-ites are the ones responsible, but we have fixed that problem."

The crowd cheered.

"I wish we could go on right now," Vicki said.

"Five minutes," Conrad yelled.

Carl Meninger checked monitors and different audio and video meters. The control room was crowded and getting hot. He asked someone to turn up the air-conditioning.

Carl's boss walked in and surveyed the scene. "Everything all right?"

Carl nodded but kept his eyes on the equipment. "We've checked out every possible way they could get in. There's no chance they'll do it this time."

Carl took a deep breath. He hoped he could get away before the GC arrested him. He glanced at his watch.

Three more minutes.

Vicki sat straight and pulled her hair behind her ears. It had been a long time since she had cared about her looks. Shelly applied Vicki's makeup and said, "Perfect."

Dr. Damosa announced the special musical guests and said they would be performing at the Gala the following week. The crowd cheered again.

"But first, the real reason we are here. We have been talking about your responsibility as citizens of the Global Community. In order to live in peace, you must help us work for peace."

Damosa's speech slowed. The camera focused on the man's eyes, and Vicki felt uneasy. He spoke softly, as if he wanted to put his audience into a trance.

"This is getting weird," Shelly said. "You think he can do what Carpathia did?"

"You mean put people under some kind of spell?" Mark said.

"I wouldn't put it past him to try," Vicki said. "How much time?"

"Two minutes," Conrad said.

"We need to start now. Is there any way to call Carl?"

————————————

Carl watched Dr. Damosa and sensed a change in the room. People behind him stopped talking. Damosa's voice was mellow, inviting, and evil.

Carl breathed a prayer for the kids in Illinois. He couldn't let this go on a minute longer. He raised his leg slightly and touched the button underneath the control board.

————————————

"You're on," Shelly whispered to Vicki.

Vicki looked up and saw herself on the monitor. She

smiled. "Hi, it's Vicki B. again. I know many of you heard about me from the last meeting, but you didn't get to see me, so the Global Community invited me back."

Vicki stood and crossed her arms. "Actually, that's not true. Right now, there are technical people trying to figure out how we're doing this. I really don't understand it myself, but I do know this. Dr. Damosa and the other GC leaders don't want you to hear what I have to say."

———————————

Panic. Chaos. People in the control room went into a frenzy when Vicki came on the screen. Carl's boss grabbed him by the shoulders and shook him. "Get that girl off there!"

Carl glanced at a side monitor and saw Dr. Damosa at Teddy Kollek Stadium. The man glared at the screen behind him and ran off the stage. Seconds later the phone rang.

Carl shouted orders and hit switches on the control board, but nothing worked. Vicki Byrne was on the air.

———————————

As Conrad put the kids' Web site address on the screen, Vicki quickly explained the truth about God. Vicki used Janie's life as an example.

"A friend of mine used to buy into the Enigma Babylon One World Faith. She had done some bad stuff in the past and wanted to follow God. But it wasn't until she understood who Jesus was and what he did for her—"

A ringing stopped Vicki midsentence. She tried to

concentrate and keep going. Someone ran downstairs and burst through the door. It was Darrion. "They're here! The GC are coming up the driveway!"

Conrad turned off Vicki's microphone. "Let's go."

"No," Vicki said. "Turn my mike back on and get out of here. I have to finish."

Conrad frowned. "Hurry," he whispered as he turned the microphone back on.

The others climbed down to the secret passage that led to safety. Charlie was the last in the group. He looked at his painting, then at Vicki. "I'm not leaving without you."

Vicki checked the monitor. She was still on. She had to finish her message and get out before the GC stormed the schoolhouse.

25

SWEAT trickled down Vicki Byrne's forehead and her heart galloped. The moment the kids had dreaded was here. The Global Community had discovered their hideout.

Vicki was frantic about getting to safety but also excited about speaking to thousands, perhaps millions, of kids around the world as she interrupted the GC's top education man.

Phoenix barked at the warning bell, and Darrion rushed into the house to quiet him as the kids scrambled into the secret passageway. Everyone was gone now except Charlie. Vicki waved at him to leave, but Charlie crossed his arms and stood by the door. He whispered, "I'm not leaving without you. Finish your talk."

Vicki turned back to the camera and smiled. "It looks like this is my last chance to speak with you. The Global Community is asking us to move out."

Vicki had to sit still because there was no one to work the camera. She peeked at herself on the monitor across the room, took a breath, and continued.

"I was talking about my friend who bought into Enigma Babylon One World Faith. She's been in a lot of trouble—used drugs, lied to her friends, and wasn't a nice person. She thought God couldn't forgive her, so she didn't try to change."

Charlie walked out of the room and quickly returned. "They're pulling up. Hurry."

"Maybe you think with all the people who have disappeared or died that it really doesn't matter what you do with your life. I want you to know it does.

"There's a God in heaven who loved you enough to die for you. You're not just a number to him. You were created to know him and live for him. And like he did for my friend who messed up her life, he can change you from the inside out."

A rumble shook the schoolhouse, and Vicki feared the walls would fall in. "If you want God to change your life, pray with me right now."

Judd, Lionel, and Sam stood outside Teddy Kollek Stadium and watched the huge monitors. Judd had gasped when Dr. Neal Damosa, the GC's top educator, lowered his voice and tried to put the audience in a trance. But when Vicki interrupted him, it was all Judd could do to keep from cheering.

As Vicki talked, Judd watched the kids nearby. One

tall boy who looked no more than fifteen said, "Not her again! That girl is a Judah-ite!"

Another shushed him. "If the GC didn't want her back on, she wouldn't be up there."

Lionel put a hand on Judd's shoulder. "Something's wrong."

Judd studied Vicki's face. When he first met her more than three years earlier, Vicki looked a lot older than fourteen. Now, at seventeen, she had grown into a mature young woman. But Lionel was right. Her eyes darted off camera. Someone said "driveway," but Judd couldn't hear the rest.

"Aren't your friends in a secure hideout?" Sam whispered.

Lionel stared at Judd. "The GC has found them."

Judd pulled his friends to the back of the crowd near a fence. He put one arm around Lionel, the other around Sam, and bowed his head. "God, you know the trouble Vicki and the others are in. They need your help right now. You've done incredible things here for us. Now do something incredible there."

Mark Eisman called for quiet as the kids walked through the Civil War–era tunnel. They had all heard of the Underground Railway in school. This tunnel was a secret passage that had given safety to runaway slaves. Mark hoped it would give them a chance to escape too.

The tunnel led down the hill from the schoolhouse and ended just before the river. Mark turned on a flashlight and noticed the muddy ground. When they came to the end, he turned and put a finger to his lips.

Water trickled and gurgled against the riverbank not far from them. A light rain soaked the ground at the tunnel's end. In the distance, a GC diesel truck chugged up the driveway to the schoolhouse. Mark turned the flashlight on the others and counted five: Conrad, Janie, Melinda, Shelly, and Darrion, who still held Phoenix by the collar. Phoenix whimpered, and Darrion clamped his mouth shut.

Conrad broke the silence. "We shouldn't have left Vicki."

"Charlie will get her out of there," Mark said. "We have to get to the satellite truck. If we leave before sunup, we have a chance to get back to the main road before the GC finds us."

"Wait!" Conrad said. "The computer. We left it inside."

"Too late."

"But that's the only way we'll keep track of the Web site and communicate with Judd and the others."

"We can't go back now," Mark said. "Let's get to the truck."

Mark wondered if Vicki was still on the air. A long cable ran from the back of the truck to the makeshift control room Conrad had built inside the schoolhouse. The kids would have to unhook it before they pulled away.

Mark crawled through the muddy opening at the end of the tunnel and looked back. Four GC vehicles approached with headlights on high beam. The huge GC truck led the way.

Conrad peeked out and gave a low whistle. "You think that thing's filled with Peacekeepers and Morale Monitors?"

"I'm not staying to find out," Mark said. "Quick. Everybody!"

The kids crawled out of the tunnel and headed for their truck. Phoenix barked.

"Let him go, Darrion," Mark said. "He's going to give us away."

Darrion let go and Phoenix scampered into the night.

Earlier, Mark had parked the satellite truck deep in the woods on an old logging road that snaked behind the schoolhouse. Janie slipped and fell in the mud. Shelly tried to help, but she fell on top of Janie. By the time the kids reached the truck, they were all wet and muddy.

Mark opened the back door and spotted the monitor screen. Vicki was still on, her head bowed.

"Conrad, I want you to unhook the cable as soon as she's finished," Mark said.

No answer.

"Conrad?"

Darrion wiped mud from her face. "He's not here."

Carl Meninger guessed this was the end of his Global Community career. He had started as a communications specialist in the GC Navy, where he had met John Preston, one of the kids from the Young Tribulation Force. John had shared the same message Vicki was now giving just before a meteor slammed into the ocean, creating the biggest tidal wave in history. John had given up his place in a minisub so Carl could live. It took Carl time, but he finally believed the message and became a member of the Young Tribulation Force. By that time, the GC had assigned him more responsibility, and he finally wound up in the satellite communications division in Florida.

As Vicki continued, Carl flipped switches and hit buttons like he wanted to take Vicki off the air. But a simple raise of his knee would activate a secret button he had wired the night before.

"Shut the power off!" Carl's boss yelled. "Do whatever it takes, but don't let her finish!"

Carl glanced at the screen every few moments. When Vicki began her prayer he yelled, "How in the world are they jamming us?"

"I thought you fixed this!" Carl's boss shouted, grabbing his arm and spinning him around. "I could have you executed!"

Carl had heard of Nicolae Carpathia killing people for little or no reason. GC officials who treated their employees harshly were rewarded. The media didn't publicize those stories, but Carl knew they were true.

Vicki said, "In Jesus' name, amen." She looked at the screen, smiled, and gave the kids' Web site address. "Be careful about this Gala that begins Monday. The entire event is evil. Listen and watch closely, and check our Web site during the week. I'm Vicki B. God bless you."

Carl grabbed a fire extinguisher from a cabinet and brought it down with a crash onto the console, smashing to bits meters and lights. He leaned forward and punched the secret button. The screen switched to Teddy Kollek Stadium in Jerusalem, where the crowd remained deathly silent.

When the monitor switched to the Jerusalem stadium, Vicki took a deep breath. Charlie yelled and Vicki followed. Then she glanced back and stopped.

"What are you doing?" Charlie said.

Vicki raced to Conrad's crudely made console and grabbed the laptop computer.

Charlie climbed through the trapdoor that led to the subbasement and took the laptop from Vicki. She followed, closing the door.

"Forgot a flashlight," Charlie said as darkness enveloped them.

"I remember where the door is," Vicki said.

She felt around in the dark and finally found the latch for the door. The tunnel was damp and musty, and with no light, Vicki couldn't go as fast as she wanted. She felt mud and water on the walls.

"Hold up," Charlie said.

"No! We have to get to the truck before—"

Charlie found her mouth with his hand, covered it, and whispered, "There's a light up ahead."

When Vicki finished her broadcast, Mark unhooked the cable from the truck and asked Darrion to carry it down the hill. "Throw the other end of it in the river. Maybe the GC will follow the cable."

"What about Conrad?" Darrion said.

Mark pursed his lips. "If he doesn't come back soon with Vicki and Charlie, we'll have to leave without them."

Vicki watched the light draw nearer, shining on the walls of the tunnel. Could it be a Morale Monitor?

Someone whispered, "Vicki? Charlie?"

"Conrad," Charlie said, "we're here!"

Before they could move, the ground rumbled above them. Dirt and rocks tumbled. Vicki grabbed a tree root to brace herself.

"Another earthquake?" Charlie said.

"I don't know," Vicki shouted over the noise.

Suddenly, the roof of the tunnel gave way, and mud and grass flooded in. Charlie pushed Vicki and fell under the earth and rock. Vicki crawled a few feet away, coughing and sputtering. She covered her mouth with her sleeve and tried to breathe.

"You all right?" Vicki said.

No answer.

She felt her way back on her hands and knees, frantically feeling for any sign of Charlie. She stood and reached up and felt metal and rubber near her head. And she heard voices above.

"Sunk," a man said. "All the way up to the axle. Gonna be murder getting that thing out of there."

250

Another called for quiet. "We'll get the truck out later. Get to the house! We don't want them to escape."

Something moved behind Vicki. "Charlie?"

She knelt and felt along the wall. A hand. Vicki clawed at the mud like an animal.

"Charlie!"

Carl and the others in GC satellite control sat with their heads in their hands. Carl's boss had left shortly after Vicki's final words. Carl ran his fingers through his hair. "Sorry, guys. I went over this console and the signal routing a hundred times."

A young techie picked up the remains of the console and tried to fit some pieces together.

Carl waved. "Don't worry about it. It's wrecked, and so's my career."

"You go down, we go with you, sir," another said.

Carl asked everyone to leave the room. Only the young techie was left when Carl's boss called and asked him to come to his office.

"Be right there, sir."

"Think I found something," the techie said, crouching under the console.

Carl stopped and turned. "What is it?"

"Something under here looks new. Could be how they got that girl on the air."

26

MARK inspected the satellite truck and noticed the fuel gauge showed a quarter of a tank. He grabbed their cash box and quickly counted their supply of Nicks. "Everybody get in! We're pulling out."

Shelly and Darrion stood outside the truck. Mark rolled down his window. "We have to go while their vehicles are still running."

"I'm not leaving without them," Shelly said.

Melinda joined them. "Vicki stuck with me through everything. I'm not ditching her now."

A GC diesel engine sputtered and stopped. As Mark opened his door, there was a huge thump and the whistle of air brakes.

"They're at the schoolhouse. The GC will be all over this hillside in a few minutes."

"Listen!" Darrion said.

Footsteps approached along the hillside. Seconds

later, Conrad ran to them and fell to his knees. "They drove that big truck over the tunnel and it collapsed," he gasped. "Vicki and Charlie are trapped."

"Could you hear them?" Mark said.

Conrad shook his head. "The cave-in was too deep. I tried digging, but it'll take hours for one person to tunnel through."

Darrion and Shelly started down the hill, but Mark stopped them. "What are you doing?"

"We've got to save them," Darrion said.

"Wait. If they're on the other side of the cave-in, they'll be okay. We need to get this truck out of here and come back for them."

"What if they're under all that dirt?" Shelly said.

Mark stared at the ground. "There's probably no hope if it fell on them."

"Whatever," Darrion said, and the two girls ran down the hill.

Conrad grabbed Mark's arm and pulled himself up. "Drive the sat truck out of here. I've got a rowboat tied to a clump of bushes not far away. There's a bridge about three miles down. As soon as we get Vicki and Charlie out, we'll meet you there."

"We'll wait as long as we can," Mark said.

"Let us help," Janie and Melinda said.

Conrad waved them off. "There's not enough room in the boat. Go with Mark."

Conrad ran into the darkness. Mark asked Melinda and Janie to ride in front with him. He started the truck and pulled deeper into the woods.

Vicki clawed a hole big enough for Charlie to breathe. He coughed and gasped for air. "What happened?"

Vicki told him. "Can you move your legs?"

"I can but not very much."

Without light, it was difficult to clear away dirt without it falling on Charlie. But Vicki kept at it, and soon Charlie could move his arms enough to help.

"What do we do now?"

Vicki shook her head. "We get you out."

"Do you think the others are gone?"

Vicki stopped digging and sighed. "Conrad saw the cave-in. He'll get help."

The two kept digging, but it seemed that once they got a section of dirt cleared away, another slid on top of them. Vicki grabbed the laptop and used it to help shovel more dirt.

"I've been meaning to ask you something," Charlie said. "Do you remember when I first met you in that hospital?"

Vicki smiled. "You loved to scare people and nearly gave me a heart attack. You've changed a lot since then."

Charlie lifted a stone and threw it to the other side of the tunnel. "I've learned a lot about God, but I don't understand why I wasn't taken in the Rapture."

"You know why, Charlie. You didn't believe in Jesus back then."

"I know. But God took little babies who didn't know about Jesus, and he took lots of other people who . . ."

255

Charlie's voice trailed off, and Vicki remembered when she first saw him. His speech was weird, he walked with a limp, and his body seemed out of control. He looked like a different person now. "Are you asking because you think God should have taken you?"

Charlie wiped dirt from his eyes. "People used to say I was slow. A few of them laughed and called me sick in the head. Nobody expected much from me, so I stopped trying. Then you guys came along and treated me different. I didn't think anybody could love me, but you guys said God did, and he even died for me. That blew me away."

"One of the happiest days of my life was when I saw you had the mark of the true believer."

"Me too. But I still don't understand. If I'm, you know, damaged in the head, wouldn't God have taken me with the other people?"

Vicki kept digging. "God knows everybody's heart. You knew right from wrong. You were able to make choices just like everybody else."

"So that must mean I'm not as messed up as those people thought."

"Right."

"Okay, then here's another question. Why didn't those locusts sting me when they had the chance?"

"You ask hard questions."

Someone moved near the GC truck, and for the first time a little light shone through a hand-sized hole above them. Vicki spotted the underside of the truck through the opening. The man cursed. "There's no way we're hauling those kids back in this."

When the man was gone, Vicki whispered, "Remember what Tsion Ben-Judah said about you?"

Charlie nodded. "He said God's love must be at work in my life. But that doesn't answer it for me."

"Maybe when the locusts attacked, God knew you were real close to believing. He showed you mercy."

"But if that's true, why were Melinda and Janie stung? They're believers now."

"One thing's for sure. There's nothing wrong with your mind." Vicki sat back, exhausted. "What do *you* think?"

"Well, I wonder if it didn't take those stings to kind of jar Melinda and Janie. Maybe it helped convince them of the truth."

"Remind me to ask those questions when we get to heaven. Right now, we have to get you out."

The two kept working until Charlie pulled his legs free. He collapsed, covered with dirt and mud.

A rock fell through the hole above them. Vicki saw someone's face peering into the darkness.

"It's me," Conrad whispered. "We tried digging through from the other side, but it's no use."

"We?" Vicki said. "You guys should be gone."

"Don't worry. We're meeting Mark and the others downriver as soon as we get you out."

"Can't the GC see you?" Charlie said.

"I'm under the truck. They're all over the schoolhouse and the woods. Help me widen this hole and we'll head for the boat. I sent Darrion and Shelly to get it ready."

Conrad looked up. A dog barked in the distance.

"Is that Phoenix?" Vicki said.

Conrad put a finger to his lips. Vicki stood on a pile of dirt and tried to see but couldn't.

After a few agonizing seconds, Conrad said, "One of the Morale Monitors has Phoenix by the collar. He's barking and trying to get over here."

"Good thing they didn't let him go or he'd have come straight for you."

"She's taking him inside the schoolhouse. Now help me!"

Carl tried to think as he knelt to inspect the secret button. "You're right," he said to the techie. "It's new. I'm not sure what it does, but it can't put the girl on the air. I was sitting right in front of it."

"Why don't we push it and see what—"

"And get our fingerprints all over it? That wouldn't be smart, would it?"

"I guess not."

Carl looked at the boy's name badge. "Kostek?"

He nodded. "Dave."

Carl shook his hand. "I appreciate your hard work, Dave. I'll have one of the engineers trace the wires. I'm sure it'll turn out to be nothing." The techie frowned. Before he could speak again, Carl said, "If that button put the girl on the air, I'd be the one to blame."

"Sir?"

Carl sat. "I was right here the whole time. I was the only one who could have pushed it."

Dave frowned again. "I wasn't saying—"

Carl held up a hand. "I know. But be careful who you accuse around here. Why don't you take the rest of the day off? I'll lock the room and post a sign so no one disturbs the evidence."

"Right. And I'm sorry if—"

"Don't worry about it," Carl said.

When the boy left, Carl locked the door and put a Do Not Enter sign on the window. He knelt and wiped the button clean.

Mark drove slowly on the logging road. He kept his lights off and strained to see as the first patch of sunlight came over the hill. Mark went faster as he approached an incline, but his tires spun and the truck slid to the left toward the river. Janie squealed and grabbed the door handle, but Mark was able to find solid ground and make it over the hill.

"Where does this road lead?" Melinda said.

"Conrad scoped it out a few weeks ago. Another half mile of this and we hit a dirt road. We keep going away from town until we come to the main road."

Melinda and Janie watched for GC vehicles as Mark tried to avoid deep ruts in the path. Judging from the trees, Mark guessed it had been twenty years or more since anyone had used the road.

Janie broke the silence with a question. "I'm new to this, but aren't we supposed to pray or something?"

Mark smiled. "Good idea."

Vicki stood on Charlie's shoulders and helped Conrad dig. In a few minutes, they had opened the hole wide enough for Vicki to get her head through. She drank in the clean air and kept clawing.

"Are you sure they can't see you?" Vicki said.

Conrad pointed toward the schoolhouse. "See for yourself."

The sun was nearly over the horizon as Vicki caught a glimpse of Morale Monitors scurrying around the schoolhouse. The truck kept the kids hidden from view. Radios squawked, and Peacekeepers yelled orders as they searched the grounds.

"Found the TV equipment," a man said over the radio. "This is where that girl was sitting during the broadcast."

"Find the satellite?" another man said.

"Still looking, sir."

"Search the woods behind the house. They had to use a snake to get the signal to the truck."

Vicki looked at Conrad. "What's a snake?"

"That's the cable we ran from the satellite truck into the room."

A female reported rooms full of supplies, food, and medicine. Conrad winced. "I wish we could have gotten that stuff back to Zeke before this happened."

"Hurry," Vicki said. "If they find the secret entrance downstairs—"

Something scratched at the door to the tunnel and Charlie turned. Vicki lost her balance and slid down the mound of earth.

"Give me your hand," Conrad whispered. "I think the hole's big enough."

The tunnel door opened a few inches, and Phoenix whined and strained to get through. Charlie grabbed a rock and stepped behind the door. "Get out," he whispered.

Conrad reached down the hole as far as he could. Vicki ran up the wall of dirt. She was inches from Conrad's hand when the rocks and mud gave way and she slid to the bottom.

Phoenix bounded in, jumping on Vicki and licking her face. Vicki stared at the door. In the shadows was a Morale Monitor.

27

VICKI turned to Conrad. "Run!"

The Morale Monitor stepped into the tunnel and pulled Charlie from behind the door. "Stand by Vicki."

Something seemed familiar about the girl's voice, but Vicki couldn't place her. Conrad didn't move.

"Get out of here as fast as you can," the Morale Monitor said. "You still have the sat truck?"

"Don't tell her," Conrad said.

"How did you know Vicki's name?" Charlie said.

"She's the most famous Judah-ite on the planet right now," the girl said. "Plus, we've met."

"What do you mean?" Vicki said.

The girl stepped into the light and took off her cap, revealing the mark of the true believer. "Don't you remember me? Natalie Bishop. I found you in the bathroom at the arena."

Vicki sighed and hugged Natalie. "Of course. I gave you our Web site address, but you never contacted us."

"I wanted to keep working from the inside. I got on the squad searching for you. Some people in the town nearby gave you up yesterday."

"Probably those people we took in during the locust attack," Conrad said.

"I wanted to send a message, but everything happened so fast, I couldn't. I saw your broadcast this morning. It was awesome."

"Let's go," Conrad said.

Natalie nodded. "I'll tell you more later. The other Morale Monitors think I'm keeping the dog quiet, but I figured he might lead me to you guys."

"His name is Phoenix," Charlie said.

Natalie inspected the tunnel and the cave-in. "Does this lead to the river?"

"Used to," Vicki said.

"I think you can get through this hole now," Conrad said. "Give it a try."

"Wait," Natalie said. "I'll lock Phoenix up and create some kind of diversion."

"No," Vicki said. "Come with us."

Natalie ran a hand through her hair. "Not now. Are there others with you?"

"They took the satellite truck, and we're meeting them downriver."

"Good," Natalie said, closing her eyes. "Okay, let me have a piece of your clothing."

Charlie took off a shoe and gave it to her.

"Perfect. When you hear a shot, take off."

"Promise me you'll get in touch," Vicki said.

Natalie smiled. "I still remember what you told me at the arena. I look at your Web site almost every day." She grabbed the dog by the collar and hurried through the door.

"What's going to happen to Phoenix?" Charlie said.

"He'll be okay," Vicki said. "Help me up."

Charlie put Vicki on his shoulders. Conrad leaned into the hole and grabbed her hand. It was a tight squeeze, but Conrad pulled her through. Next, Charlie handed Conrad the laptop. Charlie was bigger than Vicki, and it took two tries to get his shoulders through the small hole. Finally, Vicki grabbed one hand and Conrad grabbed the other, and Charlie squeezed through.

The three lay flat on the ground, inches from the bottom of the truck. Steam rose from the nearby river. Morale Monitors and Peacekeepers brought equipment and supplies from the schoolhouse and stacked them outside.

"What are they doing?" Charlie said.

"They're going to torch the place," Conrad said. "Darrion and Shelly are bringing a boat I stashed upriver. When we see them—"

"Not good," Charlie interrupted. "There's a bunch of those Morale guys down there."

Vicki craned her neck to see. She counted five uniformed people scanning the riverbank.

Phoenix barked inside the schoolhouse. Vicki thought of Ryan Daley. He had asked her to care for Phoenix before he died. *Ryan will understand,* Vicki thought.

Someone yelled from the back of the schoolhouse, and Morale Monitors along the river headed up the hill. Vicki watched the group walk directly toward their hiding place.

A radio squawked. "I think we've found a grave up here," someone said. Vicki recognized Natalie's voice on the radio. "I have a tennis shoe here, directly behind the schoolhouse, right at the tree line. I'm going to follow their trail."

A shot rang out. Natalie came back on the radio, excited and out of breath. "They're headed into the woods back toward the driveway! I need backup!"

Morale Monitors sprinted past the truck. Conrad grabbed the laptop computer and crawled from under the vehicle. When the GC group was far enough away, the kids headed down the hill as quietly and as fast as they could.

The logging road ended, and Mark stuck his head out the window to inspect the satellite truck. Mud was caked all over, and there were dents where the truck had scraped trees.

Mark headed west on the partially graveled road. "We'll hit a paved road not too far up and then it's off to the bridge."

Melinda fiddled with the GC radio in the truck and tuned to the frequency the Morale Monitors were using. Suddenly, a female voice said she had located the kids and needed backup.

"They've caught them!" Janie said.

"Stay calm," Mark said.

"We should have gone back to help," Melinda said.

Mark slammed on the brakes and slid in the mud.

A tree too big to drive over lay in the middle of the road.

"We'll have to turn back now," Janie said.

Carl quickly typed an incident report and gave it to his boss's secretary. "Tell him I'm going over every inch of the wiring, and I'll have a full report this afternoon."

The secretary glanced at the man's office. "He's been talking about you with someone in there," she whispered.

Carl tried not to show emotion. "I'm sure there's plenty to talk about after the past couple of days. I'll be in the control room if he needs me."

Carl hurried outside to the back of the building. He knelt and tried to peek into his boss's office. The blinds were slightly open, but all he could see was the back of the man's head. Carl heard two voices but couldn't make out anything they were saying. He crawled on all fours a few more feet and popped his head up for a second. Sitting on the other side of the desk was the techie, Dave Kostek.

Judd e-mailed congratulations to Vicki and asked where she was. He explained that all those staying at General Zimmerman's house were preparing for the first day of the GC Gala on Monday.

He sent the message and went back to his Internet search. Judd learned that in the past few weeks Leon Fortunato had visited each of the ten kingdoms to invite their leaders to the Gala in Jerusalem. Judd pulled up a video file of Leon in Africa before a vast, cheering crowd.

"We have endured rough times and much loss of life," Fortunato said. "But His Excellency is sparing no expense for an international festival like nothing ever seen before. Besides celebrating the halfway mark of the agreement with Israel, and I am so pleased he has given me permission to share this publicly with you, His Excellency is guaranteeing—you heard that right—guaranteeing an end to killer plagues. You ask how can he do this? The potentate is on record that if the two so-called witnesses at the Wailing Wall do not end their torment of Israel and the rest of the world, he will personally deal with them."

The words gave Judd goose bumps. He knew from Tsion Ben-Judah's writings that Eli and Moishe would be killed. Lionel believed that would happen in the next few days, but Carpathia had threatened them before, and the two had made a fool of him.

Judd pulled up other reports. In the various capital cities, Leon promised better services from the Global Community. "Within a decade, the only memory of the population loss will be sadness for those who have died."

"Fortunato is doing a PR campaign for Carpathia," Lionel said as he watched over Judd's shoulder.

When Fortunato kissed babies and held them high, Lionel walked out of the room. "I can't take any more."

Judd found the schedule of events from the Global Community's own Web site. Monday was the opening of the celebration, the anniversary of the peace treaty Nicolae Carpathia had made with Israel. Tuesday's main event was a party at the Temple Mount. Other lesser events were scheduled throughout the week, and then Friday was the closing ceremony.

Judd sat back and closed his eyes. Mr. Stein had taken them by the huge stage Carpathia would use, praying as they walked. He asked God to "let the truth be revealed even in the midst of a great, sinful gathering."

Judd thought of the vow his friend Kasim had made. Kasim planned to assassinate Carpathia on the first night of the Gala, and Judd knew he had to stop him.

Vicki followed Conrad down the hill to the riverbank. Charlie was close behind. All three dived into a clump of bushes at the edge of the water and listened. Vicki gasped for air as they slid into the river.

Conrad scanned the bank for any sign of Shelly and Darrion.

"Will there be enough room for all of us?" Vicki whispered.

"We'll make room. First, we have to find them."

Conrad waded a few feet out into the river and waved. Shelly and Darrion waded toward them pushing the boat, staying low in the water. When they arrived, Shelly gave Conrad a hug and whispered something in his ear.

"Hurry," Conrad said. "Natalie can't stall much longer."

"Who's Natalie?" Darrion said.

"We'll tell you later," Conrad said. "Charlie, you push the back; I'll pull the front. Everybody else in the boat and lie down."

Vicki shivered as she climbed in with Shelly and Darrion. Charlie and Conrad guided the boat downriver until they came to a curve. Then the two boys got in and pushed away from the bank.

"Nobody talk," Conrad whispered as the current took the boat.

Everyone had muddy shoes and wet clothes, but they were glad to be away from the GC. Vicki stole a glance behind them and saw the bell tower of the schoolhouse over the trees. She imagined what it was like to be a runaway slave, following the river to find another safe house and people who would help. Then it hit her. They *were* runaways, hiding from people who hated their message. A few minutes later smoke rose through the trees, and Vicki heard the crackle of fire.

Conrad and Charlie kept the boat moving with quick strokes of the oars.

Vicki noticed the current getting faster and the water choppier. "How much further to the bridge?" she whispered.

Conrad shook his head. "It took a couple of hours to walk. I'm not sure how long it will take in the water."

"So we're not far away?" Darrion said.

Conrad sighed and pointed ahead. "We're coming up on some rough water. If we make it through that, we'll be okay."

Vicki sat up and strained to see. Ahead the water slapped against jagged rocks.

Mark and the others tried to move the log, but it was too heavy. Finally, Janie found a chain inside a tool compartment, and Mark attached it to the front bumper. After a few minutes, they pulled the tree back far enough to get the truck around.

Mark listened for reports on the GC radio. A girl broke the silence. "This is Bishop. I've lost them."

Another Morale Monitor broke in. "The house is on fire and nobody's coming out. But we did find the snake from the satellite truck and tire tracks by an old road on the west side of the hideout."

A GC Peacekeeper barked orders and names. "Follow them in the four-wheel drive."

Mark stopped as they neared a paved road. A couple of cars passed before he turned left and picked up speed.

"We've got a good head start," Janie said.

Mark looked in the side mirror and frowned. "Yeah, but all that mud we picked up is leaving a trail. If Vicki and the others made it to the river, we have to hope they're waiting for us at the bridge."

Carl threw a few of his things in a small computer bag, grabbed his laptop, and walked toward the front gate of the GC Communications compound. He signed a Jeep out at the guard desk and said he was following a lead on the Judah-ites.

The guard saluted and handed him the keys. As Carl drove away, he wondered how long it would take for the GC to realize he was their man.

28

VICKI grabbed the boat and held on. She had never been white-water rafting. That was something rich kids did with their families. But Vicki had been on her share of roller coasters, and this felt even scarier. No seat belt. No life jacket. She couldn't even scream.

As they drew close to the rough water, Conrad wedged the laptop under one of the seats, and Charlie steered the boat to the middle of the river.

"Stay calm," Conrad said.

Darrion glanced at Vicki. "Are we going to make it?"

Vicki patted her on the back. "Just wait. We'll be at the bridge in no time."

"Brace yourselves," Conrad said.

The boat plunged over the first rocks. Conrad worked the oar furiously, but he couldn't keep the boat from turning. Charlie put out his oar, grabbed a rock, and held it there until the front came around.

Vicki tried to see what was coming next. The wrath of the Lamb earthquake had changed the direction and speed of the river. The farther they went, the more rocks jutted out of the water. In several places whole groves of trees had fallen into the river and created an underwater forest.

The boat rocked from side to side as they continued. "Worst part is coming up," Conrad said. "We get through this, we're home free."

Vicki closed her eyes as the water roared around them. She had heard the same sound the day Mrs. Jenness, the principal of Nicolae High, had died.

Mark drove the satellite truck as fast as he dared. He heard the driver of the GC Jeep radio that they had reached the end of the logging road.

"How could they have done it that fast?" Janie said.

"They can go twice as fast as we can," Mark said. "If Vicki and the others are waiting, we'll probably have to ditch this truck."

Carl drove like a madman through the Florida back-country. He headed north, hoping to hook up with the underground church in South Carolina, but he had no way of telling them he was coming. He had to connect with the kids in Illinois so they could get a message to Luke and Tom Gowin, who lived near Beaufort, South Carolina.

The radio crackled, and Carl's boss spoke without much emotion. Carl knew the man had to be furious. "Carl, I know you're listening. I've had a long talk with a worker who explained what he found in the control room. We've found the wiring and know how you did it. I have to admit, I don't know why. It'll go a lot better for you if you turn around and head back in."

Carl took a deep breath and held his tongue.

"I'm giving you this one chance before we send the troops out with roadblocks. You know we'll catch you. If you give yourself up now, I'll put in a good word."

You'll be part of the firing squad at my execution, Carl thought.

"You've been under a lot of pressure. Maybe you just went nuts and decided to help these people."

The only people who are nuts are people who believe Carpathia is God.

"Why did you do it, Carl? You owe your life to the Global Community. You were one of our best and brightest, and you threw your career away."

I helped a lot of people know God.

"Carl, you'd better talk now, or I'm going to assume the worst. We've heard about your friends in Illinois. The net's closing. We'll have them before nightfall. If we have to hunt you down, well, you know things won't go well for you."

There was a long pause. "Maybe you would agree to go undercover and ferret these people out? We can work a deal."

Carl couldn't stand it any longer. He grabbed the

microphone and pushed the button. "I'll never go undercover for the GC. You guys buy all of Carpathia's lies. I used to believe them too, but now I know the truth. Jesus Christ is the true potentate. I'm following him, and if you're smart, you'll ask God to forgive you."

Carl let the microphone go and scowled. "Stupid," he muttered. "They wanted you to talk so they could figure out your location."

He pulled out a detailed map kept in each of the GC vehicles and studied the roads. The GC might know where he was, but they didn't know where he was going.

———————————

Vicki knelt as they pitched forward. Rocks scraped the boat with a sickening creak. Twice, she thought a hole had opened and they were going to sink, but each time the boat bounced back. They were headed for a huge drop the boat would never survive. But would the kids?

"Go right!" Conrad shouted.

Charlie put the oar on the wrong side and Conrad yelled again. They were fifty yards from the final drop when Conrad signaled for Charlie to row for the bank. "Too steep!"

Charlie rowed desperately, trying to get the kids to the riverbank. Vicki thought about jumping over the side, but the water was too deep and the river too swift.

Charlie and Conrad fought a losing battle. No sooner did they have the boat pointed toward shore than the current swept the back of the boat toward the fall. The boat spun out of control. Vicki grabbed hands with Shelly and Darrion.

Conrad yelled, "Hang on!"

The boat plunged over the rocky fall backwards. Charlie's oar wedged between two rocks and snapped. The boat crashed against one rock, splintering the side. Then they spun around in the swift-moving current and crashed into a huge boulder, flinging the kids into a pool of water at the bottom.

Vicki bobbed to the surface and gasped. The boat stood upright, lodged between two rocks. Water cascaded around the edges. Vicki turned and spotted Shelly and Darrion swimming for shore.

"Where's Charlie and Conrad?" Vicki yelled.

Shelly turned. "Darrion's hurt. I'm getting her out."

Vicki frantically searched for the two boys. Finally, Charlie surfaced and gasped. "Help me!"

Vicki swam to him. Charlie beat at the water like a child first learning to swim. When Vicki came close enough, Charlie grabbed her around the neck and nearly pulled her under.

Charlie spit out a mouthful of water. "I don't swim too good!"

"Relax," Vicki said, tearing Charlie's arms away. "Let me hold you and I'll get you to shore."

Charlie went limp, and Vicki dragged him to the riverbank. When he could safely stand, he coughed and collapsed next to Darrion and Shelly.

"Why didn't you tell us you couldn't swim?" Vicki said.

"I didn't want to be a wimp. And I didn't plan on going over Niagara Falls."

Darrion had a bloody gash on her forehead. "I hit one of those little rocks as I went in the water. I'll be okay."

Shelly stood and screamed for Conrad. Vicki put a hand on her arm.

"Look over there," Charlie said, pointing.

Conrad was making his way back up the rocks to the boat. It stood like a wooden soldier, trapped between the rocks.

"What's he doing?" Shelly said. "He's going to get killed."

Conrad fought the rushing water and disappeared behind the boat. Moments later he reappeared holding something under his arm. When he got in the water, he held it above his head with one hand and swam with the other.

"It's the laptop," Charlie said.

The kids were all amazed that the machine had survived the crash. When Conrad pulled himself out of the water, Shelly ran to him and slugged his shoulder. "You scared me to death! You risked your life to save a computer?"

"Calm down. I'm okay," Conrad said. He checked Darrion's wound and made sure everyone was all right. "I'm sorry about the waterfall. It didn't look that bad when I walked by here a few weeks ago."

The kids rested a few minutes; then Vicki helped Darrion stand. Vicki could tell she was in a lot of pain. "I wish I had some aspirin," she said.

"There's some in the sat truck's first-aid kit," Shelly said. "Let's go."

It was after 11 A.M. when Mark reached the bridge. The Jeep was gaining on them every minute. Several locals walking by the road had seen the truck and waved as they passed. Mark knew it was only a matter of time before the GC caught up.

Mark stopped and looked upstream. Nothing.

"What if they don't show?" Janie said.

"Like I said, we'll have to—"

Something banged on the back of the truck. Mark looked in the side mirror and saw Charlie carrying Darrion.

Janie and Melinda rushed to open the truck while Conrad and Vicki sat up front. Mark drove quickly across the bridge.

Vicki explained what had happened with Natalie in the tunnel and how they had escaped. Mark told them about the Jeep that was only a few minutes behind.

"What now?" Conrad said.

Mark shrugged. "The GC will cover this area pretty soon. We should find a car."

Vicki opened the glove compartment and counted their Nicks. "There's not enough to buy something that would hold all of us."

Mark wound through the two-lane road into Illinois farm country. Few homes had survived the earthquake, but those that had were farmhouses.

"If we keep driving in daylight they're gonna find us," Conrad said. "We should stash the truck and head out after dark."

"Maybe Carl can help us," Vicki said. "Where's the phone?"

Mark stared at Conrad. "Do you have it?"

"I thought you were bringing it."

Mark rolled his eyes. "Great."

"It's okay," Vicki said. "I brought the laptop."

"If the GC find that phone and trace its calls, Carl's toast and so are the others we've called."

"We have to worry about getting out of here," Vicki said. "Then we can alert the others about the phone."

Mark turned up the radio as the Peacekeeper in the Jeep reported. "Just spoke with some locals. We're not far behind them."

Vicki leaned forward and looked out the window. "Pull over. I have an idea."

Carl was an hour from the Georgia state line when he stopped for gas at a small station. He tried the kids' cell phone, but again it was listed as unavailable.

Carl ran into the station and found a young man behind the counter reading a magazine. When Carl barged in, the boy nearly fell back in his chair.

Carl flashed his identification and said, "Has the Global Community been in contact with you?"

"No, sir. Why should they?"

"There's been an escape. GC officer stole a Jeep like

the one out there. This is exactly the kind of place where he'd fuel up."

"So you want me to keep an eye out for him?"

Carl wrote his own cell phone number on a scrap of paper. "I'm going to gas up and head west. I think he's on his way to Alabama. If you see any GC in this area, call me immediately."

The boy took the paper and studied the number. Carl handed him enough Nicks to pay for the gas and ran to the pump.

"Here's your change," the boy yelled when Carl was finished.

"Keep it!"

Carl turned on his phone and dialed the kids in Illinois as he raced along.

A female answered on the second ring. "Hello?"

———

As Conrad rode the rickety bike toward the road, Vicki closed the barn door. "We're going to stay in here until dark."

"Where's Conrad going?" Shelly said.

"He's riding along the road so that when the GC come along, he can tell them which way we went."

"Great idea," Charlie said.

Vicki checked Darrion's wound, but the others had already bandaged it and given her aspirin for the pain. Darrion said she was fine and wanted to rest.

Mark called from the other side of the barn. "Here comes the Jeep. Let's hope they buy Conrad's story."

Looking through the small spaces between boards, Vicki watched the Jeep speed past Conrad and nearly run him off the road. It slowed, backed up, and stopped.

As Vicki squinted to see what was happening, someone walked past the barn a few inches from her face. A man wearing a Chicago Cubs hat opened a smaller door and stepped inside. He carried a shotgun.

"You people stay right where you are."

29

VICKI gathered the others and stared at the man. He looked the satellite truck over, took off his hat, and scratched his head. "Why'd you park this thing in my barn?"

Mark looked at Vicki. She took a step forward and said, "We needed a place to rest until tonight. I promise we'll be on our way as soon—"

"I heard something on the radio 'bout somebody stealin' a big old truck from the Global Community. There's a reward for anybody finding it."

Vicki glanced at the others. Janie turned pale and shook. Charlie put an arm around her.

"How much?" Mark said, trying to smile.

The farmer ignored him and looked at Darrion. "What happened to your head?"

"I hit it on a rock. It's okay."

The man spit on the floor. "You got any guns or weapons of any kind?"

Vicki shook her head and looked at Mark. "We don't, do we?"

"No."

The radio squawked in the truck. "We just talked with a kid who says the truck went by here a few minutes ago headed south. We're on it."

The farmer squinted at the kids.

Just then Conrad pushed the bike into the barn and stopped when he saw the man.

"You got any more people, or is this it?"

"This is all of us," Vicki said.

"You hungry?"

The kids all said they were, and the man led them out of the barn toward the farmhouse. Cornstalks stood brown and brittle in the field.

"It's been a pretty dry summer," Mark said.

"Yep. My wife says God's not too happy with us right now."

Janie turned. "She believes in God?"

The man waved the gun toward the house. "Just get on inside."

A dog barked at the door. Cinder-block steps led to a rickety screened-in porch. A child's toys were stacked in the corner.

"Ginny?" the man yelled.

A heavyset woman opened the door and stepped outside. A long braid of brown hair hung down her back.

Vicki and the others gasped when they saw she had the mark of the believer.

Carl hesitated, wondering if he should hang up the phone or talk. The voice didn't sound like any of the kids from the schoolhouse.

"Hello?" the girl said again.

"Where's Vicki?" Carl said.

"Who is this?"

"I could ask you the same question."

The girl sounded peeved. "I don't have time for this. Are you GC or Young Trib Force?"

"Both."

"Good. I'm Natalie, a Morale Monitor. I'm at the schoolhouse now." She gave Carl an update about Vicki and the others and said, "Your turn."

"I'm the guy who got them on the air. I'm trying to get to South Carolina and meet with some of Vicki's friends there. Do you know where they're taking the truck?"

"No idea," Natalie said. "I led the GC on a wild-goose chase into the woods. Now I'm watching the schoolhouse burn."

"You'd better get out while you can," Carl said.

"I'm okay. I do have some good news."

"What's that?"

"If Vicki and the others can stay out of sight until Monday, they'll be okay. I just saw a document in the lead Peacekeeper's vehicle. It calls for a freeze on arrests or detainment, even of enemies of the Global Community, until after the Gala."

Vicki learned that Bo and Ginny Shairton had lived on the farm for nearly twenty years. They had tried to have children but couldn't and had adopted a girl from overseas five years earlier.

"When Amelia disappeared, my world just about fell apart," Ginny said. "I guess I could have run away from God, but somehow I thought he was drawing me closer to him. That's when I came upon the Web site of Tsion Ben-Judah. I prayed the prayer not long after that and have been trying to convince Bo here ever since." Ginny looked at him and smiled. "He's been holding back for some reason."

Vicki asked to see Ginny's computer, and the woman led her to a pink bedroom in the front of the house. Ginny ran her hand across the bedspread and sat. Teddy bears were lined up in front of the pillows.

"This was her room. I couldn't bear to take her things out of the closet or change the color of the walls. Bo thought I was going crazy, but I felt like I was closer to her somehow. I moved the computer in here and looked for answers. That's when I read Dr. Ben-Judah."

Vicki logged onto the kids' Web site, www.theunderground-online.com and looked for any new messages. Ginny's computer was slow, and with each click of the screen more and more e-mails popped up. Some had seen her broadcast at their satellite school and wanted more information, and many others reported they had prayed Vicki's prayer.

Vicki scrolled through the messages and called the others. One message marked "urgent" caught Mark's eye. Vicki opened it and read the message from Carl out loud:

> "Don't know if the GC can see this, so here goes. I'm on the run. Just talked with N.B. at the s. She has your phone. I'm trying to hook up with your friends T. and L. Can you have them call me? You know the number.
>
> "One more thing. Stay out of sight until Monday, the opening of the Gala. The GC will effect a freeze on arrests, even for people like you, at the start of the Gala week. Stay hidden until then and you'll be able to travel safely.
>
> "Thanks for any help you can give. JC is the true P.
>
> CM"

"What does all that mean?" Ginny said.

"It's from our friend Carl," Vicki said. "Natalie has our phone back at the schoolhouse. Carl's trying to get to South Carolina to hide out with Tom and Luke Gowin."

Vicki hit the forward button and copied the message to Tom and Luke. She included Carl's cell phone number and an idea for a possible meeting place.

Ginny went to the kitchen, and the kids gathered around the computer. "I think it's clear what we have to do," Vicki said.

Mark nodded. "We hide out here for a couple of days, then stick with Darrion's plan about Wisconsin."

"Can we trust the GC to stand by their freeze?" Conrad said. "I mean, if they see that satellite truck, are they just going to wave at us?"

Vicki scowled. "We'll have to travel at night."

Ginny returned. "I've talked it over with Bo, and he agrees with me. We want you kids to stay as long as you'd like. Permanently if you want."

Vicki smiled and took Ginny's hand. "That's sweet."

Bo walked in and put an arm on Ginny's shoulder. "And if you decide to go, you're not takin' that monster out in the barn. You can have my Suburban. It's old and uses oil, but it'll seat nine and there's room in the back for supplies."

"I don't know what to say," Vicki said.

"I do," Charlie said. "We ought to pray and thank God for everything he's done."

The kids and Ginny knelt by Amelia's bed. Darrion began, and then everyone spoke in sentence prayers, thanking God for giving them the schoolhouse, for safety, and for keeping them together. Mark prayed for Carl, and Vicki prayed for Natalie.

Finally Charlie prayed, "And, God, we thank you for these two people who took us in and gave us some food. I don't know what's holding Mr. Bo back from praying to you, but I ask you to help him do it real soon before it's too late."

Vicki looked at Bo, thinking Charlie's prayer might upset him. Instead, the man put a hand on the boy's shoulder and knelt. "I've always believed in the good Lord. I thought that was all you had to do. But my wife has changed so much since she read those messages on the computer, and I've seen it's real with you kids. Real enough to stand up to the Global Community."

Bo leaned forward and put his hands on the bed. "I've never been a prayin' man, so I'm not exactly sure what to say."

"It's easy," Charlie said. "Do you believe you've done bad things?"

"Sure. Nobody's perfect."

"Do you believe Jesus died to pay for the bad things and that he rose from the dead?"

"Yeah."

Charlie looked at Vicki. "Go ahead," she said.

"Pray with me," Charlie said. "God, I'm sorry for all the bad things I've done, and I ask you right now to forgive me. I believe you loved me enough to die for me on the cross. I ask you to come into my life and save me and be my Lord today and forever. Amen."

Bo whispered the prayer as Charlie prayed. Ginny smiled, tears streaming down her face. When he was finished, Bo looked at his wife, then at each of the kids.

"I'll be dogged. You people weren't kiddin' about that thing on your forehead, were you?"

Late Saturday evening, Carl reached Beaufort, South Carolina. He had talked with Tom Gowin by cell phone and agreed on a time and place to meet.

The smell of salt water and the incoming tide overwhelmed him. He loved being close to the ocean. He had taken back roads away from the water, but now he sat back and enjoyed the aroma of the low country.

His cell phone rang. It was the boy at the gas station in Georgia. "You told me to call if I saw any GC. A couple carloads just asked a bunch of questions and left."

"Did you tell them about me?"

"Of course. I told 'em you were already on that guy's trail headed toward Alabama."

"Good," Carl said. "Did you tell them I asked you to call me?"

"I didn't think to do that, sir," the boy said. "Do you want me to go after them and—"

"No, it's okay. I'll call them if I need to get in touch. Now do one more thing for me."

"Name it."

Carl pulled up to the site of the old Christian radio station, where the kids had first met Tom and Luke, and parked near the back. "I noticed you like to read."

"Everything I can get my hands on."

"Have access to a computer?"

"Sure."

Carl told the boy to find www.theunderground-online.com Web site and read what it says. "If you have questions, call me back."

A few minutes later, Carl heard movement in the bushes. He stepped out of the Jeep and whistled twice. Tom and Luke Gowin stepped out of the dark and shook hands with Carl. "You're safe now," Tom said.

Luke got in the Jeep and started the engine. "You go with Tom, and I'll put this in our motor pool."

"What's that mean?" Carl said.

Tom smiled. "He's going to drive it off the dock so the GC won't find it. Get it? Motor pool?"

Carl chuckled. It was the first time in a long time that he felt safe enough to laugh.

30

LIONEL shook Judd awake early Sunday morning, excited about what he had seen on the local news. "How would you like to see Mac McCullum today?"

Judd rubbed his eyes. "What are you talking about?"

"Carpathia and the regional potentates are in Tel Aviv. They won't fly here until tomorrow. But news reports say the GC pilots are giving tours of the Phoenix 216."

"That's probably just for dignitaries."

"I think it's first come, first served. General Zimmerman said he'd provide the car and driver, and he offered to call one of his contacts in security and arrange the VIP treatment."

Judd jumped out of bed and threw on his clothes. "Mr. Stein okay with this?"

"He said he thought it'd be good for us to get away for a few hours."

"What about Sam?"

Lionel shook his head. "He's helping Yitzhak with something."

Judd grabbed his shoes. "Let's go."

General Zimmerman's car was equipped with everything from a television to bulletproof glass windows. There was an intercom to communicate with the driver and ice-cold sodas in a small refrigerator.

The traffic coming toward Jerusalem was incredible. Already a million visitors had packed the city, and it looked to Lionel like there would be hundreds of thousands more by day's end.

The trip to Tel Aviv went quickly, but Lionel couldn't help noticing signs of devastation. The GC had done a good job of cleaning up dead bodies slain by the horsemen. But those who were still alive looked like walking shells. They had lost husbands, wives, children, and friends. And now, Nicolae Carpathia was throwing a party. Lionel shook his head.

When they reached Tel Aviv, the driver got as close to the airport as he could and parked. The terminal was jammed with people waiting to see Carpathia's plane, so Lionel and Judd walked with him to the tarmac of Ben Gurion Airport.

Judd sighed. "Let's get out of here. There's no way we'll get in with all these people."

The driver held up a hand. "Not so fast. You've come a long way. Let me try."

Lionel and Judd waited by a fountain as people of all ages snaked through the terminal. People spoke Italian, German, French, Spanish, and a host of Middle Eastern languages. Some wore the ornate ceremonial dress of their native country. A few young people with backpacks looked like they were hiking through Israel.

The driver returned, smiling. "You're in luck. Come with me."

They walked around the lines to a security door at the side of the terminal. The driver showed a piece of paper to a guard, and the woman scanned them with a metal detector. When they were outside, another guard led them to one of Carpathia's planes.

"We want to see Captain McCullum's plane," Judd said. "He's a friend of the family."

The guard used his walkie-talkie and took them to the front of a line. Others behind them grumbled. "What's so special about them?" Lionel heard one person say.

As they entered the plane, Lionel recognized Mac McCullum's drawl over the plane's intercom. He was showing the current group the instrument panel and answering questions.

An older man raised a hand. "Is this the plane that was attacked in Africa? I read about that in the paper."

Mac smiled. "No, I'm afraid that plane, the Condor 216, was destroyed. This plane was actually a gift given by the head of Enigma Babylon One World Faith, Peter Mathews. It was renamed the Phoenix."

Judd raised a hand. "How did you survive that attack, sir?"

Mac squinted and finally recognized Judd and Lionel. "That's a story for another tour. Now if you'll move to the middle of the plane, one of our stewards will show you the executive cabin."

As the group moved back, Mac grabbed a radio and said, "Hold that next group a couple of minutes. I've got some company up here."

Mac took Judd and Lionel into the cockpit and closed the door. The three shook hands, and Judd explained how they had gotten to Tel Aviv. Lionel told Mac about Mr. Stein's plan to preach during the Gala.

"That's pretty gutsy, telling people about God in the middle of a purely evil party."

Judd asked if Mac had flown Leon Fortunato during his recent travels.

"Yeah, it was the same spiel everywhere we went. Fortunato buttered up each regional potentate with big promises a thousand Carpathias could never keep."

"What's going on behind the scenes?" Lionel said.

"Something's up with that Peter Mathews guy. He thinks this Gala is going to net him more followers, but Carpathia and Fortunato have it in for him. Don't be surprised if he's not around much longer."

"Really?" Judd said. "I thought they were working together."

"They tried, but I guess even the Global Community isn't big enough for Carpathia *and* Mathews."

"What does Carpathia say about the Gala in private?" Lionel said.

"He's about to jump out of his skin, he's so excited. He says it's going to be their finest hour, whatever that means. He told the staff yesterday morning they should pamper themselves with all the physical pleasures they could find. You know, the old 'if it feels good, do it' routine."

"How are Captain Steele and Mr. Williams and the others?" Lionel said.

"Actually, you could pray for them. The GC is holding a friend of theirs. They think she's somewhere in France."

"She?" Judd said. "It's not Hattie Durham, is it?"

Mac stared at him.

Judd reminded Mac that he had met Hattie Durham on the scary flight to Europe the night of the disappearances. The kids had run into her a couple of times after that, and he knew the adult Trib Force wanted her to become a believer. Lionel and Judd said they would pray for the secret operation to rescue Hattie.

Mac's radio crackled and the guard outside said, "Captain, the people are getting very restless out here."

"Okay, send 'em up." Mac put an arm around Judd and opened the cockpit door. "Sorry to have to cut this short."

"Before we go," Judd said, "I need some advice." Judd explained the situation with Kasim, and Mac closed his eyes as he listened.

When Judd was through, Mac took a deep breath. "We know the big guy is going down at some point. Tsion believes it's going to be by a sword of some sort, but there's no way to know what that means for sure. If this Kasim is anything like his sister, he'll follow through with his plans. With all the security, he's committing

suicide if he walks in with a weapon. The GC will probably execute him for even trying to kill Carpathia."

"What should we do?"

"Stop him," Mac said.

People crowded inside the plane. Mac opened the
cockpit door and said, "You two enjoy the Gala. Hope to
see you real soon."

Judd and Lionel walked by the crowd and gawked at
all the electronic gear.

The earlier group was gone, so a steward led Judd and
Lionel through the rest of the plane. "These rooms are for
the pilots. When they're on the ground for an extended
time, they're able to sleep or just relax and wait for their
next assignment. This is the conference room where the
potentate or the supreme commander entertain leaders
and dignitaries."

"What are all those monitors along the wall?" Lionel
said.

"For the potentate and his staff. They keep up-to-date
with the latest news from GCNN or tap into different
satellites."

"You mean they watch movies?"

The steward smiled. "No. They keep track of what's
going on in the world. The potentate can go live on every
television and radio outlet from this room. It's very
important they have constant communication."

Lionel noticed the next group stepping into the cockpit area. Mac McCullum spoke over the intercom. "Sorry
to keep you folks waiting. Instead of the nickel tour, we're
gonna give you the quarter version."

"If you'll follow me," the steward said to Judd and Lionel.

Judd grabbed Lionel's arm and looked toward the front. "What is it?"

"I think I saw Kasim in that tour group," Judd whispered.

"Gentlemen?" the steward said.

Vicki was awakened Sunday morning by activity outside. The girls had shared the master bedroom. The room was dusty and Vicki had sneezed half the night, but it felt good to be in a real home again. Vicki dressed without waking the others and slipped outside.

Mark and Conrad were cleaning out the Suburban behind the house. There were scraps of lumber, chains, gasoline cans, and old blankets in the back.

"We're going to need to air this out before we leave," Mark said.

Vicki looked at the barn and noticed the door was open. "Who's down there?"

"Charlie and Bo are trying to figure out what to do with the satellite truck," Conrad said. "I think they've taken a shine to Charlie."

"Excuse me?" Vicki said.

"Ginny and Bo really like him. You should have seen the breakfast they made. Charlie must have had ten pancakes and a whole carton of eggs."

Vicki walked to the barn. The sun felt good on her skin. She hadn't realized how dark it was at the schoolhouse with all the trees surrounding the place. Here in the open land, things felt fresh.

"I'm thinking we can take it apart and use it," Bo said. "What we can't use, we'll bury."

Charlie shook his head. "You don't know the GC. If they find pieces of this truck on your land, they'll arrest you and your wife. I don't want that."

"Charlie's right," Vicki said. "We should get this out of here and as far away as we can."

Bo scratched his head. "There's a junkyard on a back road about ten miles from here. You don't pass many houses that way."

"Good. I'll get Mark and Conrad."

The kids decided not to take anything from the truck, and Mark drove it to the junkyard. Conrad followed him in the Suburban. The other girls awoke, and Ginny served them breakfast.

"We're going to have us a Sunday worship service as soon as those boys get back," Ginny said.

Vicki noticed a cloud rising over the road. She looked out the kitchen window and let her fork fall to the table.

Coming up the driveway was a GC Peacekeeping vehicle.

Judd stayed at the bottom of the stairs waiting for the other tour group. Lionel paced. "So what if it was Kasim? He can tour the plane like everybody else, can't he?"

"What if he's planting a bomb in the plane so Carpathia doesn't even make it to Jerusalem?"

Lionel squinted. "Where would he get a bomb?"

"I'm just saying, that's how serious Kasim is about this thing, and he could be endangering other people's lives."

The group walked down the steps single file. Judd saw one man who slightly resembled Kasim, but no one else. "Maybe he's hiding on the plane."

Lionel shook his head. "Come on, let's go home."

Judd reluctantly followed and got in General Zimmerman's car. He kept looking at the plane and wondering. The first thing he had to do when they returned to Jerusalem was find Kasim.

31

VICKI and the others hid in the cellar as the GC Jeep approached. Charlie remained outside with Bo, hitching something to the tractor. Ginny closed the cellar and told them to keep quiet. Vicki looked through spaces in the rickety door.

"Where are they?" Darrion whispered.

"Still outside," Vicki said.

Ginny quickly cleared dishes from the table and opened the front door. Two GC Peacekeepers walked in, tipping their hats. One was thick and pudgy, the other tall.

"Can I get you some breakfast?" Ginny said.

"Thank you, ma'am, but—"

"I'm starving," Pudgy said. He looked at the eggs and biscuits still on the table. Ginny got a plate and put it in front of him.

Bo and Charlie walked inside and sat. Charlie looked around the room, and Vicki closed her eyes. She hoped he didn't give the kids away.

"We're looking for a satellite truck that a bunch of teenagers stole," the tall one said.

"Satellite truck?" Ginny said. "We saw a long, white thing yesterday evening. I thought it was an RV."

"I didn't see it," Bo said.

Charlie chimed in. "I heard something rumbling along the road, but I didn't get a good look at it."

"See?" Ginny said. "I told you I wasn't seeing things. It was long and had something weird-looking on top."

"That must have been the satellite dish," Pudgy said as he spooned a heaping of homemade jam on his biscuit.

"Which way did it go?" the tall one said.

Ginny took him to the window and pointed. "That way. I ran to tell Bo about it, so I didn't see if it turned off at that other road or kept going straight."

The Peacekeeper sucked air through his teeth and looked at Bo. "Mind if we have a look around?"

Bo laughed. "You can plow under my scorched corn if you want. I don't care. Charlie, take these men outside."

Pudgy pulled his chair closer to the table. "If it's okay, I'll just—"

"Stay," the tall one said.

"Should I take him to the barn?" Charlie said.

Vicki froze. There was a note of fear in Charlie's voice.

Bo laughed. "I know it's a mess in there, but I don't think that's against the law. Show him anything he wants to look at."

Vicki and the others tried to stay as quiet as they could. She wondered if anything had been left behind after Mark and Conrad drove away.

"You don't have any apple butter, do you?" Pudgy said.

Ginny smiled. "I sure do." She moved past him and stopped. "But it's in the cellar. You don't mind waiting, do you?"

"Not at all, ma'am," Pudgy said.

Vicki and the others moved as far back from the door as they could. When it opened, light from upstairs shone on their feet. If Pudgy turned around, he would see them.

Ginny walked past the girls and whispered, "You mice just stay quiet down here." She grabbed a jar and headed upstairs.

Pudgy giggled as Ginny opened the jar. "I made this last fall. One of my best batches."

With a full mouth, Pudgy said, "I almost forgot how a home-cooked meal tasted. The GC gives us three squares, but it's nothing like this."

"What's going to happen when you catch these kids?"

Pudgy took a long drink of milk and wiped his mouth with his sleeve. "These are the worst kind. They follow that Ben-Judah guy. The one redheaded girl interrupted our satellite signal. We're mostly after her, but we'll lock all of them up."

"How many do you think there are?"

"Our informant said at least four and probably more. We'll keep hunting till we find them."

"Then what happens? Some kind of prison?"

"Reeducation camp is what we call it," Pudgy said. "But their life's never going to be the same. You have more butter?"

Ginny got some as the tall man returned. Charlie came in first and sat down.

"Your boy here was telling me those tracks out in the barn are probably from your tractor."

Bo shook his head. "I don't remember any tracks. But if there are, it's probably from the hay baler."

The tall one turned to Ginny. "What time did you see the truck come by?"

Ginny looked at the floor. "It was just after supper, I think."

The tall one handed her his card. "If you see or hear anything, please call me."

Pudgy grabbed two biscuits and followed the man outside. "Thanks for the breakfast, ma'am."

The tall one turned. "I don't see any other vehicle on your property. How do you folks get around?"

"My Suburban," Bo said. "A couple neighbor boys borrowed it this morning."

The two got in their Jeep and drove away. A few minutes later, Conrad and Mark returned. "I saw that GC Jeep in the driveway and we hid. What did they want?"

Vicki told them and Mark winced. "We should get out of here as soon as it's dark."

Everyone agreed except Charlie. "If those GC people come back and I'm not here, they'll know something's up. I can't leave."

Mark stepped forward. "Then you'll have to make a choice, Charlie. Go with us or stay here."

Judd couldn't believe the traffic returning to Jerusalem. The drive took three times as long as their trip to Tel Aviv.

The driver stopped for sandwiches, and Lionel and Judd ate hungrily.

The television in the car picked up the latest from the Global Community News Network. A reporter stood next to a scaffold where the gigantic outdoor platform was almost complete.

"This site will be the main stage for the opening ceremony tomorrow night here in Jerusalem," the reporter said. "Tomorrow, metal detectors will be set up as Global Community Security Forces keep a tight check on the massive crowd. Already, it's estimated that nearly two million people will attend the opening session, and hundreds of millions will watch by television and listen by radio.

"As you can see, the workers are putting the finishing touches to the stage and the sound system that will boom the music and speeches to the crowd."

The camera zoomed in on the stage with its vast green canopy. Messages in different languages were printed across the back. Judd couldn't make out the words, but he recognized the huge sparkling logo of the Global Community.

Lionel turned the sound down and leaned forward. "You want me to go with you to Kasim's place? That's what you're thinking about, right?"

Judd nodded. "I'd appreciate it."

Judd used the car phone to check in with Mr. Stein and make sure he didn't need Judd or Lionel. Mr. Stein was happy they had gotten to see Mac McCullum, and Judd told him about the plane. Judd called Yitzhak's home and asked to speak with Jamal, Kasim's father.

"I have heard nothing from my son," Jamal said. "Do you know where he is?"

"We're going to find him now," Judd said. "He took a weapon from the General's house and I have to return it."

"We will pray," Jamal said.

Judd and Lionel thanked the driver as he let them out near the Wailing Wall. Kasim's apartment was less than a half mile away.

People milled about, trying to get a look at Eli and Moishe, the two prophets of God many blamed for the suffering of the past few years. The crowd didn't want to get too close. They had heard and seen the reports of people burned to death by those who threatened the two.

The GC had placed massive television lights over Eli and Moishe. Satellite dishes, cables, and cameras filled the space in front of the two witnesses.

"I wonder if they have this much giz at the stage we saw on TV," Lionel said.

Judd was thrilled to see Eli and Moishe again. He wanted to stay and hear them preach, but he knew he had to find Kasim.

Judd and Lionel had walked this same route in the past, but they were surprised at all the new businesses. They passed bars, massage parlors, fortune tellers, and even pagan sanctuaries.

"Can you believe this?" Lionel said. "Chicago had these kinds of places, but you had to go out of your way to find them. This junk is out in the open for everybody to see."

Lionel was right. These weren't run-down stores in the bad part of town. Gleaming storefronts advertised everything sinful. One busy shop run by a group of witches offered to cast spells. If you purchased one, the second was free. Many shoppers bought charms guaranteed to hurt the two witnesses. A block away, a bar played music so loud Judd couldn't believe people could go inside without losing their hearing. The lyrics of the songs were so evil, Judd took a side street to escape the noise.

Judd and Lionel quickened their pace and finally made their way to the festival site, where in less than twenty-four hours, Nicolae Carpathia would speak. Judd found Kasim's building and waited until someone went inside. He darted behind the man and caught the door before it closed. "I don't want to scare Kasim off by ringing the buzzer."

Lionel followed Judd up the stairs. They reached Kasim's apartment and caught their breath. As Judd started to knock, someone screamed inside.

"So that's the way you want it?" a man shouted. "You want us to kill you?"

Vicki sat at the kitchen table with Charlie. The others crowded around. Conrad put a hand on the boy's shoulder.

Finally Vicki said, "What's going on?"

Charlie took off a hat Bo had given him and sighed. "I've always wanted to live on a farm and do outdoor stuff. And these people are so nice. They've treated me like I was their son."

Bo stepped forward. "We'd be awfully proud to have you stay. I could use the help."

Charlie smiled. "Plus, if those GC guys ever come back,

they're going to wonder what happened to me. They'll ask questions. And . . . and I could help teach Mr. Bo more about the Bible and get on your Web site and show them around."

Vicki nodded and put a hand on Charlie's arm. "If you decide to stay, I don't know if we'll be able to come back for you."

Charlie took her hand. "I don't want to leave you guys. You've been so good to me. You put up with all my questions." Charlie shrugged. "For some reason I think God wants me to stay here." He turned to Ginny. "I can sleep on the couch or even out in the barn—"

Ginny waved a hand. "We're going to fix up Amelia's room for you."

"No, you can't—"

"It's time I let go of that little girl. I'm going to see her in heaven someday. I know that for sure. There's plenty of room for you in there."

Vicki wiped away a tear. Charlie sat forward and said, "Oh, I didn't think about you, Vicki. I didn't mean to hurt your feelings."

"You didn't," Vicki said. "I'm happy you've found a place to stay before the Glorious Appearing. But I'm going to miss you."

Charlie stood and put an arm around Vicki. "If you ever need me, you know where I'll be."

Judd wanted to break down the door and help Kasim, but footsteps from inside approached, and he signaled Lionel to move away. The two found a closet down the hall and ducked inside.

Judd left the door open a little and saw two burly men walk out of Kasim's apartment, past them, and down the stairs. When they were sure the men were gone, Judd and Lionel crept toward Kasim's apartment.

The door was open slightly and Judd walked inside. The apartment was dark except for light coming from the street. In the distance Judd saw the huge stage where the opening ceremony was to be held. He picked up a pair of binoculars on the windowsill and read the writing printed on the backdrop. The largest read One World, One Truth: Individual Freedom for All. Judd scanned the plaza. Everywhere the Global Community could find a space they plastered the slogan Today Is the First Day of the Rest of Utopia.

"Judd, in here," Lionel whispered.

Judd hurried into the tiny bedroom and found Lionel kneeling beside Kasim's body. Judd flicked on a light. Kasim's mouth was bloody and his face bruised. Lionel felt Kasim's neck for a pulse.

"Is he dead?" Judd said.

32

JUDD was relieved to discover Kasim wasn't dead. He helped Lionel carry the boy to the bed. Lionel got a cool rag and wiped blood from Kasim's face.

"Who do you think those guys were?" Lionel said.

Judd shrugged. "I don't know, but at least we know Kasim wasn't in Tel Aviv today."

Kasim awoke a few minutes later and cried out. Lionel left and returned with two cans of soda. "There was no ice, so I figured this would help."

Kasim took a can, wrapped it in the wet rag, and held it to his head. "I didn't think they'd ever find me here."

"Who were those guys?" Judd said.

Kasim sat up. "I bought a gun and some other things from the black market. They—"

"What's the black market?" Lionel said.

"It's like an illegal store," Judd said. "You tell somebody what you want and how much you want to pay, and they get it for you."

313

"And these guys don't like to wait for their money," Kasim said.

"Why didn't you give back the gun?" Judd said.

Kasim held the can tight to his forehead. "Please, I don't want to talk about it."

Judd looked around the apartment for General Zimmerman's rifle. He walked close to the bed and said firmly, "Give me the gun."

"Your friend will get his precious weapon back tomorrow night."

"Not good enough," Judd said. "I want it now."

Kasim moaned. "You said you'd keep this between you and me. Why did you bring Lionel into it?"

"I talked with one of Carpathia's people today and—"

"You what?!"

"He's one of us. He said the GC will execute you if they discover your plan."

"They're not going to—"

"If you don't give me the rifle, I'm telling them myself."

Kasim stared at Judd. "You'd do that to a fellow believer? Someone who wants to rid the world of that evil man?"

"You're not thinking clearly," Judd said. "And if you did get away with it, they'd trace the weapon to General Zimmerman and he'd be in trouble."

Kasim pursed his lips and stood. "Help me turn the bed over."

Lionel and Judd flipped the bed and found General Zimmerman's rifle taped underneath. Kasim ripped it off the mattress and handed it to Judd. "Now leave."

"Come with us," Judd said. "We want to—"

"Leave!"

Judd and Lionel wrapped the rifle in a blanket and hurried outside. They thought of stashing it somewhere, but they were afraid someone would find it. They walked along backstreets and alleys until they came to the Wailing Wall.

Once again Eli and Moishe spoke to the crowd about the forgiveness found only in Jesus Christ. A few jeered at them, but most listened.

"You're going to get yours," one man muttered.

As Judd and Lionel walked away, Lionel said, "That guy's right. Carpathia is supposed to make war with them in the next few days."

Judd shifted the rifle to his other shoulder and said, "I'm not looking forward to that."

The two avoided any contact with GC Peacekeepers or Morale Monitors and slipped into General Zimmerman's house unnoticed. Judd crept upstairs and returned the rifle. He said good night to Lionel and fell into bed. Since Judd had learned of Kasim's plan to kill Carpathia, Judd hadn't slept well. This night, he fell asleep as soon as his head hit the pillow.

While Mark and the others tried to rest before their trip, Vicki spent the evening with Charlie, reliving their adventures. Charlie recalled how difficult it had been to carry Ryan's body all the way to New Hope Village Church.

"I wish you could have met our pastor, Bruce Barnes," Vicki said. "You would have really liked him."

"I've liked all your friends," Charlie said. "I wish I could have known you before all the people disappeared and everything."

"I was a different person back then. I'm not sure you would have liked me that much."

Charlie smiled and looked at the floor. "That Judd guy likes you."

"What do you mean?"

"You two yelled at each other, but I could tell he really likes you."

"You notice a lot of things you never talk about."

"Yeah, like Conrad and Shelly. They like to hold hands when nobody's looking."

"Really?" Vicki said. "I didn't know that."

They talked about the other kids in the Young Trib Force, and Charlie grew serious. "I've been reading as much as I can about what's going to happen next. It's going to get bad, isn't it?"

Vicki nodded. "We're in a seven-year period of trouble. The first three and a half years have been awful. The last three and a half years will be worse."

"Are we going to die before we see Jesus coming?"

"I don't know. A lot of believers will be killed for their faith in the next couple of years. I hope we all make it to the end."

"Are you ready to die?"

Vicki took a deep breath. "I guess. I mean, I don't want to, but if it's the difference between obeying God or obeying the GC, I'm ready."

Charlie nodded. "I used to lay awake at night in my

old house and worry about it. Sometimes I'd shake just thinking of all the different ways you could die. Now it doesn't bother me so much. I don't want it to hurt, but I know as soon as I'm gone I'll be in heaven."

"I look forward to you meeting Ryan and Bruce," Vicki said.

"That'll be great," Charlie said. He stared out the window. Vicki noticed how bright the moon and stars were in the country. Charlie scrunched his eyes and said, "Do you think we'll be able to know each other in heaven? Will we know those guys in the old Bible and the disciples?"

"You mean Old Testament?" Vicki said.

"Yeah, like David and Moses and people like that."

"I think we'll recognize each other, and we'll be able to talk and ask people's names. Who do you want to meet in heaven?"

"There's so many; I can't name them all. Like that Paul guy and Peter and that prophet man who had the fight with those guys on that hill."

"I don't think I know that story."

Charlie quickly gave an overview of Elijah's confrontation with the priests of Baal. Vicki was amazed at Charlie's grasp of the story. "Was that Elijah?"

"Yeah, he asked the other religious people if their god was asleep or on a trip. That was cool. I want to meet him and ask him what that was like. How about you?"

"I'd like to meet Ruth. Her story is so sad and then romantic. And Mary, the mother of Jesus."

"Yeah, and Joseph too. I want to find out what happened to him."

Charlie and Vicki talked about what they might see on television from Jerusalem during the week. She encouraged him to keep in touch through the kids' Web site.

Vicki showed Charlie everything she knew about the Internet, including how to send urgent messages to the others. She found a note from Carl saying he had made it safely to South Carolina and that Luke and Tom Gowin said hello. Vicki wrote a message back, showing Charlie how to reply to incoming messages.

The others stirred as Ginny and Bo carried boxes of canned goods and other food to the back of the Suburban. Vicki protested, but Ginny patted her on the back and said, "You kids are starting all over again."

"Where are you headed?" Bo said as he loaded cans of oil into the car.

"It's probably best we don't tell you specifics," Mark said, "but it's north. We'll stay there until things cool down a little; then we can figure out our next move."

Bo hugged Vicki. "If you ever need a place to stay, you know where we are."

The kids climbed into the Suburban and Mark started the engine. Charlie stood by Vicki's window patting her arm. "Gonna miss you."

Vicki choked up and couldn't speak. Finally she said, "We'll see each other again."

Mark backed out, turned, and headed toward the main road. Dust billowed behind them. Vicki saw Charlie in the moonlight, waving good-bye.

Judd awoke the next morning and smelled breakfast cooking. He went downstairs and joined the others, who were talking about the opening session of the Gala.

Mr. Stein paced as he ate. "The Global Community has just announced there will be no arrests or detainments during the Gala."

"What about their enemies?" General Zimmerman said.

"No one will be arrested or detained until after the Gala," Mr. Stein said. "The supreme commander announced that this morning."

Judd looked at Lionel and Sam. "That means Vicki and the others have a chance to hide if they haven't been caught."

Sam nodded. "I found an e-mail from someone named Charlie this morning. He said to tell you that everybody got out of the schoolhouse."

"Yeah," Lionel said, "but Vicki's picture is plastered all over the Internet. They better find a good place to hide, because when this Gala is over, they'll be looking for her."

Mr. Stein went over his plans for the day. Already, witnesses were handing out pamphlets to attendees of the Gala. "I don't think there is any sense in holding a meeting during the actual opening ceremony tonight. Everyone wants to see what Carpathia will say, and the noise from the musical groups will be heard for miles.

"Instead, we will conduct our first meeting this afternoon, just before the dinner hour, under a tent the General has loaned us. The GC, under their banner of tolerance and goodwill, has approved the site. We need help passing out invitations to that gathering."

Judd, Lionel, and Sam volunteered. Judd said, "What should we do about the opening session? Is it okay to attend?"

Mr. Stein nodded. "I would like for us all to be there so we can take advantage of any opportunity that might come up. In a crowd of this size, there will be people who are truly searching, even in the midst of this sinful gathering."

Mr. Stein put his plate in the sink and crossed his arms. "My friends, we are now at the devil's party. He does not want us to succeed. But you and I know the one who has forgiven us is much greater than the one alive in this world."

Everyone stood around the table and prayed. Afterward, each took pamphlets and invitations to pass out. As Judd was leaving, General Zimmerman pecked him on the shoulder. "Might I have a word?"

"Sure," Judd said, following him through the meeting room.

"I need to ask you a question, but you have to promise me you won't think I'm accusing you."

Judd nodded. "Go ahead."

"Yesterday one of my servants came to me and said there were items missing from my weapons collection. I noticed this morning that the missing rifle had been returned. Do you know anything about it?"

Judd told the General what had happened with Kasim and that he and Lionel had brought the gun back late the evening before.

General Zimmerman listened carefully and put a hand on Judd's shoulder. "Thank you for telling me the truth. Was that the only thing he took?"

"I didn't see him with anything else," Judd said.

The General put his hands behind him and looked away. "All right. I appreciate your honesty."

"What's missing?" Judd said.

"A special item I purchased a few months ago. If your friend found it that night, he could have easily put it in his pocket and you wouldn't have seen it."

"Is it a gun?"

"No, it's a high-intensity laser that can be used as a sword."

Vicki and the others drove north in Bo's Suburban. Though Mark and Conrad had cleaned it, the car still smelled like a barnyard. The kids kept their windows rolled down.

Darrion sat in front with a map. She had told the others about her parents' cabin in Wisconsin before they found the schoolhouse. Now it seemed like the perfect spot to hide.

Mark tried to find the least traveled roads. Bo had gassed up the car from his underground stash of fuel, so they wouldn't have to stop for gas. Everyone agreed the best route was away from Chicago, so Mark drove west before heading north toward Rockford. When they crossed the Wisconsin border at Beloit, Mark found a main road that went east.

"Where is this place?" Conrad said.

"Closest town is probably Lake Geneva," Darrion said. "I hope I'm not taking us here for nothing."

"What do you mean?" Mark said.

"The earthquake could have wiped the place out. I was going to come here with my mom but . . ."

Vicki put an arm around Darrion. The girl's mother had died in the wrath of the Lamb earthquake. Each of the kids had lost so many friends and family members in the last three years, it was hard to keep track.

"If we'd have come up here like we planned, she'd probably still be alive," Darrion said.

Mark drove through the night, the cool air rushing through the car. Vicki kept watch for any sign of the GC.

33

AS LIONEL and Sam passed out invitations to the meeting that afternoon, the voices of Eli and Moishe echoed through the streets. Every time Lionel heard these two, he felt goose bumps. Today their message seemed even more urgent as the prophets tried again to get people to embrace the truth of God.

Sam showed Lionel a shortcut to the Wailing Wall. Hundreds of thousands crammed into the area before the preachers, curious to see the two.

Sam climbed to a place where they could look down on the gathering. Lionel noticed many people kneeling by the fence directly in front of the witnesses.

"Those must be new believers," Sam said.

Others in the crowd jeered and mocked the witnesses as they spoke with great emotion. Lionel thought Eli was near tears as he shouted, "How the Messiah despaired when he looked out over this very city! God the Father promised to bless Jerusalem if her people would obey his commandment and put no other god before him. We come in the name of the Father, and you do not receive us. Jesus himself said, 'O Jerusalem, Jerusalem, the one who kills the prophets and stones those who are sent to her! How often I wanted to gather your children together, as a hen gathers her chicks under her wings, but you were not willing! See! Your house is left to you desolate; for I say to you, you shall see Me no more till you say, "Blessed is He who comes in the name of the Lord!"'"

The crowd fell silent, and no one moved as Eli continued. "God sent his Son, the promised Messiah, who fulfilled more than one hundred ancient prophecies, including being crucified in this city. Christ's love compels us to tell you that he died for all, that those who live should no longer live for themselves but for him who died for them and was raised again.

"We are Christ's ambassadors, as though God were making his appeal through us. We implore you on Christ's behalf, be reconciled to God. God made him who had no sin to be sin for you, so that in him you might become the righteousness of God. I tell you, now is the time of God's favor, now is the day of salvation.

"Salvation is found in no one else, for there is no other name under heaven given to men by which you must be saved. Though this world and its false rulers promise that all religions lead to God, this is a lie. Jesus is the only way to God, as he himself declared, 'I am the way, the truth, and the life. No one comes to the Father except through Me.'"

Now it was Moishe's turn. He stood and yelled, "This world may have seen the last of us, but you have not seen the last of Jesus the Christ! As the prophets foretold, he will come again in power and great glory to establish his kingdom on this earth. The Lord is coming with thousands upon thousands of his holy ones to judge everyone, and to convict all the ungodly of all the ungodly acts they have done in the ungodly way, and of all the harsh words ungodly sinners have spoken against him.

"His dominion is an everlasting dominion that will not pass away, and his kingdom is one that will never be destroyed. Come to him this day, this hour! God is not willing that any should perish but that all come to repentance. Thus saith the Lord."

Now the two prophets stood shoulder to shoulder and spoke in unison. "We have served the Lord God Almighty, maker of heaven and earth, and Jesus Christ, his only begotten Son. Lo, we have fulfilled our duty and finished our task until the due time. O Jerusalem, Jerusalem . . ."

The two stood before the fence and stared at the crowd, not moving or even blinking. Soon people grew restless and called for more preaching. Others yelled insults at them. One man near Lionel shouted, "Carpathia's coming tonight. He promised to shut you up and he has!"

Lionel tugged at Sam's shirt and they walked away. "I think we just heard the last words of Eli and Moishe."

Vicki and the others arrived at the Wisconsin hideout midmorning on Monday. The roads were terrible as they neared Lake Geneva, and several times Mark had to back-track and try another route.

Darrion had referred to the place as the family's cottage, but to Vicki it looked like a palace. It was built into the hillside in the shape of an *A*. Mark parked as close as he could, but downed trees prevented them from going up the driveway.

The kids inspected the doors and found all the locks secure. A huge pane of glass had broken on the second floor, but it didn't appear that any looters had ransacked the place.

Since Darrion didn't have the key, the kids propped a dead tree against the side of the house. Conrad crawled through the second-floor window and let the others in through the front door.

Sheets covered the furniture and there was dust every-where. Mark noticed cracks in several walls, but the cottage looked safe.

"You didn't tell us there was a basement!" Shelly said.

"I'll give you a tour," Darrion said.

She took them through the cottage, showing them the things her father had built into the home. "My dad designed the whole thing. There's a lot of hidden stuff." She opened a door in the living-room wall, revealing a huge television screen.

"The Gala should start soon," Conrad said.

Mark flicked a few switches and shook his head. "Nothing works."

"It's solar powered," Darrion said. "My dad unhooked it when we were gone."

Conrad found the brains of the solar contraption and hooked up the cells. "It'll probably take a day or two to store up enough energy. We'll have to watch on the laptop or listen in the car."

Judd stood at the back of the tent and listened as Mr. Stein told his story to the crowd. A few still clutched invitations, but most thought the tent was part of the Gala and wandered inside.

Judd had rushed to Kasim's building earlier that morning and buzzed his apartment. When no one answered, Judd tried to force the front door open, but people came into the hall and yelled at him, so Judd left.

He walked onto the plaza and watched Kasim's window. There was no movement inside, and Judd worried that the men from the black market had returned. He was also concerned about the stolen sword. Would Kasim try to use it on Carpathia? Judd tried the apartment several times throughout the morning but didn't get an answer.

At the end of Mr. Stein's talk, a few came forward to pray. Many left muttering about "the crazy Judah-ites." Mr. Stein asked Lionel and Sam to take the new believers back to General Zimmerman's home. Judd excused himself and walked toward the main stage. Huge towers held giant speakers that would boom the music and speeches to an expected two million people.

Judd noticed metal detectors on both sides of the stage and GC security guards milling along the sides,

watching the crowd. Sound technicians and camera oper-
ators ran across the stage checking cables and micro-
phones.

Judd walked through the crowd to the front and spotted someone underneath the stage. The man moved
slowly toward the back. Judd shielded his eyes from the
sun and shouted, "Kasim!"

The man turned and Judd cringed. It was a member of
the GC sound crew. "Sorry. Thought you were somebody
else."

Judd went back through the crowd to Kasim's apartment. He buzzed again, but there was still no answer.

Lionel and Sam were amazed at the new believers. Each
had been searching for the truth and had prayed that God
would show it to them at the Gala. When they arrived at
General Zimmerman's house, the General offered to let
them stay and learn about God while they were in Jerusalem.

As Lionel and Sam were about to go, the General
pulled them aside. "You've probably heard what
happened to my famous neighbor."

"Dr. Rosenzweig?" Lionel said.

"Yes. He was taken away by ambulance yesterday
morning. He could not get out of bed. Couldn't speak.
He is better, but they think it was a stroke."

"That's awful," Lionel said. "What'll happen to him?"

"He may be confined to a wheelchair for the rest of
his life."

Judd found a place where he could see the stage *and* Kasim's apartment window. The first act of the Gala opening was a Latin band. Dancers in tight costumes writhed to the earsplitting music. When the band finished, a man in GC garb rushed to a microphone and screamed the motto printed behind him: "One World, One Truth: Individual Freedom for All!"

The crowd repeated the sentence again and again, and people jumped into each other. The man at the microphone said, "Potentate Carpathia is scheduled to arrive within the hour!" People screamed and shouted, and Judd had to hold his ears.

"Would you please help me welcome The Four Horsemen!"

Judd watched a huge video monitor to his left as the popular rock 'n' roll band ran onstage. People filled the plaza and spilled around behind the stage and into alleys and empty parking lots. The crowd was like an ocean, rising and falling with movement. Some at the front held up their hands and started a wave, and quickly those behind them picked up the cue and continued it to the back.

As the sky gradually darkened, Judd watched Peacekeepers moving around the edges of the crowd. How could they possibly keep control of this many people? Security at the side of the stage sent each musician and dancer through metal detectors.

When Z-Van and The Four Horsemen finished, Judd noticed a weird sound. At first he thought it was coming from the speakers; then he saw paper flying in circles atop the crowd. A line of helicopters appeared over the buildings, and the people erupted. The choppers landed on either end of the stage, and all ten regional potentates and several other dignitaries trotted onstage.

Carpathia was an evil, but brilliant man. He had divided the world into ten regions, each with its own supreme leader, or potentate. With the increasing death and destruction around the world, Carpathia looked to these leaders to keep their regions under control.

As the potentates hurried to their spots onstage, GC security forces followed and formed a half circle around the podium.

When everyone was in place, a final chopper arrived, carrying Nicolae Carpathia. The crowd went wild as he walked onstage and shook hands with the invited guests. When he sat in a chair that looked like a throne, the others sat.

Carpathia rose again and again as the applause and cheers continued. Judd noticed the security staff standing straight, eyes forward, not smiling or talking. They were focused on protecting their leader with their very lives.

To conserve the laptop battery, Vicki and the others listened to the radio in the Suburban. They searched for the clearest signal and found that every station aired what came from Jerusalem.

Leon Fortunato spoke first. "Welcome, fellow citizens of the new world." The crowd screamed with delight.

Darrion shook her head. "The population's been cut in half and we're supposed to party."

Fortunato said he would introduce each regional potentate. "But first, to seek the blessing of the great god of nature, I call upon the assistant to the supreme pontiff of Enigma Babylon One World Faith, who also has an announcement. Please welcome Deputy Pontiff Francesca D'Angelo."

"You think this woman dresses as silly as Peter Mathews?" Shelly said.

The crowd grew deathly quiet, and the kids strained to hear what would come next. It was the voice of Nicolae Carpathia. "You will not remember that I have interrupted," Nicolae said.

Vicki shivered.

Carpathia's voice sounded hypnotic. "You are about to hear of a death that will surprise you. It will strike you as old news. You will not care."

"What's this all about?" Mark said. "Who died?"

Vicki shook her head. "I wish we could see what's happening."

———

Judd couldn't believe Carpathia was using his mind-control powers on two million people. He wondered if those watching by satellite would react the same way.

Carpathia sat and Ms. D'Angelo said, "Before I pray to the great one-gender deity in whom we all rest and who also rests in all of us, I have an announcement. Pontifex Maximus Peter the Second died suddenly earlier today.

He was overtaken by a highly contagious virus that made it necessary that he be cremated. Our condolences to his loved ones. A memorial service will be held tomorrow morning at this site. Now let us pray."

Judd couldn't move. Peter the Second was dead? So Mac McCullum had been right. Carpathia had somehow killed Mathews.

The people around Judd acted as if nothing had happened. The crowd politely applauded Ms. D'Angelo's prayer, then cheered each subpotentate and their speeches—which all seemed the same to Judd. Finally, Leon Fortunato introduced the man of the hour, Nicolae Carpathia.

The roar from the crowd was the biggest yet as Carpathia waved at the masses with both hands and walked back and forth onstage. Judd shook his head and looked away. He spotted someone near a stairway that led to metal detectors. As the crowd cheered on, the man turned. It was Kasim.

34

JUDD did a double take. The man near the stage wore a robe and a turban over his head, but Judd was sure it was Kasim. Judd didn't see the laser, but the robe was roomy enough to easily hide it.

Judd hustled into the cheering crowd. Onstage, Carpathia moved back and forth, making sure the cameras caught his smile. Nicolae was now thirty-six, and if Judd didn't know who he really was, he would have thought him charming.

Judd looked over the heads of those in front of him, trying to keep an eye on Kasim. The ovation for Carpathia lasted several minutes. He calmed the crowd just as Judd made it to the edge of the stage.

Kasim was gone.

Vicki couldn't believe how one man could talk so effortlessly for forty-five minutes. She thought listening to the radio would be boring, but he was able to keep their attention with only his voice.

Carpathia spoke about the difficulties of living in a world that faced death and catastrophe and "nature's worst." He became emotional when he talked about the many who had died, and he expressed grief for those who had lost friends and family members.

"Give me a break," Mark grumbled.

The crowd responded to every sentence, every phrase with long periods of applause and shouts of support. As the speech continued, Carpathia seemed to get more and more energized.

"Around this vast plaza you see these words on lampposts and walls and fences: 'Today Is the First Day of the Rest of Utopia.' I commit to you here tonight that I will do everything in my power to bring you Utopia. We will see perfection in society, in politics, and in everyday life."

The crowd went into a frenzy and Carpathia again called for quiet. "Our goal over the last three and one half years has been to unite the world. We have done that with our currency. We have built a one-world communications system. We have even brought people of different faiths together under one banner of religious thought.

"Look behind me. 'One World, One Truth: Individual Freedom for All' is not just a slogan. We have made it a living, breathing reality."

Judd frantically looked around for Kasim. He squinted into the darkness under the stage. It was ten feet high and there was plenty of room to hide, but GC Peacekeepers stood nearby.

Judd moved a few paces and noticed a Peacekeeper watching him, so when Carpathia finished a sentence, Judd clapped and whistled with the rest of the crowd.

As Nicolae neared the end of his speech, he leaned against the side of the podium with one hand, crossed his feet at the ankles, and put his other fist on his hip. When the camera zoomed in on the man's face, the crowd reacted to his arrogant look with whistles and more applause. They knew he was about to make a bold statement.

Carpathia held the pose for almost a minute, then stepped behind the podium and gripped it with both hands. "Tomorrow morning, as you can see on your program, we will reassemble near the Temple Mount. There we shall establish the authority of the Global Community over ev-er-y geographic location."

As cheers rose behind him, Judd slipped back into the crowd and moved to his left. He had to find Kasim.

"Regardless who is proclaiming this or warning that or taking credit for all manner of attacks on this city, this area, this state . . . I will personally put an end to the religious terrorism perpetrated by two murderous impostors. I, for one, am tired of superstitious oppression, tired of drought, tired of bloody water. I am tired of pompous so-called prophecies, of gloom and doom, and of pie in the sky by and by!"

The crowd reacted to Carpathia's energy and seemed to gain momentum as the evil world leader continued.

Judd pushed and shoved the cheering people and scanned faces. He stood on the edge of the sidewalk and spotted Kasim thirty feet away, staring straight at Carpathia. Kasim didn't cheer, clap, or respond in any way. Judd rushed toward his friend.

As the noise died, Carpathia roared, "If the Jerusalem Twosome does not cease and desist tomorrow, I shall not rest until I have personally dealt with them. And once that is accomplished, we shall dance in the streets!"

Only two people now stood between Judd and Kasim. Judd pushed a man out of the way as the crowd rushed toward the stage. Two million voices rose as one. "Nicolae, Nicolae, Nicolae!"

Kasim reached inside his robe.

"Have fun tonight!" Nicolae shouted over the noise. "Indulge yourselves! But sleep well so tomorrow we can enjoy the party that shall have no end!" Carpathia stood near the edge of the stage, waving, smiling, and soaking in the praise of the crowd.

A few feet from him, Kasim wrestled to break free of the surging mob. Several people screaming Nicolae's name pushed Judd forward. As Kasim pulled a metal object from his robe, Judd jumped on him, and the two rolled beneath the stage. Kasim struggled to stand, but Judd held him down.

Kasim was alive with rage. "You're trying to save that madman's life?"

Judd clamped his hand over Kasim's mouth and whispered, "I'm trying to save *your* life. Put that away."

Peacekeepers tried to push the crowd back from the

stage. Judd grabbed Kasim's robe and the two ran out the back of the stage. The thwock, thwock, thwock of helicopters sounded in the distance.

Carpathia walked down the steps to the landing area. Leon Fortunato quickly knelt and waved his arms at Carpathia as if in worship. Thousands in the crowd did the same. They dropped to the ground and acted like Carpathia was a god.

"Are you happy?" Kasim said. "You're letting him get away!"

"What were you going to do? Throw that laser at him?"

Kasim put his hand on the sword's handle. "This weapon will fulfill the prophecy."

Judd shook his head. "No, it won't. You're going to give it to me right now."

"You know what's going to happen tomorrow?" Kasim seethed. "He's going to kill Eli and Moishe!"

"Give it to me!"

Kasim pulled the silver handle from his robe and let it drop to the ground with a clank. Judd stooped to pick it up. When he stood, Kasim had run into the swarm of people.

———

Lionel and Sam helped with the new believers until late in the evening. Three teenagers had prayed with Mr. Stein, and Lionel made sure they knew about the Young Tribulation Force and their Web site. "You'll really grow if you check in with us daily and read your Bible."

Judd came in the back door and went up the stairs. Lionel excused himself and followed. He found Judd in General Zimmerman's weapon room.

Judd told Lionel what had happened with Kasim and pulled out the laser. Before he put it in the empty glass case, he held it out and told Lionel to stand back.

"It looks like something out of a sci-fi movie," Lionel said.

Judd turned the laser on, and immediately a thin beam of orange light appeared. Judd grabbed a cloth from a nearby table and tossed it in the air. He let it land on the beam, but the cloth tore in half and fell to the floor, the edges burned.

"Wow, this would have put an end to Carpathia," Judd said. He turned off the laser and put it in its case.

Sam ran into the room. "Meeting downstairs. Mr. Stein wants to see us all."

Mr. Stein welcomed the new believers and had everyone introduce themselves and tell where they were from. When they were finished, Mr. Stein led in prayer and thanked God for their new friends.

"I have asked God for wisdom about tomorrow. This will be a very difficult experience for all of us, and I would not require you to attend, but I believe it is important that we witness what happens at the Wailing Wall.

"To understand the grace and goodness of God, we must consider the suffering of his followers. If Jesus had not been crucified, there would be no resurrection. And the same goes for our beloved Eli and Moishe."

Mr. Stein took Judd, Lionel, and Sam aside later. "I

am going to go to the Wailing Wall tonight and stand watch with the witnesses. You are welcome to come."

Vicki was exhausted after their day at the new hideout. Mark had found a large piece of plywood and nailed it over the broken window. Conrad had worked on the solar panels after Carpathia's opening message. "The broadcast from the Wailing Wall won't begin until early in the morning. We should have enough power to watch it on TV."

Vicki and Shelly made dinner. While they were eating, Mark turned on the computer to check e-mails. He let out a whoop as he pulled up hundreds of messages from people who had seen Vicki during the satellite school transmissions.

"Some of these are from the first broadcast," Mark said, "but most are new."

Conrad pointed to a message that didn't list the sender's return address. The subject line simply said "Phoenix."

Mark clicked it and the kids read: *Do not reply to this. I just wanted you to know long tail is safe. We found the truck and are searching the area nearby. Hope you are all out of range by now. Will be in touch soon. N.*

"That's Natalie," Vicki said. "When did she send it?"

Mark checked the e-mail and said, "Late last night." He found another e-mail that was sent only a few hours earlier.

> *The GC has suspended all search due to the Gala. Praise God! I was assigned to question several farm owners this*

morning. I was exhausted but happy to see our friend C
with the farmer and his wife. They told me what happened.
C is doing well but says he misses you all. Long tail and I are
okay for now. Will send you a safe address to write as soon
as I can. I may need directions to your new place soon.

N.

Vicki climbed into the loft and fell into bed. Darrion had
found enough sheets and pillows for everyone. It felt good to
sleep and not have to worry about the Global Community
breaking in. Vicki thought of Charlie and Natalie and thanked
God they had all made it through safely. She thought of Judd
in Israel and wondered what he was doing. Would they ever
see each other face-to-face again?

Judd followed Mr. Stein as they waded through the crowd
at the Wailing Wall. Sam and Lionel weren't far behind.
The crowd was huge, but Judd knew by morning more
would cram into the site. Millions around the world
would watch and prepare for the evil celebration.

Some shouted at Eli and Moishe, who didn't speak
or move. Others simply watched the two, wondering
when they would preach again. Mr. Stein struggled
to get close to a few who knelt next to the fence, their
heads bowed. Mr. Stein joined them and Judd stood
close to him.

Finally, Mr. Stein spoke softly to the two and Judd
strained to hear. He was reciting Psalm 23: " 'Even when I
walk through the dark valley of death, I will not be afraid,

for you are close beside me. Your rod and your staff protect and comfort me.' "

Mr. Stein recited other biblical passages. Eli and Moishe didn't move, but they seemed to breathe in the words of Scripture.

" 'I am the resurrection and the life,' " Mr. Stein continued. " 'Those who believe in me, even though they die like everyone else, will live again. They are given eternal life for believing in me and will never perish.' "

Through the night Mr. Stein whispered verses to the witnesses. He prayed quietly for them, thanking God for sending them to warn the world of judgment. "And now we pray the same power you have given them to do miracles among us will be present," Mr. Stein said. "Empower Eli and Moishe to live for you and do your will until the due time."

Judd awoke to shouts and screams. The sun was up and dew covered the blanket on top of him. Someone had covered Lionel and Sam too. Judd rubbed his eyes and saw Mr. Stein still kneeling at the fence, now singing softly the words to an old hymn someone had recently taught him.

Judd stood and pushed his way to the back of the crowd to find one of the many portable toilets. Not far away, loud bands rehearsed for the party that would begin when Carpathia was finished with the witnesses. On his way back, Judd heard a group talking about the funeral service for Peter the Second.

"I heard they canceled it due to lack of interest," a

man said. "And that new woman, D'Angelo or whatever her name was, she's out too."

"Who needs those two when we have Nicolae Carpathia?" a woman snickered.

Judd shook his head. Enigma Babylon One World Faith had been popular with people around the globe. Now with its founder dead and the world under the spell of Carpathia, it looked like it would fade away without anyone noticing.

Judd wondered how Peter Mathews had really died. Did Carpathia shoot him? Did a hit man take out the pontiff? Judd shuddered as he elbowed his way back to the front. Eli and Moishe stood like statues, just as they had done for hours.

When he made it back, Sam and Lionel were sitting up, blankets draped around their shoulders. GC Security moved through the crowd, telling people to back away from the fence.

Mr. Stein continued to whisper a few verses to the witnesses. GC officers grabbed him and pulled him away, but one look from Moishe and the two security officers fell to the ground, stunned. Mr. Stein finished what he was saying and looked at Eli and Moishe. The two glanced at him and nodded slightly.

Mr. Stein helped the two guards up and joined Judd and the others. Judd said, "What were your last words to them?"

"I quoted Psalm 121. 'I look up to the mountains— does my help come from there? My help comes from the Lord, who made the heavens and the earth! He will not let you stumble and fall; the one who watches over you will not sleep. Indeed, he who watches over Israel never tires and never sleeps.' "

Judd wondered what was going through the witnesses' minds. The "debate" with Carpathia would begin in a little more than two hours. Would they stand up to him and speak the truth? No matter how they responded, this was the 1,261st day. The Bible said they would be overcome today.

AS THREE GC helicopters flew over the Wailing Wall, Judd looked at his watch. It was 9:59 A.M. The choppers landed and various dignitaries exited. Judd noticed there was no representative from Enigma Babylon.

Finally, Nicolae Carpathia stepped out and waved to the cheering crowd. A black box poked out of a pocket of Carpathia's expensive sport coat. There was a flurry of activity with the potentates, Fortunato, camerapeople, and lights, but Judd couldn't take his eyes off this evil man strutting toward the fence and the two witnesses of God.

A woman dabbed makeup on Carpathia's face as he hurried by. His lapel microphone picked up the woman saying, "You look wonderful, Potentate."

Carpathia ignored her and approached Eli and Moishe. They stood ramrod straight and stared ahead. Carpathia flung his sport coat onto the fence and rolled up his sleeves. The crowd responded with claps and cheers.

Judd had seen the two witnesses silence Carpathia before. They had breathed fire and consumed their enemies. But now they were up against the meanest man on the face of the earth.

Carpathia had a gleam in his eye as he stopped next to Eli. "And what do you gentlemen have to say for yourselves this morning?"

Vicki sat in her pajamas in the Wisconsin vacation home of Darrion Stahley. Everyone was gathered to watch the live coverage from Israel. The huge screen built into the wall made it feel like they were right there. Vicki could tell that the GC had paid attention to every detail. Carpathia's voice was clear. The scene had obviously been lighted by professionals. Even the crowd seemed to applaud on cue.

"You have plagued the world with your magic for too long," Carpathia said to the witnesses. "You have boasted about the suffering you have caused."

"That's not true," Conrad said.

"Why don't they say something?" Shelly said.

Vicki stared at the screen. "When Jesus was brought before the leaders what did he do?"

"He didn't say anything," Darrion said.

Vicki nodded. "That's what they're doing. They're like lambs going to the slaughter."

Judd thought of Kasim and the laser sword. He closed his eyes and imagined slicing through the metal fence and going after Carpathia himself. But more shouts from the evil man brought Judd back to reality.

"What is wrong with you?" Nicolae shouted, pacing before Eli and Moishe. "Cat got your tongues? The water in Jerusalem tastes cold and refreshing today! Run out of poison?"

Judd was among a group of believers who didn't shout or even speak. Some silently moved their lips in prayer.

But the others around them shouted at Carpathia. "Arrest them." One man screamed, "Just kill them and get it over with!"

Carpathia toyed with the silent saints. "Was that rain on my window this morning? What happened to the drought? Say, does anyone see locusts? horsemen? smoke? Gentlemen! You are impotent!"

Mr. Stein grabbed Judd by an arm and fell to his knees. "Pray with me."

Judd knelt too and bowed his head, but Carpathia's voice boomed through the speakers around them. "I proclaimed this area off-limits to you two years ago! Why are you still here? You must leave or be arrested! In fact, did I not say that if you were seen in public *any*where after the meeting of the cultists that you would be executed?"

Judd glanced up as Carpathia turned to the crowd. "I did say that, did I not?"

"You did, Potentate!"

"Yes! Execute them!"

"Kill them now!"

"I have been remiss!" Carpathia continued. "I have

not carried out my duties! How can I have allowed this crime to go unpunished? I do not want to be shamed before my people! I do not want to be embarrassed at their party today!"

Lionel bent beside Judd and whispered, "He knows."

"What do you mean?" Judd said.

"I think Carpathia's been studying. He knows the prophecy says he's going to win this round."

Carpathia walked a few paces away and shouted for Eli and Moishe to come out from behind the fence. "Challenge me! Answer me! Climb over, fly over, transport yourselves if you are able! Do not make me open the gate!"

Carpathia stood about twenty yards away from Judd. It was as close as he had ever been to the man. Even in the midst of this confrontation, Nicolae was charming and suave. Some, no doubt, followed him because of his good looks. Others had been convinced by the command he had over the devastating world situation. The only thing about Carpathia that caused anyone to wonder was his impotence in front of Eli and Moishe.

Carpathia turned to the crowd again. "Should I fear their very breath? Will these dragons incinerate and slay even me?"

Some laughed nervously, as if they had just remembered the power of the two witnesses. But the two didn't move, and they barely seemed to breathe.

"I am at the end of patience!" Nicolae scolded. A uniformed man handed him a key. He unlocked the gate, and the crowd fell silent.

Carpathia flung the gate open and ran behind the two. "Outside!"

Eli and Moishe stood still. Finally, Carpathia shoved them like they were animals. Eli bumped into Moishe as they stumbled toward the gate.

People near Judd gasped and moved back at the sight of the two. Carpathia grabbed Eli and Moishe by their robes and slammed them against the fence. He turned to the crowd and smiled. "Here are your tormentors! Your judges!" With a sneer he said, "Your *prophe*ts! And what do they have to say for themselves now? Nothing! They have been tried and convicted and sentenced. All that is left is the rendering of justice, and as *I* have decreed it, *I* shall carry it out!"

He grabbed their robes again and pulled them away from the fence. "Any last words?"

Eli and Moishe looked at each other. The two were loved by believers the world over. They had been God's representatives on earth for more than three years. They had spoken powerfully and had never backed down from the Global Community. Now, however, they simply lifted their heads to heaven.

Judd stared at their shining faces as Carpathia walked away. He had heard about the look on missionaries' faces as they faced death, but he had never seen such peace.

Carpathia kept his back to the crowd, walked over to the fence, and pulled something from his coat pocket. He stepped back until he was ten feet away from the witnesses. Carpathia pointed a high-powered handgun at Eli. Judd reached to cover his ears, but the blast came quickly. The gunshot knocked Eli off his feet and into the fence. He crumpled to the ground in a pool of blood.

Judd bowed his head in horror, unable to speak. He felt short of breath, like someone had punched him in the stomach. Mr. Stein looked at Moishe and whispered, "May the Lord of peace give you his peace no matter what happens."

Moishe knelt and covered his eyes. Judd had no time to prepare for what happened next. Carpathia quickly aimed the gun and fired. Moishe's body crashed into the fence and crumpled to the ground also, his arms and legs flopping clumsily.

Lionel fell to one knee. Sam looked like he was about to faint. They were all shocked at the violence they had just seen.

Carpathia put the gun away, slipped on his jacket, and bowed to the crowd. Suddenly people erupted in shouts of praise for their leader. They laughed and shouted, slapped each other's hands and danced, happy that their troubles were now over.

Mr. Stein helped Judd to his feet. The crowd surged forward, pushing them toward the bodies of the two men of God. Judd watched Carpathia and the other dignitaries get into the helicopters.

"You'll get yours," Judd muttered.

Vicki and the others sat in stunned silence as the camera zoomed in on the dead men. Newscasters couldn't hide their glee at what had just happened.

"You can understand why the people watching this here and around the world will want to celebrate," one anchorman said. "The potentate promised to take care of those two, and he has."

Vicki wept. Moishe and Eli lay in ugly heaps, their leathery skin and bony hands exposed. They had been untouchable, unbeatable. Now people danced and sang as the helicopters lifted off, taking Carpathia and his group to the party site.

The camera switched from Carpathia's helicopter to Eli's face. His eyes and mouth were open, and dark red blood spread on the ground beneath him. Moishe's body was an indescribable mess of blood and bone.

"Now the party starts," Mark said grimly.

———————————————————

Judd and the others slowly made their way back to General Zimmerman's house. They passed people dancing and singing, moving to the beat of the music that blared from blocks away. Some people gathered around TVs and cheered each time GCNN replayed the murders of Eli and Moishe.

A drunken man handed Mr. Stein a drink as they passed. Mr. Stein glared at him.

"What's the matter?" the man slurred. "We're done with those crazy preachers. Celebrate!"

Mr. Stein pushed his way through the crowd. At General Zimmerman's house he called a meeting of the believers. Those from Yitzhak's house attended there as well, including Jamal and his wife.

"Evil will flood the streets for the next few days," Mr. Stein said. "Those who do not know God won't be able to resist Carpathia's schemes."

A man in the back raised a hand. "Will we continue our meetings?"

Mr. Stein shook his head. "I did not know it would be this ghastly. The murders and the sinful actions of those on the street are unspeakable. Let us stay here and pray. We will have another opportunity this week to tell the truth. May God give us the strength to seize it."

Judd found Jamal and asked if he had talked with Kasim. Jamal shook his head, and Judd told him what had happened the night before.

"I was afraid he would do something like that," Jamal said. "Thank you for saving my son's life."

Judd nodded. "I'm scared of what he might do next, now that Carpathia has killed the two witnesses."

Jamal put a hand on Judd's shoulder. "Please help me find him and bring him home."

"I don't think Mr. Stein wants us to go out—"

"Please," Jamal said.

Lionel pulled up the Global Community's Web site and looked for any news about Vicki and the others at home. He found two stories about fugitive kids in Illinois, but nothing about them being caught.

He wrote Vicki an e-mail and asked for an update. He told her about being at the Wailing Wall and all he had seen. The whole spectacle seemed like a bad dream, but it wasn't, and the world would never be the same for anyone.

After sending the message, Lionel checked out the kids' Web site and discovered new material that could only have been written after the deaths of Eli and Moishe.

Don't be surprised at the murder of the two witnesses, Lionel read. He guessed Mark had written the update. *Just remember that the week is not over.*

Lionel smiled. Carpathia may have won one battle, but he would not win his war with God.

Judd left General Zimmerman's house later that evening and walked to Kasim's apartment. Along the way he passed hundreds of people celebrating the deaths of Eli and Moishe. Drunken men and women danced in the streets.

When Judd reached the plaza where the opening ceremony had been held, huge crowds were gathered to listen to musical acts. The noise was deafening. Judd found a schedule of events and noticed that Z-Van had been added to Friday's event.

Judd followed a drunken man and woman inside Kasim's building and took the stairs. Judd listened at Kasim's door, but he didn't hear anything. He jiggled the doorknob and was surprised when the door swung open.

Judd entered, shut the door, and found Kasim sitting on a wooden chair looking toward the plaza. He didn't turn when Judd entered but kept staring at the stage.

Though the windows were closed, Judd could still hear the booming music.

"Why did you leave your door unlocked?" Judd said.

Kasim had recovered well from his wounds, but his face was badly bruised. "I'm waiting for a delivery."

Judd shook his head. He didn't want to know what kind of delivery. "I'm here to take you home. Come with me."

Kasim turned, his eyes flashing with anger. "Did you see what Carpathia did to them? Those people out there are celebrating because two men are dead."

"Don't take this into your own hands," Judd said.

"What if I'm right? What if I'm the one who's supposed to eliminate Nicolae?"

Someone knocked at the door. Kasim told Judd to hide in the next room. Judd scurried inside and listened. The door opened and closed, but Judd didn't hear any voices.

Judd looked into the hallway. The room was empty.

36

VICKI and the others moved about in a daze. Though they had expected the deaths of Eli and Moishe, the violent way they had died affected them all.

Darrion showed the kids some of the secrets of the house. Her father had prepared for emergencies. She led the kids to a downstairs game room and pushed a button under the wet bar. A section of the wall moved slightly, and Darrion pushed it all the way open. Inside was a type of shelter built into the side of the hill behind the house. Along the wall, shelves were stacked with cans of food.

"Did your dad think you'd have to use this?" Mark said.

"By the time he had this built, he was getting suspicious of the Global Community. He wanted to make sure there was a place we could all come and be safe."

Vicki was amazed at the space inside the secret room. If the kids ever needed to hide, this would be perfect.

Darrion led them upstairs to the loft. A small ladder was stored under one of the beds, and Darrion propped it against the wall. She opened a tiny door high on the wall. Inside was something that looked like a telescope.

"I'm not sure how the thing works," Darrion said, "but if you put on these goggles, you're supposed to be able to see a long way and tell if anybody's coming."

"Heat imaging," Conrad said. "If somebody's hiding in the bushes outside, those will show you."

While Darrion showed them other surprises throughout the house, Vicki turned on the television to catch more reaction to the killing of the two witnesses.

A news broadcast showed Leon Fortunato speaking in front of a crowd. Music blared in the background as Fortunato said, "The time has come to recognize the truth about our potentate. He is a deity. That's right—a god. And perhaps *the* deity, the creator God and savior of all mankind."

People cheered as Fortunato listed Carpathia's accomplishments. When someone from the press asked about the death of Peter the Second, Fortunato waved his hand and looked to another reporter.

The only person who spoke about Peter was Carpathia himself. In an interview shortly after killing the two witnesses, Carpathia admitted that he was tired of the Enigma Babylon Faith and said it would not return. "Individual souls can find within themselves the deity necessary to conduct their lives as they wish. I esteem individual freedom over organized religion."

Every newscast was the same. They showed the bloated, decaying bodies of the two beloved prophets lying near the Wailing Wall. People danced around the bodies and laughed, pointed, held their noses, and mocked. Some went close enough to kick the bodies.

The party spread to other parts of the world. People created dummies that looked like Eli and Moishe and paraded them in town squares and at musical events. The dummies were hanged, stabbed, and burned while people cheered and laughed. Reports confirmed that many were exchanging gifts like it was Christmas.

Late the next night, Vicki found a commentator who quoted the latest Global Community poll. "People were asked if the preachers should be buried or remain in the street. An overwhelming 87 percent agree the preachers should not be buried. But let's be honest. The scene in Jerusalem is sickening. Put this chapter behind us. They were executed Tuesday. It's Thursday. You've had your fun. Don't let this get any gorier. It's time to get past this, to give these men a proper burial and move on."

But the celebration in Jerusalem only picked up steam. Top stars performed nonstop, and the crowds increased.

Judd kept watch for the next two days, but Kasim didn't come back to his apartment. Judd wondered if something bad had happened to him. Mr. Stein had been upset with

Judd for walking around during the Gala, but when Judd explained the situation, he understood.

The scene at General Zimmerman's house was incredible. It was wall-to-wall people, most of whom had the mark of the true believer. Mr. Stein and others spoke about what events might happen next and for everyone to be on guard for a possible GC clampdown. "They have promised not to arrest anyone this week, but be careful. They have lied to us before."

Judd watched for news of Carpathia's next speech, but the man seemed to be in hiding. Judd figured Nicolae was watching in secret, excited about all the sinful things going on.

Friday morning, Mr. Stein led the entire group of new believers to the Wailing Wall, where they could see Eli and Moishe. He was convinced that something miraculous was about to happen.

Judd had told Lionel and Sam to keep watch for Kasim. As they drew closer to the place where Eli and Moishe lay, Judd's stomach turned. He smelled the rotting corpses from a hundred yards away. People still danced and sang around the dead men, though most people couldn't stand the stench any longer and had moved their party down the street.

Judd put a handkerchief to his face and followed Mr. Stein. They came as close as the GC guards would allow.

"I don't see how people can stand so close to them," Sam said, plugging his nose.

A siren wailed a few blocks away, and Judd realized it was another band kicking off the morning's celebration.

Judd turned and saw a GC Peacekeeper talking to some-one perched in a tree. The Peacekeeper grabbed the man's robe and pulled him down.

Judd gasped. It was Kasim.

Vicki set her alarm and got up early Friday morning. She didn't want to miss what was about to happen. The others followed not long after and sat around the room in pajamas.

"You're sure this is going to happen this morning?" Mark said.

"Yes and I don't want to miss the live coverage. You can bet we'll only get one shot to see it and then they'll destroy the video."

Vicki put an arm around Darrion. The girl had wandered into the woods the day before and now seemed sad. When Vicki asked what was up, Darrion shook her head.

"Come on," Vicki whispered.

Darrion sighed. "This place brings back a lot of memories, good and bad."

"Tell me the good stuff."

"Fishing with my dad. Hiking with Mom. Summer nights when we'd leave all the windows and doors open and it'd be cold enough to see your breath in the morn-ing. We had a lot of fun up here."

"What about the bad?"

Darrion stared at the TV. "Mom and Dad were usually too busy to come here. Dad traveled and Mom didn't like to drive alone."

Mark found a live feed from the Wailing Wall.

"There was something else that happened," Darrion continued. "I don't like to think about it."

Vicki scooted closer. "Tell me."

"I was mad at Mom one weekend. Dad was out of town. I took off with a girlfriend who told her mom she was sleeping at my house, and we met these two guys. I knew I shouldn't do it, but I brought them all up here."

"What happened?"

Darrion looked away. "I've been reliving it ever since we got here. I've never told anybody."

Vicki hugged Darrion tightly. "I did a lot of bad stuff before I became a believer. Some of it comes back at the weirdest times."

"I know God forgives," Darrion said, "but how do I get it out of my head?"

"Sometimes it helps to tell somebody else," Vicki said.

Lionel grabbed Judd's arm as Judd started to run. "It's Kasim! I have to get him," Judd said.

Lionel let Judd go and turned back to the scene before them. Mr. Stein and others knelt, hands clasped, and silently prayed. A few who were dancing and drinking saw them and laughed.

"You people want to be next?" a dark-haired girl said. She lost her balance and fell, and her friends laughed.

Drunken people danced in a circle around the dead bodies. The line went one way, then changed direction and quickly went the other. Faster and faster they danced until the line fell apart. People fell over each other, laughing, tears rolling down their cheeks. One woman became sick and was hit by another who fell over her.

Sam pointed toward Eli's and Moishe's bodies. "Look what those people are doing."

A girl crawled toward the two witnesses on her hands and knees. A man sat nearby talking to her. She turned around and held out a bottle. Lionel stepped closer to hear their conversation.

"I gotta have another drink before I do this," the girl said.

"Here you go," the man said. "What number is this— 4,000?"

The girl laughed. "I think I lost track . . . three days ago."

The man laughed and took the bottle back. "What are you going to do, have a dance with the corpses?"

The girl pulled out a pair of scissors and snipped at the air. "No way. I got a business idea."

"What?"

"Hear me out. These guys have been in the news for years, right?"

"Yeah."

"So what do you think people would pay on-line for a piece of their clothes?"

"You wouldn't."

"Watch me! I'm goin' right up there and snip some of that burlap or whatever they're wearing. And the next thing you know, it'll be Jerusalem Twosome dot-com."

Lionel shook his head. He couldn't believe anyone

could be so greedy. The man helped the girl to her feet. She wobbled a little, then made her way to Moishe.

"This is awful," she said. "There are bugs all over." She swatted at a bird picking at Moishe's flesh. A rat scurried out from under him and she shrieked. She quickly plugged her nose.

"What do you expect?" her friend said. "They've been lying in the sun for three days."

She inspected Moishe's body. "I can't even find a spot that's not soaked in blood."

"Just cut it and get out of there before somebody stops you."

A dancer came close to the girl. "Watch it! This is delicate surgery, especially when my head's spinning." She pulled at Moishe's robe. "Right here looks like a good piece."

Lionel noticed movement of Moishe's body and thought the girl had rolled him slightly.

"Hey, whoever's moving this stiff better stop it!"

Lionel looked closely at the dried blood around Moishe's body. Something strange was happening. The red flakes were turning from dust to liquid before his eyes and moving back toward the body. Moishe's head wound was closing, the skin stretching over his scalp. Hair replaced itself. When Moishe took a deep breath of air, several people nearby screamed.

The girl stopped cutting the robe and stared at the dead man. "What in the world?"

Her friend shouted, "Get out of there, Cindy! Come on!"

"This . . . can't . . . b-be," the girl stammered. "These guys have been dead three—"

Before she could finish her sentence, Moishe took a huge breath and his chest heaved. He opened his eyes wide and raised his hands into the air.

The girl couldn't breathe, couldn't scream, couldn't move. Inches from her face the disgusting remains of two dead men were coming together. They were being made whole before her eyes.

Lionel heard Mr. Stein and a few others whisper, "Praise God! May Jesus be praised!"

The girl finally scooted backward and screamed. Others who were still dancing stopped and glanced at the two bodies, covered their mouths, and ran away. To them it was horrifying.

To Lionel, it was the most wonderful sight he had ever seen.

Vicki kept an arm around Darrion as the girl wept. Shelly screamed and Vicki glanced at the screen. Eli and Moishe were moving.

"It's happening," Mark said. "It's really happening."

The camera pulled back to show shrieking people running from the place. Others ran forward to see what was happening, only to stop in their tracks when they saw the dead bodies coming to life.

Eli and Moishe moved in slow motion. Their chests heaved as their lungs filled with oxygen. They struggled to their knees. It was like watching a newborn animal standing for the first time. Then they gained strength and put hands on the pavement in front of them and rose. As they stood, people throughout the plaza whimpered and moaned with fright.

Their skin, black and purple from lying in the sun, began to fade until it was flesh colored again. Their wounds healed.

Lionel couldn't take his eyes from them. The two gathered their robes, which had also become like new, and stood strong and tall. They gazed at the crowd, then looked up.

A voice spoke so loud that people covered their ears. "COME UP HERE!"

Lionel noticed the music from a few blocks away had stopped. Everyone watched as Eli and Moishe slowly rose into the air. People fell on their knees and buried their faces. Others cried out in horror as the two disappeared into a cloud. The cloud moved higher and higher until it vanished.

Lionel fell to his knees. All he could think to say was, "Thank you. Thank you for letting me see that."

Mr. Stein began to sing and other believers picked up the tune. The crowd that had been so happy now wailed and cried, drowning out the praises of the believers.

I have to get to Judd and tell him about this, Lionel thought. But just as he stood, the ground shook beneath him. Lionel grabbed the iron fence and held on. People nearby tumbled against each other. Some were thrown high into the air.

The bright blue sky blackened, and cold rain pelted

the ground. Then came the crash of buildings and the smash of metal and glass from a few blocks away.

"Earthquake!" someone shouted.

Lionel held on to the fence until the rumbling stopped. The sun shone through the dark clouds, casting a green shadow on the area.

Mr. Stein said, "We must help those who may be trapped."

While the rest of the crowd looked for safety, Lionel followed his friends into the death zone. Lionel's one question was whether Judd had survived the quake.

ABOUT THE AUTHORS

Dr. Tim LaHaye (www.timlahaye.com), who conceived and created the idea of fictionalizing an account of the Rapture and the Tribulation, is a noted author, minister, and nationally recognized speaker on Bible prophecy. He is the founder of both Tim LaHaye Ministries and the Pre-Trib Research Center. He also recently cofounded the Tim LaHaye School of Prophecy at Liberty University. Presently Dr. LaHaye speaks at many Bible prophecy conferences in the US and Canada, where his current prophecy books are very popular.

Dr. LaHaye holds a doctor of ministry degree from Western Theological Seminary and a doctor of literature degree from Liberty University. For twenty-five years he pastored one of the nation's outstanding churches in San Diego, which grew to three locations. It was during that time that he founded two accredited Christian high schools, a Christian school system of ten schools, and San Diego Christian College (formerly known as Christian Heritage College).

Dr. LaHaye has written over fifty nonfiction books and coauthored more than twenty-five fiction books, many of which have been translated into thirty-four languages. He has written books on a wide variety of subjects, such as family life, temperaments, and Bible prophecy. His most popular fiction works—the Left Behind books, written with Jerry B. Jenkins—have appeared on the bestseller lists of the Christian Booksellers Association, *Publishers Weekly*, the *Wall Street Journal*, *USA Today*, and the *New York Times*.

Another popular series by LaHaye and Jenkins is the Jesus Chronicles. This four-book fiction series gives readers a rich first-century experience as *John*, *Mark*, *Luke*, and *Matthew* narrate thrilling accounts of the life of Jesus. LaHaye's other prophetic novels include the Babylon Rising series and The End series. These are suspense thrillers with thought-provoking messages.

Jerry B. Jenkins, former vice president for publishing at Moody Bible Institute of Chicago and member of the board of trustees since 2000, is the author of more than 185 books, including the bestselling Left Behind series. Twenty of his books have reached the *New York Times* Best Sellers List (seven in the number one spot) and have also appeared on the *USA Today, Publishers Weekly*, and *Wall Street Journal* bestseller lists. *Desecration*, book nine in the Left Behind series, was the bestselling book in the world in 2001. His books have sold nearly seventy million copies.

Also the former editor of *Moody* magazine, Jenkins has contributed writing to *Time, Reader's Digest, Parade, Guideposts, Christianity Today*, and dozens of other periodicals. He was featured on the cover of *Newsweek* magazine in 2004.

His nonfiction books include as-told-to biographies with Hank Aaron, Bill Gaither, Orel Hershiser, Luis Palau, Joe Gibbs, Walter Payton, and Nolan Ryan, among many others. The Hershiser and Ryan books reached the *New York Times* Best Sellers List.

Jenkins assisted Dr. Billy Graham with his autobiography, *Just As I Am*, also a *New York Times* bestseller. Jerry spent thirteen months working with Dr. Graham, which he considers the privilege of a lifetime.

Jerry owns Jenkins Entertainment, a filmmaking company in Los Angeles, which produced the critically acclaimed movie *Midnight Clear*, based on his book of the same name. See www.jenkins -entertainment.com.

Jerry Jenkins also owned the Christian Writers Guild, whose aim was to train tomorrow's professional Christian writers. Under Jerry's leadership, the guild expanded to include college-credit courses, a critique service, literary registration services, and writing contests, as well as an annual conference. After fourteen years of ministry, Jerry has recently chosen to close the Guild.

As a marriage-and-family author, Jerry has been a frequent guest on Dr. James Dobson's *Focus on the Family* radio program and is a sought-after speaker and humorist. See www.ambassadorspeakers.com.

Jerry has been awarded four honorary doctorates. He and his wife, Dianna, have three grown sons and eight grandchildren.

Check out Jerry's blog at www.jerry-jenkins.com.